*Tales of Hardooth 9*

# SHE IS BACK!

*Dara J. Carr*

*Tales of Hardooth 9*

# SHE IS BACK!

*Dara J. Carr*

FOUNDATION PUBLISHER

Tales of Hardooth 9: She Is Back!
All Rights Reserved
Copyright © 2016 Dara J. Carr
Edited by Betty Powell and Linda S. Carr
Artwork by Eric A. Carr

Foundation Publisher
www.foundationpublisher.com
info@foundationpublisher.com
ISBN: 978-0-9996147-8-5
Library of Congress Control Number: 2021938858
Foundation Publisher and the columned logo are trademarks belonging to Foundation Publisher.

*PRINTED IN THE UNITED STATES OF AMERICA*

# SHE IS BACK!

# 1

Now that Bonarain was back, she had to be introduced to all of the Owlamites that had been born since she vanished. She was pregnant with Nadiwi at the time she vanished. Nadiwi was number 32 on the list of the eldest Owlamites. That meant that she was not familiar with practically all of them. The only ones who had been born prior, and still alive, were Mahanee and Hisang. That left 4,679 who needed to be introduced to Bonarain of the First…and a lot of history she had to learn. After tearful reunions with Mahanee and Hisang, the introductions began, starting with the eldest – Bikaropin.

"This is one that I have learned to depend on quite a bit," said Soolchakan. "He's a lot smarter than…most of us. He has been able to figure out things that most of us don't seem to be able to fathom."

The two smiled as they hugged.

Bonarain stepped back. "So you've become the teacher… in my absence?"

Bikaropin smiled. "Teacher? No. More of an advisor." He frowned. "Uh…where were you all this time?"

She hung her head. "I was trapped in this…Fortress Island."

He looked confused. "Uh…" He chuckled nervously. "Fortress Island?"

Soolchakan sent imagery of the island to Bikaropin. It was easier and faster thinking about it rather than talking about it.

After the imagery was finished Bikaropin shook his head. "Why didn't you just build a dirt ramp up to and over the wall?"

Now Bonarain looked as if she had been slapped. She turned away red faced and grimacing with her eyes closed.

"She thinks more along the lines of making complicated simple," said Soolchakan. "She has a problem with the…simplistic. I think simplistically, even though I don't have a solution. Once I think that way, she looks at it and simplifies it. She wasn't able to look at any other ideas there…so she over complicated it."

Bikaropin looked a little uneasy. He sniffed. "All…right." He looked at Bonarain and smiled. "Welcome back." He cleared his throat. "Has anyone told you about the combination of the blue and red stones yet?"

Bonarain was a little bewildered. "What…combination? What do you mean?"

"I haven't gotten her there yet," said Soolchakan. "I was waiting until some of the introductions were done and then…I was going to tell her."

Bonarain was now looking very apprehensive. "If this is something I need to know, I wanna know...NOW!" She glared at Soolchakan.

Soolchakan sighed. He started sending imagery of how the two stones could possibly bring someone back to life. Her eyes grew wider as the imagery continued. Bikaropin also sent some imagery, thus enhancing the possibilities of bringing the Owlamites buried on Zhagool back to life.

"Let's get to it," said Bonarain emphatically! "The introductions can wait. I want my sons back. I can meet everyone else...later."

Soolchakan shook his head. "We bring Kiyalee and Chyning back first..."

Bonarain was now very irate. "I WANT MY SONS... NOW!"

Soolchakan decided to end any arguments. "We bring all of them back, but we do it in the order in which they were born. I will listen to no arguments beyond that." He had used the power and now there were no arguments.

Bonarain looked off to the side a little perturbed, however she was doing some mild scheming (even though she knew it would come to nothing). "What about the living?"

Now Soolchakan was puzzled. "What?"

"What about Nadiwi? When do we look for her? I want

her back. If she's still alive...and possibly living as a slave...I want her freed...NOW! How are you going to change that?"

Soolchakan now looked a little guilty. "I understand what you're saying I just...don't know how to do it. I can...call out to all Owlamites but...how do I find her and get her to respond when she has never been taught...any of our capabilities...mental, magical or normal?"

Bikaropin cleared his throat nervously. "There may be a certain way...that you haven't considered, yet."

Soolchakan tilted his head back, raised his eyebrows and stared at Bikaropin. "I'm listening."

Bonarain was a little apprehensive. "Why are you talking to him about it? You're the *Voice of Power*."

"Because, as I said, he seems to be a lot smarter than most of us." Soolchakan gave her a semi-smug smile.

Bikaropin did not wait for another argument of pause between the other two. "You have the capability to call out to all Owlamites or just some...or just one." He shrugged a little. "I read, in the accounts after the initial attack by the Algothons that the *Voice of Power*, at that time, called out and there was a response. Perhaps that could be done again...in this case. Call out to any Owlamite that...say...has never seen your face. Since all of us here in the gorge *have* seen you...we won't pay attention. That would mean that Nadiwi is the only one who could or *would* get the message. She may be a little frightened or uneasy about responding, but...if you can make some connection with her... you'll at least know that she's alive and then...we can go from there."

Soolchakan licked his lips. He thought about it for a moment. He sighed and closed his eyes and started a mental send-out. "Any Owlamite...anyone who can hear this message... if you have ever lived in the gorge...ignore this call-out completely. I'm calling to anyone who can hear this who has never met Soolchakan of the city of Owlam. Speak to me, mentally, if you can hear me...mentally." He waited for a few moments. Nothing happened. He repeated the message more emphatically. Again nothing. He repeated it again. He waited and was suddenly surprised to get some kind of garbled response to the sending that seemed to be full of fear and not very practiced at mental communication. He cleared his throat and sent the message again.

She was sitting near the fireplace half scared out of her mind. A sudden voice had entered her head and was calling to her. She tried to block the voice, by thinking of something else, because she thought that she was imagining some crazy daydream. She went back to sewing up a hole in a pair of pants. The message came again. This time it sounded more like a command. She was used to getting commands from the family that she served, however, this was not from them. She had heard of people who could do all kinds of strange and bizarre things, like talk to your mind without speaking. Maybe this was one of them. She tried to pay more attention to her sewing because she figured that she would get in trouble if she was found doing something other than what the master had commanded. The third time the voice entered her head, she called out, mentally, for the voice to stop bothering her. Once again, and with much greater emphasis, the message came to her. She stood up. "What do you want," she said fearfully?

Ansantima, the Heyyah wife of the man who owned her, came into the dining room from her bedroom. "I *didn't* call you, Slut. Now don't speak until you're ordered to. Continue sewing!" She huffed and went back to her bedroom to take care of a crying baby.

Nadiwi sat back down and got ready to sew again.

Soolchakan looked at Bikaropin. "I think I got her," he said with a lot of surprise. "She did…respond. It has no practiced capability but…someone responded."

Bonarain looked even more hopeful.

Bikaropin chuckled. "Call her again."

"She seems very…hesitant to respond. There might be someone else there…that she fears…greatly."

Bikaropin nodded. "Then inform her of how to respond mentally."

"DO IT," said the wide-eyed Bonarain through clenched teeth!

Soolchakan took in a deep breath and blew it out. He shook his head, shrugged and decided to give it a try. He sent the message again along with some imagery on how to send mental messages. He decided that the best way to get her to respond in a positive manner was to use the *Power*.

She stuck herself with the needle as she mentally received this new message along with some very strange images. She looked at the bedroom door. She responded to the mental antagonist. **"Hello? Who are you? What do you want**?"

Now Soolchakan was the one standing there with a shocked look on his face. **"If you are who I think you are then…I am your father. I've been trying…any way that I can to contact you and…find you.**"

She swallowed hard. She noticed that her finger was bleeding from the prick of the needle. She knew that she would be in a huge amount of trouble if she got any of her blood on the pants. She held her bleeding finger against the rags that she was wearing. **"I think that…I've heard you…at other times but…I didn't know what you were doing or saying. If you're my father…what could you possibly do? Are you going to come here and buy me away from my master**?"

He hung his head. **"I am absolutely coming for you and I will free you from any bondage that you're under at this time.**"

She checked her finger to see if it was still bleeding. **"That's gonna cost a lot of money. My master likes owning me and he said that he'll never sell me to anyone. Are you sure you have enough to…make him change his mind**?"

Soolchakan looked rather solemn. **"I WILL make him change his mind.**" He nodded. "Or I'll remove his mind with a healthy blast from…some kind of weapon."

Bonarain and Bikaropin both looked rather confused over

the last statement.

Soolchakan saw their confusion. "I'm in contact with her…at least I hope that it *is* Nadiwi…otherwise we've got another Owlamite out there that we didn't know of…who *is* younger than I am."

Bonarain covered her mouth with her hands. "**Ask her if she *is* Nadiwi**."

Soolchakan grunted in disgust. "Even if she is Nadiwi, she has probably never heard her real name. We won't know…until we get there."

Now Bonarain looked worried. "How are you going to get there without a landmark of some type?"

Bikaropin chuckled nervously. "Maybe you can tell her to look around the room. Have her concentrate on something that… you probably wouldn't find anywhere else."

Soolchakan looked a little disgusted. "Like…*what*?" He scoffed. "You can find a table or chair any place. I've already read in her mind that she is sitting next to a fireplace. Big fat useless deal! How many homes have a fireplace? We don't even know which country she's in…yet."

Bikaropin thought for a moment. "Ask her if that…" He looked at Bonarain nervously. "…master…of hers…has ever mentioned any city or town that's close by."

Soolchakan pondered the suggestion. He sniffed. "**Has your…master ever mentioned any city or town that he has to go to…to get any supplies**?"

The frightened woman sat there trying to sew. She was having trouble seeing what she was doing through tears. **"My master has said...many times...that he had to go to Ymon in order to get another group of new slaves at the port**."

Soolchakan thought for a moment. He looked inquisitively at Bikaropin. "Ymon? That sounds a little familiar."

Bikaropin smiled. "Ymon? That's the capital of Slateel. A country in the far southern part of Ficara."

"Yes," said Soolchakan nodding. "Are you sure that there are no other cities or towns...anywhere in the world named Ymon?"

"She said that it was a port city," said Bikaropin with a smile. "In Slateel, the biggest port city *is* Ymon. We have a good start." He grunted. "It is a big city, but...at least we've it narrowed down to one single city."

Bonarain looked around almost frantic. "Should we go there and...start looking around the city?"

"No," said Soolchakan. "She said that he has to *go* to Ymon. That means that it would be a waste of time searching the city. We have no idea if this slaver lives north, south, east or west of the city."

Bonarain seemed even more upset. "But...Ymon is a port city. That means that one of those directions doesn't exist...if the city is on the shoreline."

"No," said Bikaropin shaking his head sadly. "The city is

not on the shoreline. There's a huge inlet that goes to the harbor where Ymon is located. The city is located all around that harbor and…yes, all four of those directions are there."

Soolchakan growled in frustration. "**My daughter, try to find something that could not possibly be at any other location. I need you to concentrate on…something that…is totally unique to your location…or you could think that it is totally unique.**"

She got up from the fireplace. She slowly walked over to a window and looked out. She looked up sadly. She concentrated on the one thing that she could think of that would not be located any other place…as far as she knew. The grotesque sight was one that could easily make her vomit. She steeled herself and stared.

Soolchakan opened his eyes in shock. He looked off to the side in revulsion. He went back to reading her mind and concentrated on the heinous sight.

Bonarain saw the disgust on his face. "What's the matter?"

Soolchakan sighed. "She is concentrating…on a Heyyah man who…has been hanged. He is…naked. He was whipped. He's been castrated. He has white hair and…a scraggly beard." He cleared his throat. "I don't think that there are very many other…of any race…who have been stripped, whipped, castrated and…hung. Even though it is…a very ghastly sight…it should be *very* unique." He swallowed. "**Do you know why that man was hung?**"

"**Master Shoolmon always picks one of any new group of slaves. He usually picks the one that…will**

**probably bring the least amount at the auction. He makes an example out of that one for the others...in case any of them have an idea of running or fighting back.**"

Soolchakan again fought back his revulsion. An innocent man who was murdered just to show how cruel and cold-blooded the slaver could be. He took several deep breaths. He looked the hanging body over several times. He hopped to Spy and then Jumped to where he was getting the same view that his daughter had. He had hit it exactly on target. He was standing in the specific spot that she was in. **"You can look away, my daughter. I have what I need.**"

She heaved a sigh of relief. She could not stand seeing any of the victims hanging from the gallows. She walked back over to the fireplace and went back to sewing.

Soolchakan looked around the big room. It was a combination kitchen and dining room. There was a long dinner table with a chair at each end and benches along the long sides. A cabinet against the wall held several stacks of plates, bowls and other assorted things that you would find in any dining room. There was a fireplace where you could heat up a big cauldron of some stew. There was also a stove near the fireplace. For many people this kitchen would seem extravagantly luxurious.

He looked at his daughter. There was no doubt that she was his daughter. She had inherited a lot of his face. She did have her mother's lips and chin. If he had any doubt about the possibility that this was one of his children, all skepticism was now gone. This had to be the long lost Nadiwi.

He memorized the stove because there were a few things about it that made it unique. He Jumped back to the gorge and hopped back to Home dimension. He sighed. "Bikaropin...I want you to get...at least twenty others. I want them armed with pulse or projectile weapons, whichever one they want. I'm going to take you to the location and...then you get your landmark. Then you come back here and get the others. We may have a problem...a *big* problem with these slavers."

Bikaropin nodded.

Bonarain walked over and grabbed Soolchakan by his arm. "I'm going with you."

He looked at her and smiled. "I had no intention of leaving you behind." He shook loose of her grip and put his arm around her. He held out his hand to Bikaropin. When he was touching both of them, he hopped back to Spy and then Jumped back to Slateel.

Soolchakan held firm to Bonarain. "Don't do anything yet. Don't show yourself even to your daughter...yet." He looked to Bikaropin. "Bring others here. Do some snooping around and find out just how many slavers we're dealing with. If they have a collection point here, I don't want to be surprised by a whole bunch of these parasites right in the middle of getting Nadiwi out of here."

Bikaropin nodded and gave an approving smile. "Good idea." He looked around. "Uh...what did you use as your main landmark?"

"That stove."

Bikaropin looked bewildered. "A stove?" He turned to look at the stove. He then nodded. "Oh! Okay, I see why. A stove with *eight* spots for cooking…that is…rather rare…especially one sitting that close to a fireplace."

"So landmark it, go back and bring some reinforcements."

Bikaropin nodded and then vanished.

Bonarain pulled away from Soolchakan. "I want to hold my daughter," she said with tears in her eyes.

"Before you do, hop her to Spy…or Observation. I don't want the first meeting with your daughter interrupted by any of the vermin that infest this place."

Her face changed from irritation to a contented smile. She walked over to Nadiwi who was still concentrating on the patch she was sewing on the pants. Bonarain tenderly placed a hand on her daughter's shoulder and hopped the unsuspecting woman to Spy.

Nadiwi was taken totally by surprise. She fell off her stool and dropped the pants. "Who…who are *you*?"

"I'm your mother. I'm Bonarain. You are my daughter – Nadiwi. I'm here to take you home. I'm here to take you away from these evil people."

Nadiwi stood up looking a little upset. "If you…are my mother…why did you sell me to these people and let them take me and put me in slavery?" She had a very hurt look in her eyes.

"They told me that you sold me to them."

Bonarain hung her head. "I had just given birth to you. I was alone when that happened." She looked up. "As I was cleaning you off…I was attacked by the slavers. I was alone against at least four of them. I killed two of them trying to fight them off but… remember I had just given birth. Most of my strength was gone. They locked me in…a place that…I couldn't get out of. Just a short time ago, your father finally found me and got me out of there. We came for you as soon as we could. I never did and never would…or could…sell…or give you away to any slaver."

Nadiwi looked sorrowfully toward the bedroom door. "They…won't let me go." She looked at Bonarain and sniffled. "How're you gonna get me out of here? Do you have enough money to buy me?"

Bonarain smiled. "Don't worry about that, Nadiwi. It will happen today." She embraced her daughter. "You are now free and we're taking you out of here today."

Nadiwi looked past Bonarain. "Who's he?"

"I'm your father," said Soolchakan softly. "I'm here to make sure that these monsters don't argue with us taking you home. If you're wondering why we haven't come for you sooner, it's because I really had no clue about you until I found your mother and got her out of that place where…" He shut his eyes and shook his head. "…well we'll give you the full story later. It is long and involved…and…it is a *long, long* story."

Nadiwi pulled back slightly from Bonarain. "So…you really *didn't* sell me to these people?"

Bonarain closed her eyes in disgust. She took a deep breath. "No! There is *no way* I would have even thought of doing something that horrible to my dear one-and-only daughter. As I said, I was weak from giving birth and fighting off four of them…I killed two of them in the process and…while I was fighting them…one of them stole you away and then…" She looked back at Soolchakan. "As he said: You'll get the full story later. Once we're out of here and we can sit down and really learn everything about each other…we'll have all the time we want."

Ansantima came out of the bedroom. "Fosk needs his diaper changed. Get in there and…" She looked around the room confused. "SLUT! WHERE ARE YOU? I DIDN'T GIVE YOU PERMISSION TO GO ANYWHERE!"

Soolchakan was affronted as he looked at the Heyyah woman. "Slut?" He looked back at Nadiwi. "Did she just call you…Slut?"

"That's my name," said Nadiwi as if it made perfect sense.

Bonarain cupped her daughter's face in her hands. "Your name is Nadiwi. I don't care what these monsters say or have said. Your name is Nadiwi. Do you understand? You never have to answer to them, or that name, again, in regards to anything."

Ansantima went to the window and looked out angrily. "WHERE ARE YOU, SLUT?" She turned back to the room.

Soolchakan was a little aggravated. He hopped his hand into Home and backhanded the slaver woman. He held back nothing when he slapped her.

Ansantima spun around from the impact and went face first to the floor. She turned over and looked very dazed. She rubbed the right side of her face as she attempted to get up. There was a rather large welt high on her right cheekbone. She had to fight to get up to her knees. She lost her balance and sat back down as she was somewhat incapacitated from dizziness.

Soolchakan hopped his face into Home. "Her name is NOT Slut! She is no longer a slave to you or anybody else. Try to argue with those facts and you'll get clobbered again." He hopped his face back to Spy leaving Ansantima stunned in more ways than one.

Bikaropin showed up with Mahanee, Hisang, Shashy and Meffin. All five were armed with pulse pistols.

"I'll be back with a few more, as soon as they're armed," said Bikaropin. He vanished.

Soolchakan turned to the newcomers. "You four start doing some reconnaissance. Find out how many more slavers, their families and how many victims they have here." He looked out the window. "I also want you to cut that poor man down. No one should be displayed like that…to anyone for any reason… especially since he has committed no crimes."

Bonarain giggled. "Unless your name is Prok."

Mahanee looked out the window. "Oh…that's disgusting!" Her body shuddered from her revulsion.

Bikaropin reappeared with Yeema, Chena, Cheesang and Dawuni. He then vanished.

Soolchakan chuckled. "Ladies, it is getting a little crowded in here. Get to your reconnaissance before we have an accident in here."

Several moments later, Bikaropin again reappeared with Basabee, Pinsong, Cymani and Soolkan. Later he showed up with Menola, Chenny, Pelox, Yarmaka, Passifi, Yakiss, Lep, Zuztay, Chejja, Yesati, Zenkin and Yaspon.

"That's enough," said Soolchakan. "I think that twenty-seven of us can handle this *bimyock* and his family."

Bikaropin smiled. "We've already got the perimeter of the compound checked out. There are five families of these monsters in the compound and fifty-nine living victims."

Soolchakan frowned. "Fifty-nine...*living*? Does that mean that there are some other dead bodies as well...other than that poor soul that was hung?"

Bikaropin nodded sadly. "Ten who have gone on...for one reason or another. Most of them were probably suicide."

Ansantima finally got her bearings. She stood up and looked around confused. She slowly staggered to the window. "SHOOLMON! SLUT IS MISSING!"

Shoolmon was nearby outside. "So is that example slave. Someone cut him down. Did you see who did it?"

Nadiwi was confused. "Why can't she see me?"

Bonarain hugged her daughter closer. "We have a capability...a power to keep ourselves hidden...even in plain sight. You'll learn all of that once we get you out of here."

Soolchakan walked up beside Bonarain. "Do it."

Bonarain was the one confused now. "Do...what?"

"Get her out of here! Take her back to the gorge...now."

Bonarain smiled weakly. "I'm still out of practice."

Soolchakan sighed and his shoulders sagged. "Bikaropin, get these two women back to the gorge."

Bikaropin smiled as he hugged both of the women. "With pleasure." The trio vanished.

A few moments later Bikaropin reappeared with Pabon, Ledak, Uma and Vantil.

"I said we had enough," said Soolchakan flatly.

"A few more couldn't hurt," said Bikaropin with an innocent shrug.

Soolchakan simply grunted in resignation and shook his head.

Ansantima huffed at Shoolmon. "Someone in here hit me and...then disappeared. I think he has Slut."

Soolchakan growled. He hopped to Home, walked over to Ansantima and backhanded her again. "I told you her name is not Slut! Don't you ever call her anything other than her true name."

Ansantima was on the floor again. She looked up at Soolchakan. "Where is...uh...my slave?"

He leaned down a little. "If you're talking about Nadiwi, she's no slave, especially in this house of horror."

Ansantima was doing what she could to stand up. "We have owned her all of my life and according to my father-in-law, she has been in this family for generations. WE OWN HER COMPLETELY! Now bring her back. You can't steal the property of a slaver without consequences. *Obey!*"

Soolchakan snarled, backhanded her again and hopped to Spy. "She must love gettin' coldcocked." He shook his head as he went to Bikaropin. "Tell everyone to let those captives out of their cells. If any of the slavers make any attempt at stopping us from freeing them...have fun torturing the slavers."

"There are five families with twenty-eight children among the slavers." Bikaropin looked out the window. "Some of the children are just infants."

"I don't care how young they are," said Soolchakan sadly. "They're being raised in a society that operates outside of the law. They operate on their own laws and that is just totally... unacceptable. I think we need to send a message to all slavers everywhere that their ideology is not allowed, and will not be accepted, in any truly civilized society."

The Owlamites that were there started upsetting all of the slavers in the large compound. Because some of the captives had been broken mentally by the slavers many of them were too frightened to leave their cells. This was creating a problem for Soolchakan and his family members who were present at the location.

Shoolmon was the head of the house for the Bohosh family. He also appeared to be the reigning kingpin in this compound. Soolchakan found that he was going to have to have a face to face confrontation with the snobbish slaver.

Soolchakan hopped to Home dimension directly in front of Shoolmon. The Heyyah man was tall and burly. He was bald and had a look about him that just gave a full statement of evil. The Heyyah was surprised when someone just appeared in front of him, however, he did not let that stop him from taking over the situation.

Soolchakan started the conversation. "Because you have taken a member of my family hostage as one of your slaves, the punishment is that you lose all of your hostages. If you don't want to lose your life, you will not argue with me."

Shoolmon snickered. "You are on my property and you have no right to order a Sector Chief around at all. I am the Sector Chief of Slateel and the only one who can give me orders is the Area Chief of Ficara. Now…here are your orders. You will bring my property back to me. Since you have insulted me by trying to steal other slaves as well, you and your family will be enslaved for at least five generations. OBEY!"

Soolchakan rolled his eyes. "I don't know, or care, what a Sector Chief or Area Chief is. The rules of the low-life scum of slavers means nothing to me. Your ancestors illegally stole my daughter from my wife. I have come here and claimed her and her freedom. You will *not* interfere with that at all. I also will not allow any of my children or their children to be enslaved by you *bimyocks* for any reason. Your rules mean nothing to me. Obey that, ya *doovoft!*"

Shoolmon shook his head and chuckled. "Some people just have to learn the hard way." He pulled a whip off his belt and got ready to use it.

Soolchakan hopped to Ghost dimension and walked away from Shoolmon. "Yes, some people do have to learn the hard way." He sent a mental message to Bikaropin. **"Warm up a pulse pistol and give me some power from it.**"

Bikaropin sent back. **"You'll have to hop to Spy... unless you want me to go to Ghost.**"

**"Hold on to that for a few. I'm going to watch his reaction when he can't whip me.**"

Shoolmon had a big grin on his face as he started (what he thought would be) the subjugation of this upstart. When the whip went right through the stranger without any bloodletting or screaming by the victim, Shoolmon was again surprised. For some reason, however, he did not get the message. For a while, he thought that if he could swing the whip harder and get closer to his victim, those actions would make a difference. The whip merely went through the stranger, each time, without any damage or pain. After about twenty attempts at a strike, the big Heyyah stood there confused, sweating and panting. "WHO ARE YOU? WHAT DO YOU THINK YOU'RE DOING?"

Soolchakan looked back at him patronizingly. "I think I am taking my daughter home and I'm also going to free any of the hostages that you have here as well." He smiled. "Any more stupid questions?"

Shoolmon bared his teeth. "You have no right to take anything from a slaver. Especially one of my rank." He growled. "Bring Slut back now. My sons like playing with her…when I am not getting my sexual gratification from her."

Soolchakan hopped to Spy. "GIVE ME POWER!"

Bikaropin had his pulse pistol on a low setting. He aimed it at Soolchakan and pulled the trigger. Soolchakan stood there absorbing the power from the ray.

Soolchakan started feeling some burning along with the tingling. "Enough!" He hopped to Home, held his hands out open toward Shoolmon and shot the energy out of his hands. Shoolmon was knocked back and thrown completely through a wooden wall behind him. Soolchakan then hopped to Spy.

Off to the side another slaver had arrived in the room and he raised his whip. He was going to make an attempt at stopping the upstart stranger. A punch in the mouth from an invisible Zuztay made him change his mind. Menola came up behind the man and kicked him in the back of his left knee, knocking him down to his knees. Another slap to the back of the head put his face on the floor.

Three other slavers were standing around with whips at the ready, however, they were not sure what to do with them because any targets that were around were also invisible or very elusive, and had a mean jab.

Chenny grabbed the whip of one of them and hopped the

whip to Spy. The slaver looked around desperately trying to find his favorite toy. He panicked when he could not find it. He ran back to his house to get another one. He was tripped by Dawuni on the way. He was flattened by a few others as he continued (what was turning into) the quest back to his house.

A few more men who appeared to be in their teen years showed up with more whips and idle threats. None of them could figure out what they were supposed to be fighting. If they were supposed to be whipping someone into obedience, none of them could find any target where they could make the attempt.

Shoolmon came back through the damaged wooden wall. He had two hand-shaped burn marks on his shirt that were smoking. He also had several cuts on his entire body from flying through, and shattering, all of that wood. He ripped his shirt away and there were two hand-shaped burn marks on his chest. He screamed in anger. "THAT SLAVE…SHE IS MY PROPERTY! Bring Slut back here…NOW! She is MY sex toy. OBEY!"

Soolchakan hopped to Ghost and started walking slowly towards Shoolmon with a menacing look on his face. Several of the slavers started lashing at him with their whips – all to no avail. They were whipping nothing but air. Whips were cracking all over the place, however, Soolchakan ignored them completely. He was now directly in front of Shoolmon. "Sex toy? My daughter is no sex toy to *h'oolyach* like you. Another thing – her name is NOT Slut."

Shoolmon growled back. "She has been my sex toy since I was a little boy. She was the sex toy of my father, my grandfather and…I don't know how many generations before that. She is my property and will be so…until I say otherwise."

Soolchakan sent out a mental message to all. "**It sounds as if we need to castrate the bunch of them. Then they won't need any sex toys**."

Mahanee responded. "**I've been sending messages to Bonarain and Nadiwi. If you're going to castrate these *h'oolyach*, Nadiwi wants to be one of the surgeons**."

Soolchakan did not think long on it. He shrugged. "**Someone go get her. I think that she deserves to do most of the cutting. Or however much cutting she wants to perform**." He smiled at Shoolmon. "Since you think that she is to remain your sex toy…we're going to remove your sex…and that way you won't need her at all. You and your sons will not have anything that you can harm her with." He chuckled. "You'll have to play with yourselves. The problem is…you won't have anything to play with either. The eunuch never does."

"**Bonarain and Nadiwi are here**," sent Mahanee.

Soolchakan nodded. "**How many are we talking about**?"

Bikaropin answered. "**There are five men and nine teenage boys. There are a few teenage girls…and I don't know how much of a problem they might turn out to be. I don't know what the hierarchy is in a slaver family**."

Soolchakan sighed. "**Don't think! Just corral them anyway. How many younger boys are there**?"

"**Eight**," sent Shashy.

"**This is gonna get messy**," sent Lep.

Soolchakan hopped to Spy. "Yes, it is gonna get very messy." He sighed again. "Why does everyone want to do it the hard way? All they had to do was leave us alone and…we would have freed those people and been on our way. Now…we have to make a mess…and still free those people." He turned to Nadiwi. He saw that she had a knife in each hand. He did not like that evil look in her eyes, however, he hoped that after "snipping" a few of the slavers, she would have some satisfaction.

Bonarain smiled. "Let's start with this Shoolmon. Since he likes examples, we'll make an example of him for the rest of the slaver *h'oolyach* to see. Maybe then they'll realize that we mean business."

Shoolmon suddenly found himself being lifted by people he could not see. He could feel hands on his arms and legs, however, he could see no one. Soolkan, Pelox, Lep, Zuztay and Pabon were carrying him to a central place in the courtyard. Shoolmon had the wind knocked out of him when he was dropped down flat on the ground. Now the Owlamite men were holding his arms legs and head down. Mahanee and Hisang came over and hopped all of his clothing into some other dimension…somewhere… else. Bikaropin hopped Nadiwi into Home dimension and now Shoolmon knew that he was in deep trouble. He saw the look in her eyes, saw the two knives in her hands and felt all of the weight on his arms and legs that were preventing him from moving. The other members of this slaver group were being held back and disarmed by forces they could not see and they were equally baffled and afraid of what was happening in front of them.

Shoolmon tried to take over even though he was currently helpless. "I am a Sector Chief!" He looked at his underlings. "No one can treat a slaver, let alone a Sector Chief like this! Stop this nonsense now or…I swear you'll regret ever having heard of me."

"Yes we can," said Soolchakan in a taunting manner. "We can treat slaver scum any way we want to."

Lep and Zuztay forcefully spread the legs of Shoolmon as Nadiwi walked up to him with the two knives. She knelt down and used one of the knives to lift her target, the other knife was used for slicing. Shoolmon screamed as he lost all parts of his masculinity in one quick painful slice.

Zuztay had absorbed some power from a pulse pistol and now used that power to cauterize the huge hole in the groin of Shoolmon. Shoolmon no longer had a penis or his testicles (and a good sized chunk of the skin that surrounded that area).

Nadiwi flipped the amputated flesh away with one of the knives and stood up. She had a very satisfied smile on her face. "I want them all. I want all of the men who forced themselves on me. Which one is next?"

Bikaropin looked around somewhat confused. He smiled helplessly. "Uh…which one is next? Uh…which one do you want?"

Shoolmon was picked up and thrown over a fence into a pen where they normally kept slaves. He lay there wallowing in pain, from the cut and burn. He could do very little to make any attempt at fighting back. When he stood up, he staggered in a rather awkward, bowlegged manner toward the fence.

Several of the slavers were trying to get at anyone they could see…or not see. Nadiwi they recognized. The others were playing with them by hopping in and out of Home dimension. The slavers were very frustrated with these odd strangers, especially since every time someone appeared out of thin air, a slaver got punched or kicked in the face - hard. They were also having a rather difficult time keeping any whip or club in their hands because somehow their weapons kept magically disappearing.

Bikaropin did not know which one Nadiwi wanted first – or next. He read her mind to see if he could pick out a face among the slavers. He saw a face in her mind and heard the name Todok. He started searching the minds of the slavers. He finally found Todok. This was the oldest son of Shoolmon. He was only 16 years old and was thinking of how he was already a Chainman Fifth Class (whatever that is), and could not be treated this way by slaves, or slaves-to-be. Bikaropin signaled to Lep, Zuztay, Zenkin and Pabon. The five of them grabbed Todok and carried him to the center of the courtyard where Nadiwi was waiting. Once again the slaver was slammed to the ground and held down by the men. His clothing was hopped into another dimension by the women. Once again Nadiwi completely removed all of his genitals with one quick slice of the knife. The wound was cauterized and the boy was thrown in the pen with his father.

Now Nadiwi wanted the 14-year-old brother of Todok. She wanted Koldyft. This youth was a Novice Slaver. He was thinking that if he could do something spectacular in this chaos then he could go up in rank quickly. His dream was crushed, or rather "slashed" when he lost his genitals to the knives in the hands of Nadiwi.

Eleven other men were sliced by Nadiwi. Soolchakan ordered Uma to get Nadiwi back to the gorge. Nadiwi was enjoying the dissections just a little bit too much. He wanted her out of there before she became too depraved (if she was not there already).

Eight more boys were castrated by the Owlamites before the mess was over. Eleven daughters and five wives were spayed by the Owlamites as well. The spaying was more merciful than the castrations. An Owlamite woman would hop to Spy, reach into the body of the female, find the ovaries, hop them into Spy and then remove them. Ten adults and twenty-eight children were all now deprived of their sex organs and any chance at future reproduction.

Now the Owlamites went to the hostages. They found out that all of this batch came from the same village in Lower Oosam. They had all been taken in a raid on their village at the same time. They were the survivors. Over 150 had died while trying to defend against the slavers. They were farmers and not as adept at fighting as the slavers. At first they were reluctant about receiving any assistance in getting back to their homes, seeing as how *everything* had been burned. After being reminded that they knew how to build a house and grow a crop, they were ready to return and try living their lives again…while making better preparations against any other slaver attack.

Soolchakan went back to the courtyard to see all of the slavers and their families drowning in pain and self-pity. All of their sex glands were in the middle of a bonfire in the courtyard. He hopped back to Home dimension. The smell of burning flesh coming from the bonfire assaulted his nostrils.

Shoolmon sat up and tried to appear menacing. "We'll get you for this," he croaked. "It is…a crime to attack any slaver… of any rank. You have defiled a Sector Chief and his family. You have defiled this entire outpost. We *will* get revenge."

Soolchakan scoffed. "Revenge for *what*? Where I come from, you can do anything you want to a slaver and…" He shrugged. "…no crime at all…no matter what you do to the slaver." He laughed. "Kill a slaver – not a crime. Steal from a slaver – not a crime. Injure a slaver – no crime there at all. Destroy the family of a slaver – again, not a crime. There is no crime in doing anything irregular, depraved, disgusting or fatal to a slaver."

Shoolmon tried to stand. He could only get up on his knees. "We will use any and all methods of finding you. We *will* find you. When we do, I will enjoy making you pay for the healers to restore what you took from us."

Soolchakan laughed on the outside. "You'll never get revenge on us. You'll never find us." He hopped to Spy. He looked around at his family members that were there. "I want this place flattened. Get all the help you need. I don't want to see two pieces of wood nailed together. I don't want to see two bricks mortared together. Either destroy everything or…take it somewhere else. I want these monsters left with *nothing*. I don't even want them to be left with any other clothing to cover their rancid *butts*." He Jumped to the gorge.

Bikaropin sighed and shook his head. "You heard him. I think that it'd be best if each one of us goes back to the gorge and gets some more assistance."

No one argued with that idea.

They each returned with at least three others. It took some time, however, by the time they were finished, no two pieces of wood were nailed together (not even the fence surrounding the now neutered slavers), no two bricks were mortared together, the foundations were completely gone or shattered, all slaves had been returned to their home (very much to their surprise), all animal livestock was sent to Lower Oosam with the ex-slaves, all dishes were shattered, all cooking vessels were on a ship in dimension #45, all weapons were sitting in Stink and all clothing was shredded and burned...or hopped to different dimensions.

The slavers now had nothing at all. The slavers did not even have their hidden fortune either. During the destruction of all of the structures in the compound, a secret underground vault was discovered. All of the contents of that vault were now in the gorge. The, formerly rich, slavers were totally destitute of absolutely anything and everything.

Bikaropin was troubled over the fact that the slavers did not seem too despondent over losing everything. Their demeanor was still one of hostile arrogance. They were planning some kind of retribution. He was not sure how they were going to do it.

He tried reading their minds to find out, however, their thoughts were more about anger (and pain) than planning. They were very determined and very unrepentant. Very disturbing. They seemed to be waiting…for something or someone. But who or what… very confusing.

# 2

Bikaropin, Mahanee and Hisang returned from the demolition of the slaver compound and went directly to Soolchakan.

"They're not grieving," said Bikaropin. "They're scheming."

"They haven't got anything," said Soolchakan looking rather bewildered. "What have they got to…" He shook his head and looked around rather baffled. "…scheme with? They have nothing."

Mahanee cleared her throat and looked a little nervous. "Maybe we should ask the one who…knows them best."

Soolchakan looked at her expecting more.

"Maybe…Nadiwi can help us with…something," said Hisang with a shrug.

Soolchakan was now deep in thought on that idea. He nodded. "People who keep slaves…they do have a tendency to treat their slaves as if they were part of the wall. They speak openly and freely around them." He looked up to the second floor of his apartment. Bonarain was up there with Nadiwi, giving her all kinds of instructions on how to live like a free person. Forget all of the bowing and kneeling – stand tall and forget being afraid of anybody or anything or…everything.

Bikaropin continued. "Over the years, she has to have heard something of their tactics and just…exactly how they would extract vengeance…even though they've been thoroughly defeated."

Soolchakan nodded. "**Bonarain, bring Nadiwi down here to the main room**."

Bonarain heard the mental message. She was somewhat miffed at this at first. She reconsidered over the fact that Nadiwi was his daughter and since she was currently the one and only living offspring, of either one of them, who was not buried in a vault on Zhagool, maybe he wanted to get better acquainted with her as well. She smiled at Nadiwi. "Your father wants to talk to you."

Nadiwi smiled back with some tears in her eyes. "Talk! I like that."

"What do you like best about that?"

Nadiwi sniffled a little. "Because for once…I can be in the same room with a man…that I don't have to have sex with… and he doesn't want to have sex with me. I love him and he loves me…without me having to do some…" She looked off to the side, bit her lip, cleared her throat and sniffed. A tear ran down her right cheek. "…something nasty and disgusting."

Bonarain felt a pang in her heart over that. She hugged Nadiwi close. "For the rest of your life, you won't ever have to worry about having sex…unless *you* want to."

"I don't want it…and I never will," she said bitterly.

"Don't make any hasty decisions now, my daughter."

They smiled at each other and then proceeded to the first floor.

The two women came down the stairs and Bikaropin stood there frowning. "Why didn't you just Jump down here?"

"*I'm* still a little out of practice," scolded Bonarain. "Nadiwi has *never* done it."

Bikaropin flushed and pursed his lips while studying the ceiling.

Mahanee decided to start the conversation while Bikaropin wallowed in his embarrassment and self-pity. "We were at the compound and we completely demolished everything. We found their family fortunes and we've confiscated all of that. What we didn't take from them we destroyed. They have absolutely nothing. We took their genitals so that they can no longer procreate. We took their clothing so they're all completely naked. We destroyed their homes so there is no roof over their heads or anything left of walls to their homes. We burned all of the lumber that used to be walls. We took their tools, so they cannot build. As I said we found the vaults with their family fortunes and we took that so they can't buy food or clothing or even find temporary lodging except something under a tree. They have nothing, yet, they're treating this situation as if it were just a minor setback. They're scheming to get back at us as if…all we did was give them a mildly embarrassing slap in the face. Maybe you can tell us something about this mindset as to why they're so unrepentant or even saddened."

Nadiwi shrugged. "They're slavers. They have a network that works as a secret society. My Master Shoolmon…"

"Don't ever call him master again," said Soolchakan looking a little disgusted. "He has nothing on you anymore and he never will again. And if he tries, I will make sure that he never can…one way or another. He will never be master to anyone… ever again…especially you."

Nadiwi smiled. "Yes. Thank you." She cleared her throat. "*That*…slaver Shoolmon is a Sector Chief. He's in charge of several other Chiefs that are all over that country…that he lives in."

Soolchakan groaned. "Maybe you better start by explaining the rank structure of the slavers. I hear Sector Chief and Chief… I've also heard Chainman Fifth Class and Novice. Maybe if I knew their hierarchy of ranks, I could understand it a little better and you'd have to explain it a little less often."

Nadiwi sat down at one of the tables and sighed. "Okay, the boys start out as a Novice, usually, at 13 years old. As a Novice, you have no authority over anybody…except the slaves… and then not much of that. You don't do anything to the slaves without the permission of someone higher. If a higher ranking slaver tells a Novice to do something they had better do it because they're not much higher than a slave. Just above that is Chainman Sixth Class. If you've done a good job as a Novice you get that rank. You don't have much more power, but now you can order other Novices about. Then above that is Chainman Fifth Class. Then Chainman Fourth Class, then Chainman Third Class, then Chainman Second Class, then Chainman First Class. Those are the main workers. The lower your number the higher your rank. Then you have the Chief. A Chief is in charge of a province…" She looked confused. "…whatever that is. All Chiefs answer to the Sector Chief. The Sector Chief is in charge of a country. The Sector Chief answers only to the Area Chief. That one is in charge of a continent." She frowned again. "Whatever that is."

Soolchakan sighed. "I see they work in geographical ways." He hung his head then glanced up at Bonarain. "One of the things that we're definitely going to need to teach her - geography!"

Hisang was a little confused. "How do you know all of this? You were a slave. How could you know about all of their ranks?"

Nadiwi sighed. "My mother told me that I'm 4,354 years old. So don't forget that until I was rescued, all of that time was spent listening to the *follof* of different slavers as they grew up… obtained higher ranks and…tried to impress me when they went from Chainman Fifth Class to Chainman Fourth Class…or higher. I watched them grow up, become more and more cruel, obtain higher and higher ranks…and then finally die. When they died, someone else got that rank."

Bikaropin broke in. "Did anyone ever kill to get a higher rank?"

Nadiwi snickered. "Oh no. You *are* a slaver, loyal to *all* slavers. You don't kill another slaver under any circumstances... unless ordered to do so by the Area or Sector Chief. If you kill a slaver, without permission, and the other slavers find out, your entire clan is wiped out. You only kill another slaver if they've killed a slaver without permission. Then, and only then, does a slaver legally kill another slaver."

Soolchakan nodded. "So how many clans were in that compound?"

Nadiwi looked up and grunted in disgust. "There was the Bohosh clan. That was Shoolmon. He and his wife, Ansantima. Their oldest son, Todok, is 16 and he's a Chainman Fifth Class. Their next son, Koldyft is 14 and a Novice. Then there's a daughter, Tweea, who is 10. Next is a son, Ongsool who is 9. A daughter, Tavaki who is 7. A son, Nokloon who is 5. A daughter, Teppet who is 3 and then the last son, Fosk who just turned one year old."

"We don't need all the names, just clans," said Soolchakan softly with a smile.

Nadiwi smiled nervously. "There is the Kekwa clan. The master of that house is a Chainman Second Class. He has two sons who are Chainman Sixth Class and then three daughters younger than that. There is the Toodochim clan. He's a Chainman Second Class. He has four daughters. Saysost clan. He's a Chainman Third Class. His oldest son is a Chainman Fourth Class. He has two more sons who are Chainman Sixth Class. He has another son and a daughter as well. Last is the Umtavock clan. He's a Chainman First Class. He has two sons who are Novices. He has four other sons who aren't old enough to go on raids yet."

Hisang was getting disgusted with the rank system. "So these people go on raids and enslave the people of their own communities?"

"Oh no," said Nadiwi. "The ones who are in that compound…if someone wants to do a raid in their area…" She looked puzzled. "Where was I…exactly?"

Bikaropin answered. "You were in a compound that was near the city of Ymon in the country of Slateel."

Nadiwi nodded. "Okay. In order for someone to do a raid anywhere in…uh…Slateel, they have to make arrangements with the Area Chief and the Sector Chief first. They then make arrangements with the Chief of the province where they're going to make their raid. The Chief and all of the Chainmen and Novices in that country help with the raid because they know the area. The people who are taken, are then moved to a completely different place. That way, they're not near anyone who knows them. They can be sold to someone who is not from their home and that way, no one shows any of the slaves any favoritism because of family relations."

"That stinks," said Bikaropin! "Take them off somewhere else…so that even if they do know the slavers, from their area, who victimized them…they can't do a thing about it because now, they're among nothing but complete strangers…as their masters and tormentors. They can't even try to make the ones they're acquainted with feel guilty at all. If it was someone that their children grew up with, there might be a bit of guilt but…seeing as how they're taken completely away, no one cares about them and they have no one who will care about their welfare."

"That also means that no one, who was abducted, can tell others in that area, which people to be aware of…as slavers," spat Bonarain.

Soolchakan growled. "So this Area Chief…Shoolmon… just needs to wait until another slaver comes along to make one of those raiding deals and…what happens then?"

"They'll tell what happened and start looking for us," said Nadiwi. "They'll use any method they can…to find us." She looked a little apprehensive.

"And they all stick together," said Bikaropin in a sour manner with his teeth clenched tight.

Soolchakan hung his head. "We're gonna have to have someone stand guard there. We'll have to have someone there all the time to watch over them and make sure that they don't find us."

Bikaropin clicked his tongue. "Stand guard and do… what? If they try to do something…what do we do to stop it?"

Soolchakan smiled. "They're gonna use any method to find us, let's use any and all methods to make sure that they *don't* find us. They'll probably start with magic. Bring some wizard who will look for us. Whoever is standing guard at the compound… has a free ticket to do *anything* to stop them."

Bikaropin stood up with an evil grin on his face. "No limits?"

Soolchakan looked at him grimly. "Protect Owlamites and the gorge...at all costs."

Bikaropin nodded. "I'll go back and take the first watch. I'll see if they're trying to set something up...and with whom."

Soolchakan sent a private thought to Bikaropin. **"Don't take too many trips there. I may need your help in figuring out what to do on this end**."

Bikaropin smiled, gave a thumbs up and vanished.

Soolchakan looked back at the ones present in the room. "We may have opened up another chapter in...chaotic messes of our lives...just like the Teltermak. This time it just happens to be...a bunch of Heyyah slavers."

Mahanee shook her head dejectedly. "Another blood bath?"

Soolchakan nodded sadly.

Bonarain shrugged. "If we're getting rid of slavers, we're not going to be losing anything important."

Nadiwi giggled and grinned brightly. "I agree."

Soolchakan looked at Nadiwi and smiled. "All right. What all do you know about this secret society and where they live...and who they are?"

Nadiwi shook her head. "I know of those ranks. I know that occasionally another slaver visits to set up a raid. When the raid is set up, all of the men, over 13, disappear for a few days. That puts the women in charge at home. When the men come back, some of them have injuries that have to be tended to. Then…life goes on…as normal."

"Normal," scoffed Soolchakan! He shook his head in disgust.

Hisang looked up. "Have you ever seen where…one or two of the men…did *not* return?"

Nadiwi thought for a few moments. "Not very often. If that did happen…I think that whoever killed, or injured, a slaver was put on trial by the slaver clans. That person was always found guilty of the unspeakable crime of defiling a slaver. The penalty was always slow death by whipping." She looked away looking nauseous. "They were usually a mess…before they finally died. Then the body was hung…until it rotted and no one could put up with the smell any more."

Soolchakan nodded. "We are going to have to teach them that killing a slaver is absolutely *not* a crime."

Bikaropin called back mentally. **"They've already got some people here to assist in getting these *bimyocks* back on their feet. They're also talking about getting some wizard in here and finding out who had the audacity to attack slavers. They want to have total vengeance upon us as soon as possible**."

Soolchakan scoffed in disgust, again. **"Meffin, I want you to relieve Bikaropin at that compound…or what's left of it. If this wizard gets there while you're there… keep him…or her distracted. Anything that you can do to upset their concentration will foul their spell**." He turned to Bonarain. "I think that you need to start analyzing the imagery of these spells. You seem to be the only one who can look these things over and figure them out."

Bonarain hung her head. "I couldn't figure out something as simple as a dirt ramp and you want me to figure out something that is complicated."

"*That* is your talent!" Soolchakan said softly. "You have problems with the simple. When it comes to simplifying the complicated…you're a genius."

Bonarain looked up. She took the compliment and smiled with her eyes tearing slightly. "When did you become so knowledgeable…and sweet?" She readied herself for the task.

"When I realized where your best talents are." He shrugged. "We can't all be good at everything. If we were…who would we talk to or go to, regarding something we don't know? Anything you want to talk about…the response would be: I know." He rolled his eyes. "Boring!"

She smiled and wiped a few more tears away. "Okay, show me the imagery. I'll take the complicated…and do what I do best." She laughed a little at her comment.

# 3

Soolchakan started sending some of the imagery to Bonarain. There were quite a few of them so he had to give an explanation with each one. While he was sending the imagery, Mahanee and Hisang were mentally following along. They would show Bonarain some references as to what was witnessed when each of the images was in the mind of the spell-caster, be it magical, orthodox, healer or demimondaine.

After two days of these studies, Bonarain finally had an analysis. "You have to study mathematics, geology and chemistry to understand the ones that fall under magical. The Major Wizard or Coalescent requires someone to be very well versed, if not a genius, in both mathematics and chemistry along with a good knowledge of geology. The Minor Wizard or Circumambient doesn't require the same expertise but...you still need to have a basic understanding of math and chemistry. The Orthodox requires less on mathematics and more on...some kind of devotion to a cause. When I say devotion...I mean that in some cases it is radically or fanatically devoted. The Environmental, which seems to be secondary to the Orthodox is still radical, but, it is radical to nature and not some...deity, unless that deity represents nature. The Healer...this requires devotion to working with anatomy.

You have the positive, the negative and commingling. The first is nothing but positive. You don't hurt anyone. You help everyone... no matter how rotten they might be. The second is nothing but negative. You don't help anyone...unless it is the person who hired you as an assassin. The third...is weaker than both because you're trying to mix positive with negative and that...is rather difficult to do because it seems to weaken both of them. That last one." She scoffed in disgust. "That demimondaine thing isn't even magic. All of it is drug induced and keeping the blood pressure up with some kind of prolonged...promiscuity."

Soolchakan sighed. "For the most part, we've already figured that out on the debauchery of demimondaine. What we want to know – can we do, or figure out, all of this stuff?"

Bonarain snickered. "Why? What we do falls in the lesser category of Magic and Orthodox otherwise known as the Hyperphysical. We have a natural ability that you can't just really learn it, you either can do it or you cannot. We can do it because it is in the genes of an Owlamite to be able to do it. We can't show anyone else, who is not Owlamite, how to do it – only those of our own race...because anyone in our race can do it. Anyone of another race...forget it. They can't learn our ways because they are not of Owlam bloodlines or capabilities."

Soolchakan looked impatient. "The question still is: Are we capable of learning and doing those spells?"

She took in a deep breath and huffed. "Yes, we can." She now looked impatient. "I don't understand why, because it would take quite a while to learn all of them. It would take a lot longer to learn those things than what we do by just sharing imagery."

Soolchakan rolled his eyes. "I am over 14,500 years old. I don't feel old. I am not getting slower. I think…that I have plenty of time to learn. Consider how old the younger ones are. They *absolutely* have plenty of time to learn. Consider, also, the more we know, the more power we have. Knowledge *is* power."

Bonarain nodded. "Yes it is. We still have a very small population. The more powerful we are…even with a small population…the less *h'oolyach* we have to take from anybody… including slavers."

He nodded. "Speaking of population…have you seen that information on the combining of the power of the red and blue stones? Have you seen how that combination is supposed to restore life?"

She bit her lip. "It scares me. Should we really be… messing with that?"

"I don't think that it'll hurt to try."

"But…who do we start with? What would happen if we screw things up and…a person ends up as…some kind of, mentally or physically, unnatural…*thing*?"

He raised his eyebrows. "I already said that I wanted to do it in the order in which they were born. That means that we start with Kiyalee."

She cocked her head to the side. "Can I make a suggestion?"

He blew his breath out impatiently. "Okay, make a

suggestion, as long as it *is* relevant."

"Let's do the first experiment on…someone who doesn't matter.  That way, if we foul it, or them, up…it *doesn't* matter."

He frowned.  "And just *whom* are you suggesting we use as our throw-away, experimental laboratory rodents?"

She smiled.  "We have ten slavers and twenty-eight of their children.  If we end up turning one, or more, of them into some kind of unnatural, or gibbering idiot…or totally deformed atrocity…who cares?"

He did not have to think long on that idea.  **"Meffin, this is Soolchakan.  Are you still at the slaver compound?"**

**"No.  Right now, Menola is taking a turn watching the *h'oolyach*."**

He grunted in frustration.  **"Menola, this is Soolchakan. Are you in the slaver compound?"**

**"Yes, why?"**

**"Is anything going on there right now?"**

**"Right now, they have some other slavers bringing food and clothing to the ones we spanked.  They're also talking about getting some Healers here to restore the lost…*organs*.  They're also talking about getting some wizard in here to find out who hurt them and where those wretched defilers are located."**

He nodded while in thought.  **"Bikaropin will be there shortly to pick one of them up."**

Menola frowned. "**Why**?"

He grinned. "**Because we need a lab rodent to experiment on. We need one of them because if we foul the experiment and one of them suffers irreparable damage…who cares**?"

Menola smirked. "**Sounds good to me**."

Soolchakan redirected his contact. "**Bikaropin, where are you**?"

"**In my apartment eating some fruit…why**?"

"**We need a rodent to experiment on. We need one of the slavers, or a member of one of the families to use for this experiment**." He went on to explain why.

Bikaropin sat there thinking. "**I think we need one who can't really fight back. I think we need one of the younger children for that purpose**."

Soolchakan sighed and turned to Bonarain. "Where is Nadiwi…right now?"

"She's working with Dawuni and Cymani on some of the Owlamite special abilities."

"Go get her."

Nadiwi was in on the conversation. "I'm still a little squeamish about my skills. Remember I wasn't able to do any of it for over 4,300 years. Why don't you have Dawuni bring me there?"

Soolchakan called out to Dawuni.  Moments later Dawuni, Cymani and Nadiwi were in the main room in Soolchakan's apartment.

Soolchakan did not like the idea of picking on children, however, he was in complete agreement with Bonarain on experimenting first on someone (or something) that did not matter.  "Nadiwi, who are the youngest girls…among those slaver families?"

Nadiwi frowned and then looked up as she was thinking.  "Let's see there's Teppet Bohosh who is three years old and Veevoo Kekwa who is four."

Soolchakan grimaced.  "Is there…someone just a little bit older?"

"There's Tavaki Bohosh…she's 7 years old.  After that is a boy and a girl who are 8 years old, then one 9 year old.  After that there are three girls and two boys who are ten."

Soolchakan steeled himself for the task at hand.  **"Bikaropin, come here to my apartment.  Get Nadiwi and take her to the slaver compound.  Find this Tavaki Bohosh and bring her to…the Chok spacecraft in 45 that we've been using for…so many purposes**."

Bikaropin finished the last of the fruit.  He took a few moments contemplating and then Jumped to apartment 12-562.  "Which one of the spacecraft do we want to go to in 45?"

"That big Chokchakchok ship we've been keeping in good condition.  I think that'd be the best place for this…experiment.

They have a big hospital bay on that ship. That's where we'll do this."

Bonarain huffed. "Everything is *big* on a Chok ship."

Bikaropin nodded. He walked to Nadiwi, took her hand and the two of them vanished.

Soolchakan took Bonarain's hand. "Shall we?"

Bonarain nodded.

Soolchakan Jumped the two of them to the medical bay on the ship in 45. Dawuni and Cymani Jumped with them.

Soolchakan looked around remembering some of the fights they had with this bunch of giant, hairy creatures. He did not have long for nostalgia because Bikaropin appeared in the hospital with Nadiwi and a rather frightened young Heyyah girl.

"We have to start this by killing her," whispered Bonarain. "Who is…going to…do the deed?"

Soolchakan shook his head. "**I can't order someone else to do this. I'll do it myself…no matter how much it hurts**." He frowned as he looked over at Bikaropin. "**Bikaropin… why do you have a…pulse pistol with you? Were you worried about that child…overpowering you**?"

Bikaropin let out a low snarl. "**Just in case you need some extra power…I brought this to feed power to you…or Bonarain. The text on those stones says that it *takes* from you when you're restoring life. If I can give something back to you…with the power of the pulse**

**pistol...why not try it**?"

Soolchakan stared at Bikaropin. "**Good idea.**" He looked down at the child. "**Did you say anything to her...like we're not going to hurt you**?"

"**I didn't say a thing to her. We just grabbed her and...here we are.**"

Soolchakan picked a rather ugly looking piece of surgical equipment off of a tray. He hopped to Spy. He walked around behind the sniffling, frightened girl. He closed his eyes and tried to think of something that would justify his next act. He could think of nothing rational or even slightly reasonable. He clenched his teeth, hopped back to the spot in 45 and rammed the big blade into the child's back as close to the cardiac area as possible. She grunted in surprise and fell to her knees on the floor. "Check her pulse and let me know when she...is...dead." He walked over to a trash container and threw up.

Bikaropin picked up one of the mechanical devices and turned it on. He started scanning the child. "The thrust was accurate," he said quietly. "She died...almost instantly. The brain activity is rapidly diminishing...there's no circulation...no respiration." He looked over at Soolchakan. "She...is dead."

Bonarain was sickened as well. "Do we start now?"

Soolchakan shook his head. "No! We wait until tomorrow. That way...we know that she has been completely dead... for at least a day. Then we'll start the procedure." He turned to Bikaropin. "Tomorrow, bring more than one pulse pistol. I may need some help and...so will Bonarain." He cleared his throat. "If this doesn't work...properly...or even if it does...we may need to get...one or more of those ten-year-olds for...further experimentation."

Bikaropin nodded. "Tomorrow." He picked the lifeless body up. He placed the corpse on a gurney that was designed for one of the big Chokchakchok people. The tiny body seemed to be lost on the giant table. "Tomorrow."

All of the Owlamites went back to their apartments.

Bonarain went to Soolchakan as he was brooding. She shook her head. "What is your problem? You've killed a lot of Heyyah and Axswain and Cacktash and Teltermak and...lots of others. What's the problem with that one?"

He gave her a bitter glare. "The day it becomes easy...to kill anyone...especially a child...is the day that I cease to function with any form of morality in my heart and soul."

She nodded. She then went back to Nadiwi to give more instructions in Owlamite capabilities.


Soolchakan was the first to arrive at the Chokchakchok ship. He simply sat there staring at the body. Even after the others started arriving he did not move. He could not understand why this killing was bothering him more than others. He did remember what he had told Bonarain though. Killing should never be easy. If it is necessary to save your own life than so be it. It was still not easy to just commit cold blooded murder.

Bonarain was able to Jump to 45 by herself. She was

now back in practice at hopping and Jumping, or at least doing everything she could to get back into the practice. She brought Nadiwi with her.

Mahanee, Hisang, Bikaropin, Shashy, Meffin, Soolkan and Pelox all showed up for the experiment.

The corpse was placed on a smaller table. Since they had no idea what might happen, if the resurrection actually did occur, Bikaropin and Soolkan tied the girl down to the table. Mahanee and Hisang each turned the pulse pistol power packs on. They put them to their lowest setting. Soolchakan went to one side of the table and Bonarain to the other. Mahanee was behind Soolchakan and Hisang stood behind Bonarain.

Soolchakan took a deep breath. "Let's get this thing started. We don't need any long speeches…just…start."

Soolchakan and Bonarain both leaned over the body close to the upper torso. They held their stones up and immediately the two stones pulled together. Together they started glowing purple and purple rays were coming out of the merging.

**"Start concentrating on…giving life to the girl,"** sent Soolchakan. He closed his eyes.

Bonarain nodded. She closed her eyes and thought only about seeing this child with her eyes open and being alert.

Suddenly all of the purple rays that were coming out were all going down to the dead body. They were rapidly going all the way from head to foot. In a very short time the girl started stirring.

Bonarain opened her eyes. She looked rather shocked. Her

knees buckled a little. She had to hold herself up against the table. Soolchakan opened his eyes. He looked more concerned than shocked. He leaned against the table. Both of them then started sagging to the floor. Mahanee and Hisang aimed the pistols at the two and pulled the triggers. Soolchakan and Bonarain began absorbing the power from the pistols and both were able to stand back up. Both of them were still breathing harder.

Tavaki opened her mouth and started gasping for air. She was writhing on the table as life was back into her body. Everyone there was a little stunned when they saw this phenomenon happening in front of them. When the breathing became less labored, Tavaki opened her eyes. She had a wild and frightened demeanor as she looked around at all of the Owlamites standing around her.

The two stones separated. Soolchakan and Bonarain backed away, both covered in perspiration.

"**That was…unusual**," sent Soolchakan.

Bonarain cleared her throat. "**Very unusual. I wonder if that's what we're going to go through for all of them**." 

"**We'll know more…later**," sent Soolchakan.

"**Right now, let's get her off of the table and see how she functions…mentally…after being dead for a full day**," sent Bikaropin.

Pelox untied her legs while Bikaropin untied her arms. They then assisted her in getting off of the table. She fell flat on her face. She was helped back to her feet. Any movement or walking she did was extremely awkward, unbalanced and very unsteady.

All of the Owlamites tried to read her mind. All they got was a bunch of gibberish. Her mind was completely confused. She seemed afraid, however, she did not know what she was afraid of. She wanted to go…somewhere, however, she did not know where or why or what to do when…or if she got there. She recognized nothing around her in a rational manner. She had no thoughts of family, friends or home.

Soolchakan turned away and gritted his teeth. **"Go get those three ten-year-olds. We're going to have to experiment further**."

Nadiwi started sending thoughts. **"Actually…there's five of the ten-year-olds. Three girls and two boys**."

Soolchakan nodded. **"Fine! Bring all of them**."

Nadiwi looked at Bikaropin. He smiled helplessly, nodded and took her hand. The two of them vanished. Mahanee, Hisang and Pelox went with them. Shashy. Meffin and Soolkan stood there looking rather nervous for a few moments. Shashy and Soolkan vanished while Meffin continued caring for the young Heyyah girl.

Bikaropin and Nadiwi reappeared with a boy in tow.

**"This is Chanjim Umtavock**," sent Nadiwi.

Soolchakan did not care who he was. He looked around. **"Where are the others**?"

Bikaropin responded. **"The other children have been taken to different places on this ship. That way, none of them know what's going to happen to any of them and... well they're just going to have to be ignorant until we start...using them.**" He looked away nervously.

Soolchakan closed his eyes. **"So do it.**"

Bikaropin clenched his teeth. He grabbed the boy's head and with a quick jerk, broke his neck. The boy slumped to the floor. He picked the body up and placed him on the table.

Several monitors were connected to the body in one way or another. They watched as all of the bodily functions shut down. When there was no more beeping or reaction by any of the monitors they all looked to Soolchakan.

Soolchakan walked over to the side of the table. **"Let's go ahead and try it with this one now.**"

The results were the same. Soolchakan and Bonarain had to receive power assistance from the pulse pistols. The child woke up and had no lucid thoughts or physical coordination. His broken neck had been healed. They brought each of the other children in and tried again with each one. All the results were the same. Now they had six Heyyah children who were mentally trashed and physically incapable of doing anything on their own, including walking or feeding themselves.

Bikaropin sat there looking at the children. **"May I make a suggestion**?"

Soolchakan was sitting in a chair with his head tilted back

and his eyes closed. He did not move. **"If you think that it is in any way productive - yes."**

Bikaropin looked around anxiously. **"From what you've told me...about these stones, they seem to work best when...all four of them are in play. Since you have the red and the blue here...I guess that the yellow and green are...still with the bodies of Kiyalee and Chyning."**

Soolchakan still did not move. **"They are."**

Bikaropin scratched his head. **"Since Kiyalee and Chyning aren't capable of using them right now... maybe you could loan the two stones to...Mahanee and Hisang. They could give it a try with all four stones... together."**

Soolchakan opened his eyes and frowned at Bikaropin.

Bikaropin continued. **"There is still a lot of that text from that ship. Traitor was able to translate some of it, but, not all of it. Maybe...with all four stones together... the yellow and green could...in some way...enhance the actions of the blue and red."**

Soolchakan was rather uneasy about this thought. He had been wearing the red stone ever since he obtained it from that odd ship. The thought of allowing someone else to wear the stone was just unheard of. He could not imagine taking the yellow and green off of Kiyalee and Chyning. There was a lot of the needed text that had not been translated. Traitor was the only one who had been able to translate what they had. He had no intention of asking for her help in translating the rest of it. That would tell her that she was needed. He did not want to give her that privilege at all… ever. "**I have a different idea.**"

Soolchakan Jumped back to his apartment. He picked up a lantern. He then Jumped to the vault on Zhagool where the body of Kiyalee was entombed. The air was a little stale and he had forgotten how cold it was there. He quickly placed his hand on the sarcophagus, hopped to Spy and Jumped it to the medical lab on the Chokchakchok ship.

Soolchakan sighed. "**We have to test his theory. We're not going to take the stone from Kiyalee…we're going to…bring her back and…see if her yellow stone… reacts with the red and blue.**"

Bonarain felt a little fear over this plan, however, she had nothing that could be called a better suggestion. It seemed logical, if not desperate. She felt uneasy about loaning her stone to someone else as well. Even when she had ended up naked inside that fort, the one thing she never took off was her stone. Taking the stone from Kiyalee or Chyning, even though they were dead, seemed rather heinous as well as unthinkable.

The concrete tomb was left in Spy. The desiccated body of Kiyalee was placed on the gurney. Everyone took their place. Soolchakan and Bonarain leaned over the body and faster than anyone could think about it all three stones seemed to grab each other. Together they turned a translucent brown and brown beams were coming out of the trio of stones. As soon as Soolchakan and Bonarain started concentrating on the body of Kiyalee all of the beams now started shooting into and enveloping her. There were several movements as the beams were striking her especially in the upper torso. Kiyalee's jaw fell open and despite the fact that the body was completely desiccated, they heard her gasping for air.

Bikaropin noticed that both Soolchakan and Bonarain were starting to buckle at the knees. He sent a mental message to Mahanee and Hisang and they pulled the trigger on their pulse pistols. Soolchakan and Bonarain started absorbing the power from the guns and were able to stand back up.

The gasping for air from Kiyalee became stronger, but less labored. She was breathing rapidly. Eyelids that had shriveled from drying up were suddenly back in place covering the formerly empty eye sockets. Kiyalee opened her eyes and looked around in shock and fear. When she recognized Soolchakan and Bonarain, she calmed down considerably.

The process continued as each one of Kiyalee's legs and arms started filling in with musculature and returning to a normal color. She still had a look of bewilderment on her face as the healing continued.

Finally, just as quickly as the beams had been aimed only at the body of Kiyalee, they were now shooting all over the room again. Soolchakan leaned back from the table and his stone fell away from the joining. Bonarain leaned back as well. Her stone left the yellow one and all of the scintillating light show was over.

Kiyalee looked around puzzled and was still panting. "What's going on?"

Soolchakan wiped perspiration from his forehead. "You

were killed...by the Teltermak. You were killed in 1816 ATUT. We just brought you back."

Kiyalee chuckled cynically. "You mean injured!"

Soolchakan shook his head. "No, you were killed." He took a deep breath. "You were killed in 1816 ATUT. It is now the year 5474 ATUT. We found out from...a source that I'll tell you about later, that the red and blue stones can bring someone back to life. You remember that Bonarain disappeared in 1120 ATUT. I found her. Once I found her, we decided to start bringing our people back."

Kiyalee looked around in disbelief. "If that's true...then... am I going to get the five of my children...who I guess were murdered by the Teltermak...back as well?"

Soolchakan sighed and hung his head. "Momatak and Loov were murdered after you were." He looked up. "All seven of your children were killed and...yes, we will be bringing all seven back."

"Do I get my children now?"

"You get them back in the order they were born. That includes the children of Bonarain and Chyning. All will be brought back in the order they were born."

Bikaropin interrupted. "I don't know if you've noticed or not but...she *is* totally lucid. The yellow stone did make a difference. I don't know what the green stone is going to do but... we definitely have progress using the yellow in conjunction with red and blue."

Kiyalee started sniffing. "What is that...*smell*?"

"It's your clothing," said Bonarain. "You've been dead for well over 3,700 years. The clothing that you were buried with... still smells like a rotted corpse."

Kiyalee looked at her body and saw the rotted fabrics. "Yuck! I *really* need a change of clothing." She sat up on the gurney. She hopped off of the gurney and fell flat on her face.

Bikaropin nodded and smiled. "The yellow stone helps with the brain. The green...it just *might* do something about the equilibrium."

Soolchakan hung his head. He was tired, however, he felt that it was necessary, right now, to bring Chyning back. He sighed. "I'll...go get Chyning. Someone else...get rid of Kiyalee's tomb."

Mahanee looked around with a frown. "Where is it?"

"In Spy," said Soolchakan. He hopped back to Spy and Jumped back to the vault on Zhagool. He looked at the concrete tomb that held Chyning. "Okay, smart-alec. You're next. Time to see if Bikaropin was right." He sighed. "I hope he is." In spite of how tired he was, he was going to see this through. He hopped the tomb to Spy and Jumped with it to the Chokchakchok ship.

There were several of the Owlamites milling around. Bikaropin, Mahanee and Shashy assisted in getting Chyning's body onto the gurney.

Soolchakan looked around. "Where's Kiyalee?"

Mahanee smiled. "She was taken back to her apartment

to get something to wear. Nadiwi, Hisang and Meffin are helping her."

Soolchakan nodded. "Uh...why does it take three?"

Mahanee shrugged. "Remember, she's a little clumsy right now."

He walked over and sat down on a chair. He looked around at some of the other chairs in the room. "Did someone refurnish this place?"

"Yes," said Bikaropin. "All of the furniture in this place was just *way* too big for any of us. We put some smaller chairs and tables in here so we could function easier in here."

Soolchakan grunted in approval. "So now we just wait while Kiyalee is primping."

Bikaropin smiled. He held up a pulse pistol. "Did you want some power while you're waiting?"

"No. I think I'll wait until I need it. I might have to blow a hole through the wall if I get too much power from that thing."

Bikaropin chuckled as he powered the pistol down and thrust it in the holster.

Bonarain walked over and sat down next to Soolchakan. "How many Owlamites are we talking about...murdered by the Teltermak?"

Soolchakan did not move. "In three different wars with those monsters...we're talking about 2,882 Owlamites that we have to bring back...minus one...since we now have Kiyalee."

Bonarain groaned and placed her fingertips against her forehead. She dropped her hands to her lap. "How many do you think…we can get done…per day?"

Soolchakan shook his head. "Who knows? We might start…with four per day. After we've had a little practice…who knows?" He shrugged.

The quartet of women returned to the Chokchakchok ship. Kiyalee was doing a few stretching exercise with her arms and legs…while sitting on the floor. The other three women were looking at hem lines to make sure that the shirt and pants fit correctly.

Kiyalee looked around cheerfully. "Hisang informed me of a few things that happened…back then and a few that happened while…I was out. When are we going to work on Chyning?"

"That depends," said Soolchakan. "Did anyone bother to bring something for Chyning to wear?"

Hisang and Meffin both grimaced in embarrassment. Nadiwi giggled.

Soolchakan stared at the three women for a few moments. "Well…go get something! *Now*, would be nice!"

Hisang and Meffin vanished.

Bonarain stood there snickering. "You seem to learn certain simple things rather quickly."

Kiyalee looked up. "Hey Bonarain, where were you all that time?"

Bonarain looked down at the floor and blushed. "I was stuck inside the walls at Fortress Island. I couldn't get out because...I didn't have any tools to build a ladder or scaffolding with. I was just...stuck."

Kiyalee scoffed. "Why didn't you just shove a bunch of dirt up against the wall and build a dirt ramp?"

Bonarain's face turned even redder as her lower jaw hit her chest. She clenched her eyes shut. She huffed a few times. "I just...didn't...think of...that," she said through clenched teeth.

Kiyalee turned to Soolchakan. "Isn't she supposed to be smart?"'

Soolchakan just sat there chuckling while Bikaropin was off to the side doing everything he could to keep from laughing out loud. A few of the other women were looking around with reddish faces from clenched lips. They were attempting to not laugh as well.

Hisang and Meffin returned and could only stand there looking confused as to why everyone (except Bonarain) was snickering.

Of course Kiyalee was a little confused about all of the giggling as well. She shrugged and shook her head.

Soolchakan regained his composure. "Let's get to it! Chyning is waiting."

Chyning was placed on the table. Soolchakan, Bonarain and Kiyalee (with some help from Hisang and Meffin) came up close. All of their stones jumped at each other. Then the green stone joined in. The four stones turned into a golden orb and gold beams shot out of the complete ball. All three of them concentrated on bringing life to Chyning. The majority of the beams were now all going into the body of Chyning. A few went to Kiyalee. The torso of Chyning started swelling up. Her face started filling out. She started breathing. The breathing was labored at first, however, it was very soon rhythmic and even. Her arms and legs filled out. Chyning opened her eyes. She looked around suspiciously. Soolchakan, Bonarain and Kiyalee started sagging. They were given power from pulse pistols and they were able to stand up again.

Chyning coughed. Then croaked a little as she spoke. "Are we going after whoever killed Sona?" Then she looked a little surprised. "BONARAIN! When did you get back?"

"We have a lot to tell you," said Soolchakan. "Right now, we need you to get up and then…we'll start the explanations."

The four stones fell away from each other.

Chyning sat up and noticed her clothing. "What…is this… foul smelling mess?"

"That's part of what we have to tell you," said Soolchakan. "The Teltermak murdered you in the year 1804 ATUT. Bonarain was found just a little while ago and we found out that these crazy stones…when working together…can bring people back to life. Right now…it is the year…5474 ATUT."

Chyning propped herself up on her elbows and looked at Soolchakan shocked. She was speechless.

Hisang came up to the table. "Would you like to change your clothes?"

Chyning simply nodded, still with a dumb look of confusion on her face.

Soolchakan sighed and hung his head. "Sona...and all five of your other children were murdered by the Teltermak." He looked up. "With the aid of the four stones, we will be bringing all six of them back to life."

Chyning looked around a little dazed. She frowned and turned to Bonarain. "Where were you?"

Bonarain flushed and sighed. "I went to Fortress Island. I wanted some fresh fruit. I didn't want any more of that hydroponics...chemically grown fruit. I wanted the real stuff. I got trapped inside."

Chyning frowned harder. "How...did you get trapped... inside?"

"Some...slavers showed up...in a boat near the door. I... had just given birth to Nadiwi and...they grabbed her. They were going to take me as well but...I fought them and killed two of them. They closed the door and barricaded it and...I was stuck."

"You couldn't get out of there...by any means at all?"

"I didn't have tools to make a ladder or scaffolding."

Chyning scoffed. "Then use dirt and make a ramp! What's so hard about that?"

Bonarain flushed, squawked and vanished.

Soolchakan growled. **"Bonarain, where are you**?"

She did not want to answer, however, it was the *Voice of Power* asking. He could force her to answer. **"I'm in my bedroom**."

Soolchakan looked around the Chokchakchok sick bay. "Take care of Chyning and…I'll be back as soon as I can." He Jumped to the apartment. He went to the door to Bonarain's bedroom. "I need to talk to you."

"GO AWAY!" She hung her head in misery.

"I'm not going away, we need to talk."

She did not want to even think about any of what was happening right now. All she could do was drown herself in self-pity over the fact that everyone else was coming up with that dirt ramp instantly and she had never thought of it in over 4,300 years.

"We're going to talk," said Soolchakan. He hopped to Spy and walked through the door. He hopped back to Home. "Stop feeling bad about yourself. Remember, I told you, you can come up with explanations for the most complicated things, but…you have a hard time with the simple."

She turned her back to him. "You already said that."

"Yes I did. I have something else to say now. You remember that saying, that all things happen for a reason? Well this *did*! I want you to think. That one who betrayed us…people of her own race. She didn't know that you were still alive. She had no clue that Nadiwi existed. If she had been successful in her plot to kill all Owlamites who were older than her so that she could become

Drey Sssorg, you and Nadiwi were still out there. Both of you older than her. She didn't know anything about Fortress Island, so she didn't know where to look for you. She would've never become Drey Sssorg because you were still alive. Even if the power could not find you, because of the void at Fortress Island, it would have gone to Nadiwi. It would have been some time before she was able to find out and try her dastardly deed against Nadiwi, if she had ever found Nadiwi. Still...there you are. She couldn't ever be allowed to obtain the power...not as long as you were alive and because she had absolutely no clue where you were... you were safe from her plotting. It all works out...for the good."

Bonarain turned around and sighed. She wiped tears off her cheeks. "Where is she?"

"Who?"

"The traitor!"

"She was banished to a ship in 45."

Bonarain frowned in confusion. "And...she...stays there?"

"She was commanded to stay there by the *Voice of Power.*" He chuckled. "She was given the commands that she cannot go anywhere. She cannot harm herself in any way at all. She is stuck there for the rest of her life. Only when there is a chance that she might become the Drey Sssorg...only then will she be executed."

"Why didn't you execute her before?"

"She said that she would rather be dead than be subservient to me...or any other Drey Sssorg. I decided to *not* give her what she wanted."

"I wanna see her."

He frowned. "Why?"

She grinned. "To let her know that her plot has, not only, been completely foiled, but it never had a chance to begin with."

He closed his eyes, shook his head and sighed. "If you must. I'll tell Bikaropin to take you there."

"Why can't I go on my own?"

"Because he's the only one with a really good landmark inside her prison ship."

She nodded. "Okay." She sniffled and wiped her nose. "What do we do now?"

"We go back to the Chokchakchok ship and check on Kiyalee and Chyning. Then we check on those six children."

She frowned. "What are we checking on the children for?"

"To see if we can make them normal using all four stones. If it takes all four stones to bring someone back and make them normal, mentally and physically…then that's what we'll use for all the other 2,880 Owlamites that we need to bring back."

"Good idea." She scoffed and shook her head. "When did you start getting so smart?"

He snickered. "I've been hanging around Bikaropin a lot. His intelligence seems to rub off on anyone who listens to him."

She sat there chuckling for a few moments.

They Jumped back to 45 and the Chokchakchok ship.

During the process of bringing Chyning back, Kiyalee had been there with all four stones and now she had her equilibrium. Chyning was having no problems at all. They pulled the six Heyyah children out and gave each one of them a dose of all four stones and all six of the children were back to normal...if a slaver could ever be called normal.

After the last child, Bonarain sat down. "I'm...very tired. I think...we all need to get some sleep...before the next round."

Kiyalee was a little upset. "But if we start getting to work...you get Shalam and Monaha...then I get Aya. Why do you wanna stop now?"

"So we can start fresh tomorrow," said Bonarain. "Aren't you the least bit tired?"

Kiyalee hung her head and nodded. "Yeah, I'm tired, but..." She hung her head. "I guess a little sleep wouldn't hurt."

"I agree," said Chyning with a yawn.

Soolchakan grunted in agreement. "So tomorrow we start fresh on our own children." He turned to Bikaropin. "Who is on duty at the slaver compound?"

Bikaropin thought for a moment. "Zenkin and Yesati are there. They're reporting that some wizard is on the way there...in order to find out who the culprits are."

"Make sure they don't find out anything...except that

those six children are back there."

Bikaropin nodded. "Yeah! The six children...who will probably have a really strange story to tell all of their families."

Soolchakan simply grunted in affirmation.

Bikaropin looked confused. "This...Fortress Island...that you keep referring to...uh...why didn't you just hop a shuttlecraft near there and just fly it over that wall?"

Soolchakan was now confused. "I...don't know. I never thought of that."

Bonarain grunted in exasperation. "I think...we did not do that...because the *Voice of Power*, at that time, ordered us to go to the door, in order to enter the fort. Since the *Voice of Power* ordered it...none of us even questioned it or...attempted to try a shuttlecraft...or any other way of hopping the wall."

Bikaropin smiled weakly. "Soolchakan, you now have the capability of changing that order."

Soolchakan shook his head and chuckled. He then rescinded the order that limited them going to the door and allowed a shuttlecraft to be used for any future trips to Fortress Island. "This power can be...somewhat debilitating if you don't use it correctly."

# 4

Bikaropin and Mahanee were getting ready to shuttle the six children back to (what was left of) the slaver compound. Bikaropin noticed that the genitals of the boys were intact. He sent a mental message to the other Owlamites about this conundrum.

Shashy grunted in disgust. **"That means that when they were brought back...they were repaired as well**."

Hisang looked a little perplexed. **"So what do we do now**?"

Bikaropin sighed. **"We have to re-castrate the boys and re-spay the girls...then we send them back. Then tomorrow...after all four, Soolchakan, Bonarain, Kiyalee and Chyning are rested, they are then informed of this finding**."

Mahanee shuddered in disgust. **"Let's hurry up and get the dirty work done and then get these monsters back to their monster parents. They're going to have some interesting things to tell their parents about having been neutered...again**."

The "surgery" was performed and then the children were

Jumped back to the compound. All six children gave babbling accounts of what had happened while they were in that strange place. The parents were not sure of what was fact and what was fiction. Most of it seemed just too incredible to believe, however, the stories were too consistent coming from their children. The parents knew that they were dealing with some incredibly powerful wizards. They knew the wizard that was being hired and brought here was going to have to be among the absolute best in order to determine all that had happened to them and exactly who were those audacious anti-slavery fools.

After the children had been delivered and the ones delivering them had gone back to the gorge, Zenkin and Yesati saw the procession bringing the wizard to the area. They smiled at each other as they each were thinking of different devious ways to stop the wizard from achieving his goal.

During the last few days, the slavers who had come to the compound from other areas had brought all kinds of tents, clothing and food. The place was now more of an encampment. They were preparing to rebuild after the wizard had accomplished his task. They were going to capture those impudent offenders, who had taken and destroyed everything, and make *them* rebuild the entire compound. The slavers were going to find out where those offenders came from and confiscate any and all wealth of theirs. The slavers were giving themselves an absolute guarantee that these lawbreakers would spend the rest of their lives in servitude to slavers along with any children…forever. This insult against the slavers was just too great to ignore.

Zenkin shook his head. **"They're mouths are making**

a lot of promises that their butts can't keep."

Yesati nodded. **"They sure think the world of themselves and their capabilities**."

Zenkin snickered. **"I don't know who is going to get the bigger shock - the slavers or the wizard**."

She giggled. **"Let's make sure that both get a huge, nasty surprise**."

The procession arrived. The Area Chief, the one who was in charge of slavery and slaver raids on the entire continent, was at the lead. Area Chief Thatoom Showshoo was a rather large Heyyah. He had thick curly brown hair that was graying at the temples. He was dressed all in brown. He had several scars on his face and hands. He was very upset over the fact that one of his Sector Chiefs had been attacked, robbed, defiled and mutilated in his own compound along with his entire team. There was going to be some heavy retribution for that unacceptable transgression against a professional slaver.

The other main character in the procession was the High Grand Wizard Henteskim. He was a tall skinny man who had a scowl on his face. He was wearing long flowing dark green robes. He had a thin mustache that hung down below his chin. Other than the mustache, he had no hair on his head at all – even eyebrows. He was charging a fortune for his services. He was riding in a very large, ornate, primarily red and gold carriage that was so heavy it took ten equines to pull the monstrous thing. He brought his carriage because there was no way that he was going to be forced into sleeping in some shabby little tent. He liked his comfort and there was none in any tent. The lower life forms could reside in a tent…along with the vermin that crawled on the ground. He *will* be luxuriously comfortable. He had worked too hard on his status to be reduced to sleeping outside…ever again.

The rest of the procession consisted of more slavers (with slaves) carrying tents and supplies for the people of the compound and the ones bringing the provisions.

While all of the new equipment was being set up, Henteskim listened to the stories from the "victims" of the scandalous attack against the compound. He also listened to the tales of the kidnapped children. Most of it was boring complaints. There were some things, however, that were very interesting. He decided to have a new conversation with the Area Chief. He did not want to have a meeting inside any of those shabby tents, so he invited the Area Chief into his carriage.

Thatoom entered the lavish carriage and sat down in a chair that looked more expensive than any chair he had ever seen in his life. "What is it that you wanted to talk about?"

Henteskim smiled. "I am fascinated with some of the things that I am hearing about these criminals. They are obviously of a different Grand Magical Clique than the one I am a member of. They have some strange spells…that I *want*!"

Thatoom interrupted. "If you're asking for a higher fee, *that* could be a problem…"

"Oh, no! In fact, if you give me the use of their…higher wizards…for a time…I could be compelled to lower the fee… by…oh say…around 50,000…or so."

Thatoom raised his eyebrows. "Lower...the fee?" He grinned in anticipation of hearing this deal.

"I am always looking for new spells to learn. We have a library back at our home base. It is an extensive library and I've read every book there. I can do virtually all of the spells listed in all of those books. What I find fascinating about this incident is... there were some spells that were performed here...that I've never heard of." His expression turned grim. "I...*want*...those spells. If I get some new spells as a result of what happens here...yes...I will lower my fee. The spells are much more valuable to me than any amount of gold, silver or any expensive baubles."

Thatoom scoffed. "You can have all the spells you want! You get the spells and I get the slaves."

Henteskim held his hand up as if in pause. "The spells are only part of it. Whoever the spell-*casters* are...I would need them, for a time, in order to truly obtain the spells and become proficient with them."

Thatoom growled. "So...you want some of the slaves for yourself."

"Only for a short time," he said with a friendly smile. "Just long enough to obtain and become proficient in any spell that I'm not familiar with...at this time. Once I have what I need..." He leaned forward with an evil grin on his face. "Then...I will empty their minds of any magical capabilities. I will also make them..." He looked up in thought. "...totally loyal...as slaves." He brought his gaze back to Thatoom. "*Totally*...loyal slaves. Wouldn't that make them much more valuable to you?" He grinned.

Thatoom nodded while smiling. He was having a difficult time controlling his bladder. This meant even more money in his coffers. "That will make them more valuable...yes. Do you have any idea how long you would keep them?"

Henteskim pursed his lips and shrugged as he leaned back in his throne. "That...is totally unknown...at this time. It depends entirely on what spells, how many, how complicated and how long it takes to learn them. How long it takes to document them in our library. But, I am hearing of this one slave...named...Slut. According to this Shoolmon, this slave has been in their family for more generations than he can remember. If the others are of the same race...then we're talking about multi-generational slaves... that would be..." He leaned forward and opened his eyes wide and whispered. "...priceless. A slave that can be passed from one generation to the next...without having to purchase many more, or any, new slaves for a household."

Thatoom leaned back and smiled. "I like negotiations like this. Both of us will profit immensely from this grand undertaking." He nodded with nothing but avarice showing on his face. "Massive profits! I like that!" He nodded. "You will get your spells and I will get my slaves. Wonderful!"

They smiled at each other, got up and shook hands.

Zenkin turned to Yesati. "Are you ready to wipe some filthy smiles off of their greedy faces?"

Yesati gave him a look. "Their smile, their lips, their teeth, their tongue...and a few other parts of their anatomy. I'd like to do it with...semi-sharp instruments. That will make it...very painful to them."

Henteskim sniffed. "Now…if you'll leave me. I have to prepare for the spell casting that will take place…in order to find these atrocities."

Thatoom smiled. "Do you need any preparations set up by us?"

"A tent…that I will be in privately. It has to be…in the center of the area that is in question. Once I go in there…I am to be left alone…" He leaned forward looking as stern as he could. "…no matter what."

"It will be done," he said nodding. He got up and departed still grinning with greed.

Henteskim sat there chuckling. "Simple minded *paff*! I'm gonna soak you for more money than you ever thought possible. If those wizards are as powerful as I think…you'll never get them back…without paying dearly for them." He continued chuckling as he poured himself some wine. He brought the glass up to his mouth to sip - and Zenkin pushed the bottom of the glass up above his lips thus spilling the entire contents all over his face. The wizard stood there looking (and feeling) rather foolish as the wine dripped down his front. He sputtered a little as he tried to blast wine out of his nose. After some cleaning of his face, robe and sinuses, he poured another cup of wine. He ended up wearing that wine as well. He angrily decided he did not need any more wine at this time.

The next day, Henteskim came proudly striding out of his carriage wearing gray robes and a gray, very wide brim, hat. Shoolmon led him to the tent that was as near the center of the compound as possible. The flaps on the tent were up at this time. Henteskim walked around the tent pulling the flaps down.

"Once I go inside, no one disturbs me," said Henteskim patronizingly.

"Except me," said Zenkin.

"And me," said Yesati.

Henteskim walked in. He figured that he was going to have to make some sounds for his audience, otherwise they may not think that he was doing anything. He closed his eyes. He inhaled deep and loud. He exhaled deep and loud. He repeated. As he started the third inhalation, Zenkin Jumped him to the Stink planet, where he got a snoot full of the foul atmosphere of that planet. Zenkin immediately Jumped him back to the tent where the wizard stood there, for a moment, with a look of total wide-eyed horror on his face. He was then down on his hands and knees puking up everything he had eaten for breakfast…and dinner from last night…and lunch from yesterday.

The audience outside heard the retching noises going on inside. They could not understand how any form of self-purging was supposed to aid in the magical stuff, however, they were not wizards, so leave it to the one in the know.

Henteskim stood up on wobbly legs while spitting some unknown lumps out of his mouth. He backed away from the mess in the middle of the tent. He looked down at his robes to see if he had stained his garment in any way. There were a few spots that he swiped at. He also dusted off the knees. He spat several times to get more of the remnants out of his mouth. He cleared his throat several times more. He calmed himself to prepare for the spell. He tilted his head back and spread his arms out in order to concentrate on the spell.

At that time Yesati kicked the wizard in the groin - hard.

Once again there was a look of total shock on his face as he lost his concentration and every bit of air in his lungs. He once again was on his knees. This time he was holding his crotch with both hands as he now fell sideways in agony. He did everything he could to keep from moaning in pain. Even through the pain he knew that someone outside the tent would lose faith in him if he were to reveal he was in pain. He lay there rocking back and forth until the pain finally subsided. He got up and paced several laps around the interior of the tent in order to get his wobbling legs functioning properly. He exited the tent.

"The proper magical providences are not conjoining right now," said Henteskim weakly. "I…must go to my carriage and… meditate some more in order to get the proper alignment." He walked back to his carriage without saying anything more."

Shoolmon looked at Thatoom. "Is anything else going to happen today?"

Thatoom sighed. "We heard that the Healers are supposed to be here…sometime this evening. From what I understand, the cost of regenerating the sex organs of twenty-eight people is going to be…extremely high."

"All the more vengeance to take out on these people who stole Slut, and everything else I own," spat Shoolmon bitterly.

Zenkin was standing there in Spy. "Dream on, *bimyock*."

Yesati followed Henteskim back to his carriage. She was very curious to see what he was going to do as far as further preparations. As soon as he closed the door to his carriage, he crumpled to the floor and continued holding his crotch while whimpering in pain. In here, he did not have to worry about any of those slavers hearing him agonize. She sat down in one of the chairs and just snickered. She was thinking about kicking him again, once the pain had completely subsided.

For the first time in a very long time, a new Owlamite baby was born and all four of the first generation were able to hold the baby and give her a blessing. Umyana of the Seventeenth, daughter of Juhntrom and Irva of the Sixteenth was the first Owlamite to be held by all four since Fomin of the Fifth in the year 1116 ATUT.

Zenkin and Yesati reported back to the gorge. They informed Soolchakan what had happened and what they had done. After getting the briefing, Yaspon and Garya were the ones who reported to the slaver compound now. They were going to check and see how much (if at all) the wizard had recovered from the treatment that he had received at the hands of Zenkin and Yesati.

In the gorge, they were setting up for all of the resurrections that were going to be done. The first one was to be Shalam. He had claimed apartment 1-562. He was going to be brought back in his own home. The coffin holding his body was Jumped from Zhagool to 1-562. The concrete tomb was hopped to Spy, revealing the desiccated body of Shalam. They placed him on a table in the main room and started. The four from generation one leaned over the body. The four stones jumped up and joined each other forming that familiar translucent golden orb. The four of them concentrated on bringing life back to Shalam. Once again they required some stimulus from pulse weapons in order to complete the task. Once Shalam was breathing, Cymani was given the task of educating him on the highlights of what he had missed over the last 3,673 years.

They Jumped to apartment 1-1 and repeated the steps bringing Monaha back from the dead.

Since Aya was the next one and she had been the first wife of Shalam, they had to go back to 1-562 in order to bring her back in her home.

The same thing happened with Zina. She was the first wife of Monaha, so back to 1-1 to bring her back.

Next they brought back Jada, Peldom, Baktim and Zoya. By the time they were finished with eight, the four from generation one were completely exhausted. They had to be assisted back to their apartment, to their bedrooms and they all four quickly fell asleep.

Bikaropin went back to his apartment with Mahanee and Shashy. "Eight of them in one day." He shook his head. "It is gonna take a *long* time before…all 2,872 are back. Maybe…as they go along and…get more practice, they'll be able to do more than eight in one day."

"You know…," said Mahanee. "…once they bring Zormun back, I'm going back to him. He was my first husband."

Bikaropin smiled. "I have no problem with that. You were first married to Zormun and Shashy was first married to Bak. Both of you will be going back." He smiled. "After a while I'll get Inorim back. Then a little later…Pyree. I miss both of them and…I'll be glad to get both of them back. Then…as time goes on…we'll all get all of our children back as well."

Shashy snickered. "Maybe we should start moving our stuff back to our old apartments before our initial husbands show up."

Mahanee nodded. "Good idea."


The next day, Minima, Panami, Zormun, Bendarik, Zorkeen, Banama, Maramee and Amma were brought back.

Bikaropin was thinking of where he should place all of the concrete tombs that were being brought down from Zhagool. They certainly did not want to keep them in their apartments. The hope was that they would never have to use them again. It was finally decided to keep them on the big Chokchakchok ship. Those people had been giants so there was a lot of room on the massive ship. They had huge storage bays on that big ship. They might even move the caskets back to Zhagool.

Yaspon and Garya found that Henteskim was begging for help from his Clique. He had some kind of glass box that he could communicate with them over a very large distance. Yaspon and Garya decided to watch how the thing worked before committing to any sabotage on the thing. At first the people in the Clique thought he was being rather childish about requesting assistance until he explained what had happened. He had been attacked with and by things that he could not explain. He had first been personally attacked with some incredibly powerful sickness spell (which he had not been able to fight against), followed by a physical attack from someone he never saw and could not sense. He also informed them of the stories he had heard from the slavers and their children. This information was indeed intriguing to the others so they informed him that they would send help. They advised him to open up a "*Quendinta*" portal. They would be sending someone through tomorrow.

Yaspon looked at Garya. "A…*Quendinta*…portal? What in thunder is that?"

Garya shook her head and shrugged. "Do I look like someone who knows all of their *chokwad* secrets?"

He huffed. "Neither one of us knows. We'll find out tomorrow."

She nodded. "Should we ask for some assistance as well?"

He pondered for a few moments. "Seeing as how it just came up…and neither of us ever heard of that spell, I think we should."

After a few mental messages, Zuztay and Chejja showed up at the compound to assist in the observation of this new phenomenon. They also were there to observe all of the different incantations and gyrations that Henteskim went through while casting the spell. He had a very large metallic hoop in the middle of the carriage and was putting all of his attention towards this hoop.

Zuztay did a lot of intruding into the mind of Henteskim as he spouted the unintelligible words and did his strange dance around the hoop. He was able to see some landmarks in the wizard's mind that told him the home of the Clique was in Falamin – a country that was the entire southern portion of South Chilamte. Zuztay focused on the landmarks in the other place and Jumped. He found himself in a dark, cold tower on an island near the south shore of Falamin. Another wizard on this end was doing the same ritualistic chanting and dancing as Henteskim.

Several other Heyyah were sitting in the room quietly watching the one doing the dancing. They were all dressed in gray robes. Fifteen of them altogether. Nine men and six women. All had long gray or white hair. The men all had long thin beards. They were all rather thin people. Several of them had goblets of… some kind of liquid refreshment.

Zuztay decided to barge in on their thoughts. He found that four of the men and one of the women were proficient in this spell. The others were observing to see how it was done. From what he could glean from their thoughts it was a spell that opened up a portal, much like the "Jump" ability that the Owlam had. The main difference was that the Owlamites did not have to go through a long sequence of silly incantations and even sillier dancing. They also did not need that hoop.

**"Bikaropin, this is Zuztay, can you hear me?"**

Bikaropin was surprised at first, however, he did respond. **"Yes, what did you need?"**

Zuztay described what had taken place and what he was seeing now.

Bikaropin snickered as he thought about it. **"When the *bimyock* tries to go through…intercept him and send him somewhere else."**

**"Any suggestions as to where I should send him?"**

Bikaropin shrugged. **"One of the easiest places there is to send someone. Send him to that planet in dimension #10. That's the planet that was named Beasties. That'll give him something to think about and…we'll see how he reacts once he gets there."**

Zuztay nodded. **"I can do that."**

**"Let me know if anything new comes up."**

Zuztay could not think of anything new or stranger that might come up, however, he could not think of a decent argument to the request. Nothing to do now other than sit back and watch the show. Prepare for when this other wizard was ready to attempt the move. From what he was reading in the minds of the other wizards…it was going to take a very long time before the spell was finished.

The next day, Ashak, Nafee, Poolkiy, Sunok, Alam, Nafena, Momatak and Amaree were brought back from the dead. There were several tearful reunions as each one was awakened from a long sleep. Mothers held their children and then the children would then go to the spouses who were already back.

Soolchakan received a briefing on the things that Zuztay had reported. He requested a full briefing once the trick had been pulled on the one who was trying to "Jump" through the two hoops.

Zuztay watched as the hoop on his end started glowing. Prior to the glowing it had been a rather dull gray. Now it had a very bright glow where the hoop seemed to have turned gold in color. Chejja reported that the one on her end was glowing as well. The wizard walked slowly towards the hoop with his eyes closed while mumbling some more incantations. Zuztay got behind the wizard, looked through the hoop and nearly lost his lunch.

"**Chejja, this is Zuztay, I can...see you...through the hoop! As a matter of fact...I can see Yaspon and Garya as well! Get off to the side or...*somewhere* else...I don't believe this!**"

Chejja did a quick side-step to her left. "**Can you see me now**?"

Yaspon and Garya both scooted over the other way.

He got closer to the hoop. "**Only at a certain angle.**"

Chejja scoffed. "**Well I suggest that you get away**

**from that hoop because now I can see you…through the hoop**."

Zuztay grunted in disgust. He turned around, grabbed the wizard and Jumped him to the "Beasties" planet in dimension #10. The wizard did not notice because he was still concentrating on the spell and continued slowly shuffling forward - until he tripped over the root of a tree, and did a face plant in the dirt.

The wizard pushed himself up. "Henteskim, why didn't you warn me abuh…Uh?" He noticed that he was not in that fancy carriage and started looking around rather dazed. He cleared his throat. "Henteskim? WHERE ARE YOU?" He looked all around him. "Unh…where am I?" Now he sounded a little desperate and frightened as he spun around surveying the scenery.

Henteskim peered through the portal and saw only the room back at the tower. "Where is Parrok?"

Several of the members of the group in Falamin heard Henteskim and momentarily were taken aback.

One of the men stood up and grabbed his little glass communication box. "Henteskim, what are you saying?"

Henteskim looked over at his glass communication box. "Come on Kavluck! I asked what happened to Parrok!"

Now several of the other wizards got up and gathered around the hoop.

Kavluck closed his eyes trying to think. "Parrok just… disappeared…on this end. Are you saying that…he didn't come through…to where you are?"

"He's not here," said Henteskim. "I thought I saw him for a moment and then...I saw him coming towards the portal and... that Elf got in the way and...he disappeared."

Kavluck was now looking around in shock. "Elf? What Elf?"

"Uh...didn't you...see him...standing in front of the portal?"

Kavluck turned to the others who were gawking through the portal. "Someone interfered with the spell. Apparently some... Elf! Sendonisk...Challoom...FIND HIM!"

Two of the men pulled out, what looked like a glass eyeball, closed their eyes and placed the eye against their foreheads. They slowly started turning around. They could find nothing because Zuztay was currently in dimension #10 with Parrok and giggling profusely over the frustration that the wizard was going through. After a few moments Zuztay stopped giggling and was now rather curious. Parrok was attempting all kinds of spells and none of them seemed to be working...in any way at all.

**"Bikaropin, this is Zuztay. Can you hear me**?"

**"This is Bikaropin, is there anything special to report**?"

**"Yes! It seems that none of the wizard's spells are working here on the Beasties planet. He's tried several of them, including that glass communication box...and...absolutely nothing seems to be working**."

Bikaropin was a little stunned. He slumped down in his

chair while trying to think. "**Zuztay, bring him back. Let's see if he can do his...tricks...if you bring him back... here**."

"**Any specific spot you want me to take him**?"

Bikaropin snickered. "**Take him to someplace close to that slaver compound. See what happens in the confusion**."

Parrok was desperately trying to communicate with someone back at his Home Clique. He was screaming at the box to begin communications. Zuztay touched Parrok and Jumped him to a place just outside of the slaver compound. Several of the wizards covered their ears as the screams of Parrok were now coming through – *loud* and clear – through their communication boxes.

Kavluck picked his box up. "STOP THE SCREAMING, PARROK!" He froze and looked a little astonished. "Parrok...is that you?"

"Yes," said Parrok sounding a little relieved.

Kavluck snarled. "WHERE ARE YOU?"

"I DON'T KNOW," screamed Parrok!

One of the women picked her box up. "What did you see...in...at...uh...wherever you were?"

Parrok thought for a moment. "I saw...some animals... the likes of which I've never seen before. I saw trees and...other shrubs and plants...the likes of which I've never seen before.

It looked like a jungle but...I've been in the jungles of Ficara, Cifpasica and the central part of South Chilamte. This jungle was...unlike any of those."

Kavluck broke in. "How did you get there?"

Parrok snapped back at him. "I have no idea! All of a sudden...I was there. Then just as suddenly...I was...uh...where in thunder am I now?" He spun around desperately looking for something recognizable. "I think I see Henteskim's carriage. So I think...I'm close to where I'm supposed to be but...I have no clue how I got here."

One of the women broke in. "Weren't you supposed to be there...at the slaver compound?"

Parrok rolled his eyes. He bared his teeth as he snarled into his communication box. "I should have arrived *inside* that carriage. That way...none of them would know how I got there. None of these slaver types would see or know anything about the portal."

Kavluck shook his head. "Fine! Right now, you're where you're supposed to be. Go inside the compound and assist Henteskim." He looked up. "Meanwhile...the rest of us have to try and figure out...who this Elf was that was seen...in the middle of the spell."

The four Owlamites were listening intently to all of the conversation that was going on with a little concern. They had been seen.

"I think we need to get back to the gorge and...do some

briefings on what happened here," said Yaspon.

"I agree," said Chejja. "This was just too strange."

"Yeah," said Garya. "We could see each other through that portal and...that Henteskim saw Zuztay on the other side."

Zuztay frowned. "Another thing was that...none of his magical spells worked...on the Beasties planet. I wonder why."

Yaspon shrugged. "Let's get some relief here and...go do some briefings."


They decided to get a little bolder in the resurrections. Today they did twelve. Fomin, Sodona, Chima, Sona, Na, Zar, Xatang, Polii, Zintom, Loov, Farn and Yumok were all brought back.

After all that work, Soolchakan had to sit there and listen to the briefings by the quartet from the slaver compound. He found the bit about the magic not working on that other planet rather curious. He found the fact that they could see an Owlamite, who was in Spy dimension, through this portal was rather disturbing.

Muz and Yeema were currently the ones at the compound and they were doing what they could to keep a low profile. They wanted to stay away from that *Quendinta* portal, however, they still needed to observe what was going on.

Henteskim and Parrok were currently attempting to start the spells to track the marauders who ransacked the slavers. While Yeema did what she could to distract them, Muz was searching through the carriage in order to see if he could find anything of value regarding intelligence data.

Zuztay took Zenkin and Ledak to the tower south of Falamin. The three of them were there to find out anything they could about this Magician Clique. They needed to stay away from that hoop as well.

Ledak did a little deeper probing of the minds of the Magician's Clique and found that this portal was named after one of the women of the Clique. He found that there was definitely a pecking order among the seventeen wizards and that the fourth in line – Quendinta - was the one who had invented this portal spell. That was why it was named after her. He further found out that Kavluck was the number one wizard, Henteskim was number three, and Parrok was number seven. He did a few further mental intrusions to determine where each of the seventeen were in ranking order.

All this information was sent back to the gorge for intelligence purposes. Bikaropin was looking over all of it with a little trepidation because it meant that these seventeen Heyyah were not just any wizards who practiced spells, they were capable of inventing new ones that were more powerful (and it appeared) more dangerous to the Owlamites if left unchecked. He groaned as he considered that this was another new enemy that may have to be dealt with. He now had better understanding of what the first generation had gone through for nine millennium.

After receiving all new intelligence updates, the first

generation brought fourteen of their children back from the dead. Nahama, Pomani, Zelok, Tonat, Sanapin, Sab, Machek, Jotsoom, Hamar, Zhontam, Molkan, Sodek, Mymin and Korpem were now back among the living.

The four were sitting in the main room of their apartment getting ready to go back to bed again.

Bonarain contemplated. "The ones that we've raised… they don't seem to be too interested…in procreation…yet."

Soolchakan chuckled. "Poolkiy, Pomani and Korpem have been out of action for the least amount of time. They're still rather curious as to what they missed while they were…entombed…on Zhagool. I guess that copulation is not the most important thing on their minds…yet."

"I agree," said Kiyalee. "This whole thing about…bringing us back…after all that time, I still have a lot of history to catch up on."

Chyning scoffed. "Neither you or I are catching up on much of it…since we're so busy bringing all of them back."

Bonarain shook her head. "I was out of it as well…but in a different manner. There's a lot that I've got to catch up on too."

Soolchakan got up and headed for his bedroom. "Right! The main problem we have to focus on is the fact that we still have over 2,800 of our children to bring back before any of you can really get caught up on history."

The three women looked at each other as they contemplated his last statement. Each one got up and went to their bedroom to rest. Tomorrow would bring more of their children back. Over 2,800 more resurrections was a daunting order to fill. They all knew that they were determined to do it because they wanted their children back - all of them.

The next day, Montaza of the Eighteenth was born. The first generation held another baby in their arms prior to going on to the resurrection of Balak of the Third.

Henteskim and Parrok were continuing to get pushed around by any Owlamite that was in the area. They were still attempting to find out who those pesky Elf were that were causing their grief, however, since they could not concentrate on any one of their spells they were able to find out virtually nothing.

Kavluck, Sendonisk and Quendinta were using the same spells back at their tower in order to find out anything at their end. They were equally pestered by the Owlamites there. The more the wizards tried to perform their spells, the more that Zenkin and Ledak were able to find out about the spells.

Balak, Ino, Mobor, Sazha, Zhytash, Bymin, Ozar, Na-Ima, Borim, Bak, Alamet, Lorib, Yaming and Anda were all brought back to life before the first generation quartet had to go back to bed.

Ledak reported back to Bikaropin regarding some of the things that they had found out about the Clique. Bikaropin was more curious about the fact that none of the spells that had been attempted on Beasties had worked. He told Ledak to go back. Each of the Owlamites that were spying on the Clique would choose one of the seventeen. They would Jump that person to some other planet or some other dimension in order to find out if Beasties was an unusual conundrum, or was it the wizard that was panicking and could not perform his spells.

Zuztay grabbed the fifteenth in the order: A man named Garlzyst. Zenkin grabbed number sixteen: A woman named Whaynamka. Ledak grabbed a man named Thontayn who was the seventeenth in order.

Zuztay went to a planet in dimension #21. This planet had a sentient race who had just invented their first flying machine. Zenkin went to dimension #75 to a planet that was inhabitable, however, it had no sentient race. Ledak took his victim to an island on what was left of the Doolood planet. They each kept their victims there for one day. They brought them back and then reported back to Bikaropin that none of the magic attempted on these other planets worked at all. Bikaropin found all of this very interesting. He would report all these findings to Soolchakan…as soon as he woke up.

# 5

"You're telling me that…this magic done by…wizards works here but not on any other planets." Soolchakan pondered. "How many *other* planets have you tried?"

Bikaropin was momentarily surprised with the question. He cleared his throat. "Uh…three."

Soolchakan gave him a patronizing glare. "I think you should try…maybe a few more planets…like maybe twenty or so. Also, try several more dimensions as well. If it starts becoming completely consistent that this magic only works here then we've found something to really look at closely. If it does work on other planets, or dimensions, we have to find out which ones and, act accordingly."

Bikaropin smiled. "We'll do it. As soon as you're finished today, I'll get to it."

"You'll get to it now!" Soolchakan looked at him grimly. "I don't need your intelligence to pull the trigger on one of the pulse guns for resupply of energy. I can absorb the energy, just as easily, if Shalam is holding the gun."

Bikaropin nodded. "I'll get some more help…from those

not assisting you and we'll…get to work."

Soolchakan smiled. "Thank you." He turned to Bonarain. "You ready?"

Bonarain smiled. "Bringing back more of my children? Absolutely!"

"Let's do it," said Kiyalee.

Chyning scoffed. "What're we waiting for?"


Bikaropin got help from some of the younger Owlamites who were not assisting with the resurrections. They took turns Jumping the seventeen different wizards to all of the planets they knew about in the different dimensions. The planets were near and far, however, they existed and they were used. The result was that they found that none of the wizards could perform any of their spells on any planet other than Hardooth, or any dimension other than #1. All of their magical gadgets, be they communication boxes, staffs with special spells on them, different types of armor or some unusual amulets they had manufactured – nothing worked outside of Hardooth.

Bikaropin, along with his assistants, were rather tired after all of that Jumping. He was tired, however, he was happy with the results. They did not have to assassinate all of the wizards. They could just banish them to some planet with no sentient life form and see if they could survive…without magic. It became a wonderful thought of banishing the slavers to the same planet and see just who they would force into slavery there, since it would be no one but neutered slavers and out-of-work (very elderly) wizards.

Bikaropin also began wondering if Ootgreeg was still alive in that prison of his. If none of this magic worked outside of Hardooth then, maybe, none of those longevity potions or get smart potions might not work either…possibly. No matter there, because the entire purpose of the banishment to that prison barge was his ultimate death…along with a prolonged wait for that death.

Bikaropin got the word that the first generation quartet was finished for the day. They stopped with Nesh. He raised his eyebrows and snickered. They were getting bolder. They had stopped with Anda the previous day and today they stopped with Nesh. That meant they had brought sixteen back today. They were getting stronger with practice and maybe this tremendous task would be finished a lot sooner than originally thought possible.

If they did another sixteen tomorrow, he would get his first wife, Inorim, back. He could hardly wait to welcome her back to the living. He would not be alone. Mahanee had gone back to Zormun and Shashy had gone back to Bak. Inorim would be here tomorrow and it would be just a few more days before Pyree was back again. Then the three of them would be awaiting the arrival of their children. He then realized that he would see his first two children, Namin and Judog, before Pyree would be brought back. Namin and Judog had been born, of Inorim, before Pyree was born. He shrugged in acceptance. Soolchakan had stated that they would be brought back in the order they were born - no argument.

Bikaropin hoped that there would be no more nasty

surprises awaiting any of them any time soon. He had seen enough sorrow in his time. Between two original wives and three temporary wives (temporary since the resurrections were now going on and those women were going to go back to their original husbands), he had seen twenty-five of his children murdered by the Teltermak. That was more than enough sorrow for anyone.

The first generation was standing over Boldak of the Third. He had just been brought back to life. He, like the others, was laying there looking rather confused. Why was he on this table? Why were the originals standing over him? Why were they looking at him so strangely?

Kiyalee shook her head. "His ears. Why…are they so large?"

"I see," said Soolchakan. "He was only 98 years old when he was murdered."

Now Boldak was even more confused. 'Murdered? If I was murdered…why am I hearing them and…looking at them… and…*what*?'

Bonarain looked closely at Boldak's ears. "His ears appear to be…what would be normal for someone who is over 3,700 years old."

Soolchakan saw the consternation on Boldak's face. "Don't worry, my son. You will be receiving a full explanation… from your mother and father."

Boldak shook his head. "No! My father…Monaha…

was killed…in 1804.  Now you say that…I was dead as well?
HOW?  How could my father explain anything to me without one
of those…crazy *talk-to-the-dead* things that those silly mediums
do?"

Chyning patted Boldak's shoulder.  "Don't worry.  All of it
will be explained.  You're in for an incredible education in…lives
of Owlamites and these remarkable stones."

Boldak snickered weakly…and looked even more
confused.  Boldak was led away by his parents, Monaha and
Momatak.  Momatak was already informing him of what had
happened to him and them.

The last one they brought back that day was Namaheen.
They could not tell anything from her because she had been quite
a bit older when she was murdered.  Boldak was murdered in the
first Teltermak war while Namaheen was murdered in 3478 during
the Traitor's war when she was over 1,700 years old.

Namaheen was married to Porim.  Both of them had been
killed in the Traitor's war.  One of the children of that pair was
Dawuni, who had survived all three wars.  She led the two of them
away along with their parents. Dawuni was in the middle and had
her arms around her parents. Both of them gave her their (shocked
and) undivided attention as she started educating them on what
had happened since their deaths.  Porim remembered Namaheen
being killed because she was killed in 3478.  He was now informed
that he had been killed the next year.  Both of them, like all of the
others who had been resurrected, were confused and a little scared
over what had happened and were not sure what to make of this

new situation.

Soolchakan looked over at Bonarain. She had the list of which one was next to be brought back. "Who is the next child... we'll be bringing back?"

Bonarain looked at the list with tired eyes. "The very next one we'll be doing. The first one tomorrow – Ponipa...why?"

He nodded. "I'm wondering, if she'll look, as mature as Boldak. How old was she when she was murdered?"

"She was 76."

Kiyalee stretched. "Are there any other younglings... tomorrow?"

Bonarain nodded. "A few. Fywinn was 65 when killed, Bornam was 66, Damel was 53 and Layis was 52."

Chyning yawned and then frowned. "Are there any other younglings from the first Teltermak war?"

Bonarain nodded again. "Those should be *very* interesting." She looked up from the list. "Byrib...he was 25 when murdered. Yotam...she was 19." She opened her eyes wide. "Banabar! He was only 6 years old...when murdered. If he shows...growth... that is anything close to Boldak...then...I don't know what to think...about what we're doing."

"It has to be the stones," said Soolchakan. "It seems that they'll be bringing people back...and aging them...according to how old they would have been...if they had never been killed."

Bonarain smiled apprehensively. "I think that we should

wait…until we see what they look like before we make that assumption."

"I agree," said Kiyalee. She yawned. "You said that we don't get to Byrib, Yotam or Banabar tomorrow, so, we worry about them the next day."

"Right," said Bonarain. "Tomorrow we finish with Faroog."

Chyning chuckled. "Faroog? He is Hisang's husband. She'll be happy."

"Right," said Soolchakan. "Bedtime!"


Bikaropin was a little happier now. Inorim was alive again. He had led her away from that table and had done a lot of explaining in a very short time. Inorim was looking around in shocked amazement as she was receiving a lot of unbelievable information in a very short time from him and her parents. She was told that she would be able to accept it a lot more, once her children started coming off of that table…alive.

When Inorim arrived at apartment 2-34, she now had to accept the fact that something had happened to her. All of her possessions were in boxes that were old and falling apart. Most of the clothing was rotten and crumbling. She would need an entirely new wardrobe. That evening, Inorim clung hard to Bikaropin as he gave out instructions to others on abducting the wizards and taking them to other planets and dimensions that had not been tested yet. She felt like a lost child. Her husband and parents seemed to be the only thing that was helping her keep her sanity.


Soolchakan woke up and called Bikaropin. Bikaropin showed up with a rather shocked looking Inorim.

Soolchakan looked at Inorim and smiled. "Don't worry, my child. All the others are just as upset and surprised as you. You'll understand it better...once you start reading all of the memoirs and...getting updated on what you missed."

She swallowed with a look of fear on her face. "I hope so. It just seems...so incredible...that...I was dead and now... because of those...*stones*...I'm alive again. It seems like...just yesterday when..." She looked off to the side bewildered. "I don't...remember anything. It seems like I was asleep the whole time and...not dreaming or...*nothing*!"

Soolchakan nodded. "You remember nothing, from when you were, not with us?"

She shook her head. "It just seems...that I woke up from a deep sleep. I don't remember anything. I don't..." She shook her head again and just looked off to the side.

Soolchakan nodded. "Apparently, that part of the scriptures, from the Great Maker, are true when it says that...for a time, we will be asleep, awaiting the great resurrection of all the true family of believers."

Bikaropin cleared his throat. "Uh...you called me here for...what?"

"Oh...yes." Soolchakan blew his breath out. "Okay! You said that those wizards couldn't do any spells...on these other planets. We're able to...Jump and Spy and Observation and... Ghost...on all these places. Why are we able to do it - but they are not?"

Without being noticed, Bonarain had come into the room. "I think I have the answer to that."

Soolchakan raised his eyebrows. "Oh?"

Bikaropin chuckled. "I'm listening."

Bonarain looked off to the side and started. "Remember that there are nine different types of magic?"

"Actually there are ten," said Bikaropin.

Bonarain gave him a disgusted look. "Demimondaine is *not* magic! It is a vulgar use of drugs and sex." She scoffed. "Don't put debauchery in the same category as the arcane."

Bikaropin nodded with a guilty look on his face. "Fully acknowledged."

Bonarain loudly cleared her throat. "The wizards, both major and minor, use all kinds of mathematics and chemicals in order to perform their tricks. We...just use our minds. If we try using those same mathematics and chemicals...I don't think we'll be able to do any of those tricks on other planets as well. We use our minds in order to do our special skills. There's no dead spots on those planets for that."

Bikaropin huffed. "So what...is so unusual about our

planet…where we and the wizards…and the clergy and the healers can do these crazy things but…*they* can't on other planets?"

Soolchakan pointed a finger at Bikaropin. "Wait! Have you tried…sending some of those clergy and healers…to the other planets? I thought we were just pestering the wizards."

Bikaropin blushed and turned red-faced. "Uh…no! We haven't sent any clergy…or healer…yet." He looked a little concerned and smiled weakly. "Should we?"

"If you want the answer to the questions as to whether or not those people can do their tricks on other planets…yes!" Bonarain smiled and shrugged. "How else will we know?"

Bikaropin licked his lips while pondering. He cleared his throat nervously. "I'll get on that…right away."

"Excellent," said Soolchakan! "Meanwhile, we've got some more of our children to bring back."


Ponipa, Fywinn, Bornam, Damel and Layis looked as if they had physically matured, even though they had been dead. They all looked like full adults even though both Damel and Layis had been in their fifties when murdered.

Soolchakan watched as the last one of the day, Faroog, was led off by his two wives Hisang and Maramee. Maramee had been killed as well and had been educated by Hisang while waiting for Faroog. Now the three of them were going to be waiting for their children to be brought back so they could educate them as well.

"That is what makes all of this worthwhile," said Kiyalee. "All of the ones who are being reunited in a manner that none of us ever dreamed possible."

"We still need to keep an eye on them," said Bonarain. "We're just getting started in this...adventure. We still don't know...all of the ramifications or...possible problems that could occur...from what we're doing." She looked concerned as she turned to Soolchakan. "We also need to keep an eye on Kiyalee and Chyning."

"I wonder," said Chyning. "You said that Bikaropin can't find another planet where the wizards can do their spells. I wonder...if the stones...can work...on other planets."

Soolchakan looked a little concerned at first. "We did the first experiments on the Chokchakchok ship. That place is *not* on this planet, or dimension, and the stones worked just fine... there." He looked down at his stone. "I wonder if...they work on...some completely different...existence...or...if it comes from our minds."

The four of them pondered that thought for quite a while.

Finally Chyning broke the silence. "Is someone still causing those wizards a lot of grief at the slaver compound?"

Soolchakan grunted in disgust. "Do you ever read anything...on any of the reports?"

Chyning closed her eyes and flushed. "What'd I miss?"

"The slavers are getting very upset over all of the - no results so far - from the wizards," said Bonarain. "They're talking about going to another Wizard Clique in order to get their wishes fulfilled."

Chyning gave a guilty smile. "Are we gonna pester them as well?"

Kiyalee scoffed angrily. "Whaddaya think?!" She looked off and scoffed again. She shook her head. "Let's get ready for tomorrow's work!" She glanced back at Chyning, huffed and Jumped to her bedroom in apartment 12-562.

Bonarain gave Chyning an annoyed look and Jumped to her bedroom.

Soolchakan sighed, shook his head and Jumped to his bedroom.

Chyning sighed helplessly as well. "Maybe I *should* read more," she said helplessly. She shrugged and then Jumped.


Kavluck looked through some of his possessions. He was trying to find something that he could use to thwart all of the problems that his Clique was having with whoever the pestilence was that had ransacked that slaver compound. He needed to keep the slavers happy because they had supplied him with all kinds of slaves he could use as personal servants and experimental victims.

The rest of the Clique was with him as far as keeping slavers happy, however, none of them could figure out the who was causing all of this grief or how. All of them were of one accord, however, they were all equally in disarray.

Two of the women, Sky and Mimdinsa, came to chambers.

"Peppa and Allk are missing again," said Sky indignantly.

Mimdinsa looked a little sullen. "Vivnova and Oorsk are back but…neither one looks like they want to talk about anything."

Kavluck clenched his teeth. "Why don't they want to talk?"

Mimdinsa scoffed. "Because they were somehow taken… *somewhere*, stripped of their dignity, capabilities and…some of their magical artifacts as well." She shook her head. "Oorsk had set up one of those…impenetrable glyphs. Somehow… this…enemy got through, pulled him to another one of those strange places and…none of his spells, charms, amulets or other possessions worked…AGAIN!"

Sky looked down at her hands. They were heavily bandaged. "I set up a spell to blast *Hand Fire* on the thugs. All of a sudden, I find myself in some…unknown place. I didn't recognize any of the plants…or animals…OR INSECTS! I opened the cloth, smeared the catalyst on my palms and…all I got was my own skin being burned by that phosphorus. I couldn't throw the spell. All I could do was try to bury my hands in the dirt and put out the fire in my palms."

Kavluck frowned. "Are you saying that Oorsk set up one of the strong protection glyphs?"

"No," said Mimdinsa. "He set up the *Death* Glyph. No one should have been able to get through that without… something horrible or detrimental happening to them. When it was penetrated…nothing happened to the vandal. Oorsk was stuck in some place…where, again, none of his spells worked."

Several Owlamites were sitting in Spy listening to the conversation.

"A Death Glyph!" Pelli turned to Beetha. "That sounds nasty."

Beetha frowned. "Who took that *bimyock* Oorsk off to that other planet?"

"I don't know," said Inotami. "I just grab whichever one Bikaropin points to and run them off to the place he wants me to take the *doovoft*. I haven't bothered taking any roll call of any of them." She giggled. "I don't really care what their name is."

Corena snickered back. "Unless Bikaropin wants us to know it, the names of these wizards is wholly unimportant." She shook her head. "The only thing we're worried about is…do their spells work…somewhere else?"

Chipshak walked in. "I just got back with one of the *doovofts*. I wonder what he's going to say to their kingpin."

At that moment, Hozhozek came staggering in. He looked rather haggard and very upset. He held up a twig. "Does anyone recognize this plant? I was taken to another one of those… PLACES! I couldn't do anything magical so…I ripped this off a bush." He turned to Sky. "You know a few more things about botany than most of us. Do you recognize the leaves on this thing?"

Sky sadly shook her head. "Over the last few days, I've

seen more plants, I have no idea what they are or..." She cocked her head to the side. "I have no idea if they're poisonous or not... useful or not."

Hozhozek dropped the twig as if it were on fire. "Poisonous?" He looked down at the fallen twig. "Is it possible that...?"

"It is entirely possible," said Kavluck. "Remember that there are three plants that Sky has in her *special* garden...that no one touches without very thick gloves." He looked down at the twig and then to the hands of Hozhozek. "Since you're not dead...we can only hope that it is not some kind of thing that kills you slowly. I suggest that someone burn that thing as soon as possible...unless there is some absolute proof that it is not dangerous."

At that moment, they heard some very loud cursing coming from another room.

Hozhozek sighed in consternation. "Sounds as if Gralzyst is back from his latest misadventure. I wonder what he has to report."

Gralzyst came stomping into the room with a wild look in his eyes. "They...whoever *they* is...passed right through a Protection Glyph, a Warning Glyph AND a Death Glyph." He grabbed an amulet that hung from a silver chain around his neck. He pulled the necklace off and threw it into a corner of the room. "That thing didn't help either." He looked around desperately. "Has anyone figured out who this pestilence is yet?"

Kavluck slumped down in a chair. "If I could answer that,

I'd know what to do about it. It has to be one of the other Cliques but…" He shook his head. "…for the life of me, I can't think of another Clique that is…" He clenched his fists. "*Any* Clique that is so…powerful that…we're so completely helpless against them."

Corena giggled. "Ya hear that? We're a Clique."

Inotami blew a raspberry. "I don't wanna be part of any Wizard Clique."

Sky turned to Kavluck. "Should we…try the *Team Spell of Finding?*"

Kavluck rolled his eyes. "Before we could do that…we'd have to find some Glyph that…these monsters can't get through. We'd have to be uninterrupted for a full day and a half in order to get the spell working completely." He stroked his chin. "You think that there's a possibility that…*they*…will leave at least six of us alone…for that amount of necessary time?"

Sky looked around helplessly. "We have to try… *something!*"

Kavluck looked up with a rather sarcastic smile. "I'm completely open for any suggestion THAT WORKS!"

"Yeah, I think we've got them completely frustrated," said Pelli.

"Oh thank you so much for that obvious observation," said Chipshak sarcastically.

Pelli stuck her tongue out at him.

Soolchakan assisted Efor off of the table. Efor was turned over to his wife Palakim who had been resurrected only one day earlier. The parents of Efor, Naban and Mila were there as well. Meffin was there to help Palakim and Efor in the education of "what-happened-while-I-was-dead" information.

"Next is Byrib," said Bonarain. "He was only 25 when he was murdered. If he turns up as a full grown adult then…I'd say that these stones are really doing something that…we are completely incapable of understanding…the how or why."

Kiyalee huffed. "Yuh THINK?"

The body of Byrib was brought in. They stared down at the small shriveled corpse. They all looked at each other nervously wondering what was going to happen once they started the procedure on him.

Chyning looked off to the side. She saw Poolkiy and Oanin standing there looking very anxious. "What do you two want?"

Poolkiy frowned looking rather confused. "I'm…waiting for you to…bring my son back," he said still looking perplexed.

Chyning looked back at the body. "Oh! This is your son?"

Kiyalee snarled through clenched teeth. "When are you going to start reading…ANYTHING?!"

Chyning cleared her throat with a red face. "Let's get it done," she said looking a little guilty.

They leaned over the corpse and started concentrating. The

four stones jumped up and joined. The, now familiar, shimmering gold rays started shooting out. They were all thinking about bringing the boy back and were all four eagerly waiting to see what would happen. The rays enveloped the corpse and all they could see was the golden glow. All four of them started getting weak in the knees. The ones behind them noticed the slumping and opened fire with the pulse guns. The four started absorbing energy from the rays and were able to stand up again. The shimmering glow started elongating as if it were stretching the body. They did not hear the normal gasping for breath yet. The glow finally stopped growing and now they could see the body on the table. The body was that of a full grown adult. Finally the labored breathing started. The eyes opened and Byrib was now alive again –and full grown. The shimmering rays continued on a little longer than normal. When the rays stopped, the four stones fell away from each other and the first generation quartet were all panting and perspiring heavily.

Soolchakan looked back at Uruduns. "Why did you stop… with the pulse pistol?"

Uruduns looked down at the pistol. He looked back up cautiously. "You…it looked like…you didn't need any…more energy." He cleared his throat. "Uh…do you?"

Soolchakan simply nodded while looking somewhat disgusted.

Bonarain wiped some of the sweat off. "Yazhayki, I need some more energy as well."

Kiyalee waved her hand at Witsatay. "Don't just sit there

like a lump! Give me something as well."

Chyning simply gave Chamachay a dirty look.

Now all four were getting more power from the pulse pistols.

As soon as he had enough, Soolchakan signaled to Uruduns to stop. "In the future I think…we need to tell…whoever has the pulse pistols, that a child…especially a small one…will require a great deal more energy than any adult."

"I'll write that down…right now," said Bonarain. She went to a computer terminal and entered the information.

Poolkiy and Oanin retrieved their son Byrib from the table. It was a little unnerving seeing someone who was physically very young when he was killed, now as a fully mature adult. They realized that they were going to have to give him more than just the normal indoctrination regarding what had happened. They were also going to have to give him a crash course in mental maturity as well as his newly acquired physical maturity.

Kiyalee groaned. "Oh…*h'oolyach*! Byrib was 25 when he was killed. The next one, Yotam…she was 19." She looked back at Witsatay. "Don't let off of that gun until I tell you… understand?"

Witsatay nodded.

Bonarain looked around at the others. "That goes for all of you." She then turned to the door. "Baka? Chera? Are you ready to get your daughter?"

Baka and Chera were standing there with looks of anticipation on their faces and tears in their eyes. They both nodded.

Soolchakan sniffed and wiped his brow. "Bring in Yotam."

They went through the same tribulation with Yotam. They had the same light show and they were all panting and perspiring after it was over.

Kiyalee went to a chair and sat down. "How many more children do we have today?"

"Just Banabar," said Bonarain. "After he is done...we won't have to worry about any children...for a while."

Chyning was leaning on the table looking exhausted. She looked up. "Is Banabar next?"

Yeema came up with the list. "No, he's not. You have Ayino, Ometik and Ranip before you get to Banabar."

Soolchakan wiped more sweat off his face. "They'll seem easy compared to what we just went through."

Yeema snickered nervously. "That thing about Banabar... is only one problem."

Soolchakan hung his head. "Uh-oh. What else?"

Yeema looked down at the list. "You've been doing sixteen per day for a few days now. If you do sixteen today...the last one is Eena of the Fifth."

Chyning shrugged. "So what's the problem?"

"Eena is...the older of...twin sisters. Are you going to do Eena today and...leave Sana until tomorrow?"

Soolchakan closed his eyes and grunted. "Why don't we see how we feel...after Eena? If we feel like...one more then... we'll do one more."

Yeema looked a little concerned. "You might...wanna wait...until tomorrow for both of them."

Bonarain now looked a little upset. "Why?"

"Because right now, Palakim has her plate full working with her husband Efor. Eena and Sana are her children. Do you really want to put three of them on her...the day after he was brought back?"

Bonarain walked up and put her arm around Yeema's shoulder. "Yesterday you got your husband Nog back. Today, you get your daughter Shana. When do you get your next child back?"

Yeema looked at the list. She looked up with a smile. "I'll get Nankee back tomorrow."

Bonarain nodded. "Is that too heavy a load for you?"

Yeema clenched her lips trying to hold tears back. "I guess not," she sniffed.

Kiyalee grunted. "Are we finished with that conversation? Can we get back to our work at hand?"

"By all means," said Soolchakan. "Onward and forward with Ayino."

After what they went through with Byrib and Yotam, the work on Ayino, Ometik and Ranip almost seemed easy.

As usual, Mahanee was there to welcome back any of her children. She cried tears of joy as she helped Ometik off of the table. Ometik was the ninth of her twenty-two children brought back, who had been killed during the three wars. They almost had to shove them out of the room in order to continue. Usually, they had been going to the apartment where the victim had lived. That became a little too much with all of the apartment Jumping and resurrections. Now, it was all done in one centralized area.

Banabar was every bit the challenge that Byrib and Yotam had been. Once the procedure was finished on him, Azar and Meffin were more than ready to take the very confused Banabar back to their apartment and begin his lessons in history...among other things.

By the time they got to the fifteenth one of the day – Shana, they were physically spent.

"I'm sorry," said Soolchakan. "The twins will have to wait until tomorrow."

"I agree...completely," said Kiyalee.

Chyning was almost asleep already.

Soolchakan turned to the four who had been assisting by feeding them power. "I think that...we'll need the four of you to Jump us back to our apartment. Today was extremely difficult and...I don't want to miss the target."

Uruduns looked concerned. "I...don't have any form of

landmark…for your apartment."

Bonarain shook her head sadly. "Then we'll just walk."

"No," said Kiyalee. She smiled at Uruduns. "All you have to do is picture the front door of your apartment. Now, see it with the number 12-562 on it instead of…whatever your apartment number is. Is that simple enough for you?"

Bonarain felt really stupid again. 'Simple,' she thought. 'Why can't I think of something simple?'

Soolchakan smiled. "Just do it one at a time though, *please*. I don't want to have any of us *join* accidentally in front of my door. I hate to think of what might happen if we do. Coordinate with the one that goes ahead of you."

All four got to the bedrooms safely.

Osakisha looked down at the fallen (and cursing) Henteskim. "How long are we supposed to keep aggravating these silly *bimyocks*?"

Ohway kicked Henteskim in the ribs…again. "As long as they keep trying to find us. If they give up and go home, stop looking for us and go on to other things…then we leave them alone."

Hotherette giggled. "Until then, we have all kinds of fun and find out just how cruel we can be."

"We especially want to keep them away from that big hoop in that carriage," said Yoozoma. "When I heard that they can look through the thing and…actually see us in another dimension, I just…I didn't know what to think."

Hotherette looked out a little peephole in the carriage. "Hey! Who is that?"

Ohway slapped Henteskim down again and headed for another peephole. "What are you talking about?"

Both Osakisha and Yoozoma were peering through other peepholes.

Hotherette was looking slightly north. "I see that Area Chief, Thatoom Showshoo coming back and he's got two strangers with him."

Thatoom was riding a large equine. The two Heyyah strangers were sitting in the driver's seat of a very large carriage that seemed to be moving by itself.

The one on the left was a very beautiful, rather thin but very buxom woman. She appeared to be wearing just too much makeup. She was dressed in a long shimmering scarlet robe. Her long blonde hair hung in curls down below her shoulders. She was looking around the entire area, taking in everything she saw as the carriage moved slowly. She was holding onto a long staff that she was moving slightly. It appeared that the staff was being used to somehow guide the self-propelled carriage.

The one on the right was a rather old looking and rather pale, skinny man. He was dressed all in light brown - shirt, pants, boots and a wide brimmed hat. He had equally long hair, however, his was thin and completely white. He had very thick bushy eyebrows. For once, one of the male wizards came here with a clean shaved face. He had a long staff as well, however it was just sitting there between his knees. He appeared to be totally bored with (and ignoring) everything going on around him.

Henteskim got up. He looked rather troubled. "Huh? Whu…what's going on?" He ran to the door of his carriage. Before any of the Owlamites could stop him he was already outside. He saw the newcomers. "WHAT ARE THEY DOING HERE?!"

Thatoom scoffed. "They're here because you don't seem to be making any progress. If you can't do it, maybe they can."

Henteskim clenched his teeth. "WE HAVE A CONTRACT!"

Thatoom dismounted from his equine. "A CONTRACT THAT, SO FAR, YOU HAVE FAILED TO FULFILL!" He pointed at the newcomers. "Maybe they can get *some* results. You, so far, have nothing."

Osakisha clicked her tongue. "Uh-oh. I believe we have another set of wizards to contend with."

"I hope they don't have another set of those wretched hoops," said Yoozoma.

"Only one way to find out," said Ohway. "I'm going to do a quick search of that new carriage."

"I'll join you," said Osakisha.

The four of them were in Spy dimension, so walking out of the carriage was no problem.

Osakisha was walking towards the new carriage. "Hotherette, you start reading that new woman. Yoozoma, you get the man. Ohway and I will see if there's anything in that carriage that could possibly cause us some new problems."

Ohway shook his head. "I think…we should notify someone back at the gorge. If these people are from a different Wizard Clique then we might be in need of reinforcements."

Osakisha nodded. "Excellent idea. You thought it up - you do it."

Ohway did not hesitate. **"Bikaropin, this is Ohway, can you hear me**?"

Bikaropin looked up a little surprised. The newest one brought to the table for resurrection was being put in place. He responded. **"This is Bikaropin, I hope that this is important. We're getting ready to start today's rounds of bringing back the dead. What did you need**?"

**"We've got some fresh blood here at the slaver's compound. It appears that they're wizards but…they don't look like any of the ones that we saw here…or in Falamin**."

Bikaropin hung his head and sighed. **"I'll get some help out there**." He thought for a few moments. **"Senbower, this Bikaropin, can you hear me**?"

Senbower was sitting at the table with a mouthful of food. He shrugged. **"This is Senbower. What did you need? Our shift at the compound doesn't start until midday**."

"**Change of plans. It seems that the slavers have called on a different wizard Clique to assist in finding us. I need you to get your family and assist Ohway's family as soon as you can get there**."

Senbower chuckled. "**It had to happen sooner or later. The wizards that are there are getting nothing so...I'd hire a different group as well**."

Bikaropin nodded. "**Right**." He went back to getting Eena on the table.

Soolchakan had been eavesdropping on the conversation. He shook his head. "I wonder where this bunch is coming from."

Bonarain frowned. "What are you talking about?"

Soolchakan shrugged. "The slavers have hired a new group to try to find us. According to Ohway, the new representatives just got there."

Kiyalee grunted. "Are we gonna be needed there?"

Bikaropin shook his head. "I already sent Senbower's family to assist Ohway's family. If there's any concern, we'll let you know."

Chyning sighed. "Yeah! They get all of the fun now, while we get all of the work."

Bikaropin sneered at Chyning. "Considering the fact that my son Judog is one of the ones listed for today's round, Inorim and I are kinda looking forward to what is going on *here*."

Chyning smiled. "Good point." She looked down at the

corpse. "Okay, Eena, get ready."

At the end of the day, Bikaropin now had another one of his children as well as his second wife, Pyree, back.

"They all say the same thing," said Soolchakan while looking irritated. "Nobody can remember anything. It seems as if they just woke up from a long sleep. They're a little disoriented and weak, but...they're functioning as if...I don't know."

"That's what it was like," said Kiyalee.

Chyning nodded. "I don't remember nuthin' between 1804 and 5474." She sighed.

Soolchakan just shook his head. 'I wonder why,' he thought. He bit his lower lip while concentrating on the puzzlement.

# 6

Senbower rubbed his temples. "This is getting monotonous. They all have memories of towers but, they all seem to be in different places. The view from their windows is...always different."

"I figured it out," said Vanva. "They do have different towers...all over Ficara. The team from South Chilamte has just one tower. They have everything there. They don't seem to have any other place to fall back on...in case of disaster. They're relying on the fact that their island is too difficult to get to."

Eela scoffed. "So if that one tower goes...they're stuck with nothing."

"Judging from the scenery...viewed from the windows of each of the rooms of this woman, Kokee, I'd say that this Ficara Clique has a tower in each one of the countries on the continent of Ficara," said Pesitenee. "When you read her mind and check on her memories, all she can do is concentrate on the plants."

Vanva nodded. "A lot of those plants are rather unique to certain areas."

Senbower chuckled. "That woman, Kokee, is very

interested in Botany.  She likes to use a lot of the different petals, leafs and sap for some of her spells.  It seems that she is very good at those spells."  He looked at the man.  "That one, Huth, he doesn't care about plants.  He cares about chemicals.  If he could make a chemical from a plant then he'll do it.  If not…hang the plants, go to chemistry and geology."

Osakisha walked up to the other group.  "I take it that you got the same thing we did.  They have towers all over Ficara and each of their twelve members has a bedroom and an experiment room in each one of those towers."

Pesitenee huffed.  "These magical types sure like their tall towers."

"Why not?"  Osakisha shook her head.  "Put them in the right place and they're easy to defend.  If you have several towers, you have some kind of escape route planned.  Just make sure that you don't leave anything behind that is truly valuable to you at any one location.  That way, if you have to run you don't have to worry about forgetting something.  Plus, a tall tower helps in seeing any enemy from a distance.  A good plan would be to leave the lower floors uninhabited and filled with traps.  That'd slow any invaders down considerably, especially if the traps are noisy and painful.  Plus, when you're up high - it is very easy to look down on others."

Hotherette joined the group.  "That continent Chief… Thatoom.  He's finished with the briefings to Kokee and Huth. The two of them are doing some conspiring with each other in their carriage.  Ohway and Yoozoma are in there listening in on their conversation. They seem to think that they have some impenetrable barrier in there. They might be able to block the other Wizard Clique out of their business, but…" She grinned. "They can't block us."

Yoozoma suddenly appeared next to the group. "We've got a bit of a problem."

Eela cocked her head to the side. "Like what?"

"That man, Huth." Yoozoma took a deep breath and shook her head. "He has some kind of crazy little lens. He can see into other dimensions with it. Right now, Ohway is doing everything he can to stay behind the man while he's looking through it, but… that thing could be a problem."

Pesitenee snickered. "Why don't we just take it away from him?"

Yoozoma frowned. "Are you sure that you wanna do *that*?"

Senbower shrugged. "Soolchakan did say that we're supposed to defend Owlamites at all costs. Taking something away from him that could reveal our presence here…and who we are…I think that could meet the requirement."

"Let's wait until he goes to sleep," said Vanva. "That way, he'll just think that he misplaced it."

Yoozoma nodded. "He did say that he was getting tired. That might be a good plan. If he thinks he misplaced it, that'll distract him, for a while, looking for it. If we swipe it…right in front of him…he'll know…" She shook her head. "The fewer clues we give them – the better off we are."

Ohway appeared next to the group. "That man is suspicious and…I had to get out of there before he spotted me."

Hotherette gave him a patronizing glare. "All you had to do was stay behind him. How's that so difficult?"

Ohway gave her the same kind of dirty look. "He started spinning around rather rapidly. I was reading his mind and it almost seemed as if he was aware of me being in there. He was turning back and forth rather quickly and then…he started spinning." He closed his eyes. "I'm still reading his mind and… he's still spinning around in there. He should be getting a little dizzy by now and…oops…he just fell down."

Osakisha closed her eyes. "Yes, I've got him." She giggled. "He is very dizzy and very frustrated." She opened her eyes looking rather perturbed. "He knew that someone was in there and he's a little upset over the fact that he can't find any of us."

"He's beginning to doubt the power of that lens," said Ohway.

"That helps," said Yoozoma. "If we can get any of them to doubt their own magic, that will be a wonderful asset for us."

Senbower got an idea. "Did he drop the lens?"

"No," said Yoozoma. "He won't let go of the silly thing. Even though he's doubting it right now, he still wants to keep it because it is still a magical item."

"Okay, so we have to wait a little before grabbing it," said Senbower. "I wonder…"

Vanva looked sideways at him. "About what?"

"Hold on a moment," said Senbower. **"Bikaropin, this Senbower, can you hear me?"**

Bikaropin shook his head. **"I'm a little busy right now, is this important?"**

**"Just one question, have we tested some of the toys that these wizards are using? We found that their spells don't work in other dimensions, how about all of their gadgets?"**

Bikaropin huffed. **"So far, all of their toys that they took with them, none of them have worked in the other dimensions…why?"**

**"Because this Huth character has a toy that could cause us no end to grief. I think we'll Jump him to the Beasties planet and take the toy away."**

Bikaropin shook his head. **"Sounds like a plan. Remember, you don't have to ask permission to cause them grief, just go ahead and do it."**

The others had been listening in on the conversation.

Pesitenee stood askance. "What about that Kokee?"

Senbower was confused. "What about her?"

Pesitenee huffed. "She is still in there. Don't you think

that if we make him disappear in front of her...she'll be a little suspicious?"

"I wouldn't worry about that," said Osakisha. "She's considering him to be some kind of *bimyock* because he got himself dizzy to the point of falling down. She's coming out right now."

Senbower smiled. "Now is the time to Jump him to Beasties and...take his little toy away." He Jumped to the inside of the carriage. He saw that Huth was still trying to get his mental faculties lined back up.

Vanva walked through the wall of the carriage. She wanted to watch what happened and see if Huth would be aware of her or Senbower.

Senbower reached out with his right hand and took hold of Huth's shoulder. A rather loud bang and several sparks came out of the robe where Huth had been touched. Senbower fell back screaming in agony clutching his right hand. Seeing as how he was in Spy dimension when he fell, he fell directly through the floor.

Vanva saw him fall and then saw Huth pull that lens up to his eye, looking to see if he could find the perpetrator that had touched him. She ducked down through the bottom of the carriage before she was spotted. She found Senbower still screaming and clutching his right wrist. She grabbed Senbower and Jumped both of them to Beasties.

As soon as they arrived, Senbower stopped his screaming. He was now just breathing rapidly and sweating. He peered down at his right hand with a very surprised look on his face. He flexed his fingers several times and kept rubbing his wrist.

Vanva knelt down and took hold of his face. "Are you all right...now?"

He looked at her. "Uh...yeah...I'm okay now." He looked back at his hand. "What happened? I'm reaching for him and... POW, my whole arm is in agony. Then...just as suddenly as the pain started...it went away. That...is very disturbing."

She sighed in relief. "He had some kind of protection glyph on his...clothing. As soon as you hopped your hand into Home and grabbed him, the glyph went off and did the damage that it was supposed to do. I figured that since their magic doesn't work in these other dimensions, then maybe, just maybe, if I bring you here, then the spell is...broken."

Senbower laid down flat. He stared at the sky for a moment. "Nice quick thinking. It worked." He chuckled. "Thank you... very much."

She nodded. "Problem now...if you go back to Hardooth... will the spell come back again?"

He clenched his eyes and sniffed. "Unfortunately...that is something we're going to have to find out." He opened his eyes. "Since the spell has been...corrupted...I hope that it *has* been completely...busted." He inventoried all parts of his right hand and wrist. "The best way to find out is...you're going to have to be the one who...Jumps me there and be ready to Jump me back... just in case the worst possible thing happens."

She nodded. "You're right." She placed her hands on his chest. "Are you ready?"

He chuckled. "No, but we're still gonna have to do it anyway."

She chuckled back nervously and then Jumped them back to their apartment in the gorge.

He sat up. "Why'd you bring us here?"

She shrugged. "If that *bimyock* is still looking through that infernal lens he might have seen us come in. If he is looking around *there*, the others that are there are hiding from him. Now, that we know that the spell is gone, we can safely go back to the slaver compound."

"After we send a report to Bikaropin and mentally check and see if everything is clear."

She smiled. "Right!"


Bikaropin listened to the report from Senbower and Vanva. He mulled it over in his mind. "This is good information to know. If he has these glyphs on his clothing and the power of those spells can be broken by going to another dimension..." He shook his head. "The only thing that I can think of is that we're going to have to Jump that entire carriage into...some other dimension. Once the spells are nullified...then we can do whatever is necessary to get his toys away from him."

Senbower shook his head. "So how do we Jump that entire

carriage without anyone noticing that a huge carriage is suddenly missing?"

"I'm working on that," said Bikaropin as he looked up at the ceiling.

Vanva smiled. "Why don't we see if there are other carriages just like that one at the other towers? If there are...we could do some kind of a momentary tradeoff. We bring one of the others there as soon as we take the primary one away. Once the spells are broken and we have the toys that we need to take away from them, we trade back."

Bikaropin sighed. "The timing would have to be *so* precise. If we're off by just the amount of time it takes to blink your eyes... we could end up making both of them join."

Senbower smiled. "Not necessarily. If we bring the substitute in Ghost dimension, the *doovofts* at the compound will still see a carriage. After we've purloined what is necessary at the other end...we bring it back and the one in Ghost is then taken to...wherever we got it from originally."

Inorim and Pyree had been listening to the conversation.

"I'd like to be a part of that," said Inorim. "I want to get back in the swing of things as soon as possible."

"You're a little out of practice," said Bikaropin. "Remember what Bonarain went through."

Inorim stood up askance and angrily huffed. "Bonarain was not...asleep! She was awake and stuck in some void where none of *our* powers work. I didn't have that problem. I can still do my…tricks."

Bikaropin nodded. "You're right. I forgot. You were in a totally different situation." He nodded. "As soon as we find a carriage that is identical…or at least a reasonable facsimile to the one at the compound…we'll do it." He smiled at Inorim. "All of us."

Soolchakan staggered over to a chair and sat down. "Haven't we done sixteen by now? I'm getting really tired."

"So am I," said Bonarain.

"I've been tired," said Kiyalee.

Chyning simply looked around dull-eyed with her jaw sagging.

"I didn't tell you the count," said Yeema. "I…was wondering…what would happen if I didn't tell you the count."

Soolchakan leaned forward in the chair. "And…" he growled angrily?

Yeema gave him a guilty smile. "La-Iya was number sixteen. "Since you finished with her…you've done Takar, Keero, Dameen and Maling. You brought twenty back today."

Soolchakan's shoulders sagged. "We're getting better at it then. That is good to know." He sighed. "Good!" He nodded. "Good to know. But for now…I'm going to go get some sleep. Twenty…for one day is good." He nodded again and vanished.

"I agree," said Kiyalee.

All of them Jumped back to their bedrooms.

Nog looked at Yeema and shook his head while smiling. "I don't know whether to smack you or kiss you for that stunt."

She smiled. "Hey…it worked out for the better." She shrugged. "They gained another four for today. They know that they can do twenty…so they may speed up the process."

Nog sighed. "Let's hope that it all turns out positive."

Soolchakan came to the location of the events. Bikaropin was already there with the concrete tomb in place. Bonarain, Kiyalee and Chyning all came in ready to get back to work.

Soolchakan waited until the concrete was gone. He turned to Bikaropin. "I keep on hearing reports of how those wizards are being manipulated so they can't perform their spells. I haven't heard about any of the Healers. They were supposed to be coming in to regenerate the *organs* that we took from the slavers. What's happening there?"

Bikaropin chuckled weakly. "Sorry. I thought I had reported that."

"You haven't," said Bonarain impatiently.

"That's another one of our dirty little tricks. The slavers have called on several different sects of Healers to come in. We watch for the Healers." Bikaropin was doing everything he could to keep from laughing. "When the Healers get within two teckpell from the slaver compound, we get hold of them and Jump them to the northeastern shores of Buzitari."

Chyning frowned. "Where's Buzitari?"

Kiyalee slapped Chyning on the back of her head. "READ SOMETHING! If you had bothered to read anything, including geography, you'd know that Buzitari is the most northeastern country on the Ficara continent."

Bonarain shook her head in disgust. "And...again...if you had bothered to read anything, you'd know that Slateel is geographically the most southern location on Ficara. The Healers aren't being taken to a different continent, they're just being taken to a different place on the same continent...as far away as possible."

Kiyalee turned to Soolchakan and smiled. "All this time and you haven't thought of using the *Voice of Power* to force her to start reading the reports? Why not?"

Soolchakan looked at Kiyalee. He then looked over at Chyning without turning his head. "I don't want to get in the habit of *forcing* anyone to do anything...unless it is absolutely necessary and essential for our survival." He sighed. "If she wants to continue being irresponsible, that's her problem." He looked at the body of Vistul. "Let's get to it."


Yatozon found another carriage at one of the towers of the Ficara Clique. It was not identical to the one that was currently located at the slaver compound, however, if no one got too close they should not notice too many differences...hopefully. The primary differences were the fancy decorations on the side and a name on the seat where the driver would sit. It was also convenient that none of the Clique members was currently at that specific tower at the time. His three wives, Zanashi, Na-An and Neffrata all went there to assist in moving the decoy carriage.

Osakisha and Hotherette were the ones who were coordinating the movement of both carriages.

"First, thing," said Osakisha, "is to hop that substitute into Ghost. Then we can go with the movement of both of them."

Yatozon nodded. "Right. I'll take care of that business right now." He reached out and touched the side of the carriage. A bang and sparks shot out of the carriage where his hand was. He fell back screaming in agony.

Since the others had been informed of what had happened to Senbower and how Vanva had taken care of the situation, Zanashi grabbed Yatozon and Jumped him to Beasties. The two of them were back rather quickly.

Yatozon stood there rubbing some feeling back in his right hand. "Okay, that didn't work. It seems that this Clique doesn't trust anybody and they have all kinds of protection glyphs...not only on their clothing but their possessions as well. What do we do now?"

Vistul had been brought back and now they were working on Fan. Bikaropin was interrupted by Yatozon and Osakisha regarding what had just occurred at the sight of the other carriage.

Bikaropin hung his head. 'Can't anyone think for themselves,' he thought bitterly. **"As I recall, I was informed that when Senbower was zapped, he fell through the floor of the carriage. Vanva told me that she went through the bottom of the carriage as well to rescue him. Why don't you try touching the bottom of each of the carriages and see if that makes a difference? They are only thinking of the top and sides of the carriage. They don't seem to think that anyone will come through the bottom. Also, if that doesn't work, try going inside. I don't think that any of them would set any booby-traps inside that they might trip over and get their own butt blasted to *h'oolyach*. Call me back ONLY if there is another problem that slows you down."**

Yatozon went under the carriage, hopped to dimension #1 and touched the underside. Senbower did the same. Neither one of them got zapped nor was there any reaction from Kokee or Huth.

Senbower now had an evil grin on his face. "I wanna to try something before we move the carriages."

Eela tried to remind Senbower that she was currently the one in charge at this location. Before she could say anything, Senbower had acted. He was back under the carriage. He reached up through the floor and grabbed Huth by his ankle. He Jumped Huth to one of the uninhabited planets in dimension #30.

Huth looked around in shock. He pulled out a leather pouch, pulled a few items out of it and attempted a few spells (which did not work). He pulled his special little lens out, placed it in front of his right eye and started turning around slowly. Senbower stood his ground. He waited until Huth had completed two full rotations. Huth had not noticed Senbower at all. More proof that none of the wizard's toys worked outside of Hardooth.

**"We now have more proof that the toys are ineffective as well as the spells. We also have some proof that they put the protection glyphs on their clothing but not their bodies,"** sent Senbower. He slapped the lens out of the hand of Huth.

Huth looked at his hand in surprise. He looked down to find his fallen lens.

Senbower kicked Huth in the groin - hard. Huth fell to the ground moaning and clutching his crotch. Senbower, again, grabbed an ankle and Jumped Huth back to his carriage. The lens was left behind. Senbower was the only one who knew where that special lens was and he didn't care if anyone on that planet found it. It did not have any magical properties there, so it was now totally insignificant.

Eela stood there with her arms folded looking rather perturbed. "All the trouble we went through to try set this plan in motion and…now you've gotten rid of the lens. What're we supposed to do now? We don't have any reason to move this, or the other coach."

Senbower shrugged. "They still have a lot of other toys. They still have some of those protection glyphs on their clothing… and possibly their toys as well. I got rid of one toy…that was on his person. Now, we can Jump the whole carriage and get rid of any other toys…and protected clothing."

Hotherette nodded. "Sounds good. We still go through with the plan."

Senbower, Eela, Vanva and Pesitenee crawled under the carriage at the slaver compound. Yatozon, Zanashi, Na-An and Neffrata crawled under the substitute. Osakisha gave the order for the substitute to be hopped to Ghost. The Ghost was then Jumped to the slaver compound and the original carriage was Jumped to the middle of the big desert on the planet in dimension #198. The decoy was hopped into #1.

Vanva stood up and was now looking at the inside of the carriage. "Uh…now that we're here…we don't know what does or does not have any magical glyph on it. What do we get rid of?"

Pesitenee giggled. "Everything!  Leave nothing and… they'll have nothing. We don't take any chances that any of this stuff was going to be used against us."

Eela nodded. "Chairs, tables, wardrobes, clothing and… all paraphernalia that is in here. It all goes."

"Yeah," said Senbower. He looked at Huth, who was still moaning in pain on the floor. "That includes the robe he's wearing. I remember getting my hand *blasted* by that thing. I'm not gonna take any chances with that wretched thing again."

It took a while, however, they cleaned out everything in the carriage except Huth.

Eela called back. **"Is that other carriage still in**

**Ghost**?'"

"**It is now**," sent Hotherette.

"**Here we come**!"

With that, the original was brought back to the slaver compound. The substitute was then sent to #198 and emptied as well. It was then returned back from whence it had been taken originally.

While all of that was going on, Ohway had been in the tent with Kokee. He had been doing several things to upset her concentration. He did everything he could to make it appear as something other than himself causing her breaks in the process. He dropped an insect down her cleavage, he made several strange noises that seemed to be coming from the outside or he touched her finger, nose or a toe. He was getting tired of being covert. He decided to end her spell-casting for the day with one substantial act. She was trying hard to keep her concentration and ignore any outside noises or other distractions. He reached to the back of his neck, got a finger full of his sex mucus and liberally striped her forehead with it.

She gasped in shock. Her eyes and mouth were now wide open with a very strange look on her face. She grabbed her crotch with both hands and looked around in surprise. She went to the main entry flap of the tent, opened it, saw Thatoom Showshoo standing there, grabbed him by his left arm and yanked him inside the tent.

Thatoom was rather surprised at being pulled inside, however, he did not question the act. She had given instructions that the slavers were to cooperate with anything and everything that was ordered by her or Huth in order to accomplish the desired goal. If she wanted him inside the tent – okay, fine. Now, he was being stripped – from the waist down – okay, uh…fine (he thought). Now, he was thrown down on the ground on his back. Now, her robes were going up and pantaloons down. Now, she was (rather impatiently) stimulating him sexually. Now, she was on top of him maniacally copulating with him. He did not know what to make of it, however, he was going to cooperate…no matter what. He had heard of wizardry and also those things with the demimondaine. Maybe this was a combination of both. He was not sure, however, as long as he was being pleasured… 'Might as well just lay here, cooperate and enjoy it,' he thought. 'It is sexual pleasuring.' He enjoyed it for a while until she showed no signs of slowing down. She seemed insatiable. "I can't keep this up much longer," he said through clenched teeth. "Can I get one of the other men to…cooperate with you?"

She looked down with savage eyes. "I thought you said that all the other men have been castrated," she panted. "You're the only one here…who can do this!"

'Oh no,' he thought. All of the other slavers were out searching for the very tardy Healers. The only other non-snipped man in the compound, currently, was Huth. As old as he was, he might not be able to *do the deed.*

After some time, Kokee was finally showing signs of extreme exhaustion, however, she was not slowing down. She was just a few heartbeats away from collapse. Ohway decided to show some mercy and cleaned his mucus off of her forehead.

She did collapse on top of Thatoom, panting heavily. He was still unsure if he should do anything. Ohway stood there snickering.

Kokee finally got a little bit of a second wind and slowly pushed herself up. She looked around inside the small tent. "I... don't know...what happened." She looked down at Thatoom. "I...couldn't...control myself."

He frowned. "You mean...that wasn't part of...any spell?"

She shook her head. "No! That...wasn't part of...any plan of mine...or any spell." She tried getting up and fell back down on him. She wiped some perspiration off her forehead. "I think... we're dealing with a Clique of wizards who...they're beyond my powers. We may have to bring the entire Clique here."

He groaned. "How much is that gonna cost?"

"Do you want this done," she snarled through clenched teeth?

He sighed. "It has to be done," he whined. "We were insulted beyond belief. We were attacked, we were disrespected, and we were robbed of possessions and merchandise. My people were mutilated. Right now, we're both being distracted and prevented from obtaining slaves, you for experiments and me for profit." He shook his head helplessly. "It has to be done or neither of us gets anything, positive or profitable, accomplished."

"Then help me back to the carriage. I have a way of contacting the other members of my Clique." She seemed devoid of any strength at all, however, she was finally able to get off of Thatoom (with a little assistance from him) and pull her pants up.

He crawled over to his pants and redressed himself. He got up on wobbly legs. He now assisted her in getting up and the two of them departed the tent. The rest of the people in the compound were rather mystified as to what was going on. They could not understand why Thatoom and Kokee seemed so...weak and/or inebriated. They all did remember that they were supposed to cooperate with the wizards in whatever was needed. They did not question what they were seeing. They had observed, on other occasions, that after doing some serious spell casting, the wizards did seem somewhat disabled or tired. On the other side of that, why was Thatoom looking so tired? He was not a wizard so why was he looking so exhausted? Apparently, she had somehow used him for a part of the spell. No one had the courage to ask what it was or why.

The pain and discomfort that Huth was feeling had finally dissipated. He was laying there, flat on his back with his eyes closed breathing slowly. He reached up to his chest to scratch an itch and was rather startled over the fact that he felt no clothing. He opened his eyes and looked at his body. Now he was even more distressed at seeing that he was completely naked. He got up to go to his closet and get another robe and...now he was aghast and baffled over the fact that there was nothing inside the carriage other than himself. The lamps were gone and the only light was coming in through small peephole slits in the sides of the carriage. He heard a noise at the door. He knew that Kokee was the only one (at this location) who could possibly know how to get in. He prepared himself for the shock that she was going to experience...

in just a few moments.

Kokee backed in. She thanked someone for assisting her. She closed the door and was surprised by the sudden darkness... where it should not be dark. She turned around and now she was just as shocked and baffled as Huth. "What...happened in here?"

Huth took a deep breath. "We're not dealing with any amateurs. I don't know who we're dealing with, but..." He shook his head. "I don't think that we're capable of handling this...I mean just the two of us. It may take the entire Clique."

She sank to her knees. She was still looking around the interior. "But...how do we contact them? I...we..." She closed her eyes and clenched her teeth. "I don't have anything here that I can use to contact any of them. Everything was in my special closet."

He huffed. "You've still got a few pouches full of goodies around your belt along with a few hidden pouches in your robe! Don't tell me that you have...absolutely *nothing*. There's got to be something that we can utilize for long distance communication."

She looked down at her pouches. "I'll check but...I won't guarantee anything." She dug through all of the pouches. She had to go to the light coming through the slits. She finally found one tiny little item. She held it up with a helpless look on her face.

"That is only enough for a very short message," whined Huth.

She sighed. "So what message should we send?"

He hung his head. He looked up and took a deep breath.

"Since we can only send two or three words…I suggest that we send one word."

She was aghast. "One word?"

He nodded. "Help!"

She nodded. "If I sound desperate enough…they'll contact me. They have a lot more of this where they are, to make a stronger connection…and a two-way conversation."

He shrugged. "So do it."

Eela looked at the others. "Are we gonna allow this communication?"

"We need to," said Pesitenee. "If we allow it, we'll find out who and where the others in this Clique are currently located. We'll have more information about who we're dealing with."

Eela shrugged. "Okay."

Kokee did what was necessary. The small item in her hand was crushed and rolled between the palms of her hands. It started glowing faintly as she mumbled something unintelligible. She leaned closer to the glow. "Avancha…HELP!" The glow died out.

Huth sighed. "Now we wait."

Kokee sniffed. "Haven't you got something else you can wear?"

He grunted in disgust. "Have you got another robe under the one you're currently wearing? They, whoever *they* are, took…

absolutely…EVERYTHING!'"

She looked off to the side and grimaced. She reached under her robes and dropped her pantaloons. She kicked them off and walked away. She huffed as she realized there was no place to go in here.

Huth picked up the garment and put it on. He looked up disgusted. "The crotch is…very wet."

She clenched her eyes and flushed. "Don't ask!" She walked to one side of the carriage and sat down, leaning against the wall sulking. In a very short time, she bowed her head and was sound asleep.

He was very confused.

Eela sent a message back to the gorge. They were about to get a full roll call of the Clique from Ficara.


The response to the call for help took almost half a day to respond. Kokee and Huth could do nothing but sit there and feel sorry for themselves. They had no food, drink, clothing or any other possessions in the carriage and they did not want the slavers to know of their dilemma.

Kokee looked up, bleary eyed, at a sliver of light that appeared inside the carriage. It took Huth a few more moments to notice the light. Both of them stood up and faced the light. A blurred face started materializing inside the light as it grew larger. The face took shape as it slowly rotated in the light. It was the face of an elderly woman.

"Thank Nepekeep you're here, Avancha," said Kokee. "We've been waiting quite some time."

Avancha responded in a ghostly voice. "Yes, I am here. I'm wondering…why is it so difficult to get through? What happened to your devices and…where are you? It is very dark."

Kokee hung her head. She looked up. "We're inside my carriage."

"Then why don't you light some lamps?"

"We don't have any," said Kokee! "Believe it or not… we've been robbed. Everything that was in the carriage is…gone."

Avancha now looked shocked. "How is that possible?"

"We're not dealing with any minors or amateurs," said Huth. "Not only did they clean the carriage out…they stole everything of mine…including *all* of my clothing."

Avancha giggled. "I was wondering why you were dressed that way."

"This is *not* funny," scolded Kokee. "I can't think of any person or Clique that is capable of this theft. If this gets out, our Clique is humiliated beyond belief. No one will ever let us live it down, plus they'll think that they can steal anything from us at any time."

Avancha scoffed. "Especially Penbelth. He'll make a huge deal out of it."

"He'll let the whole world know," growled Huth.

"All right," said Avancha. "What do you suggest right now?"

Kokee grimaced in frustration. "We need someone to… teleport here…to us. Bring something to…make it easier for others to come here…through the carriage. We can't show any sign of weakness…especially since the South Chilamte Clique is already here."

Avancha hung her head. "Yes, we do need to show strength. We're supposed to be replacing them because they failed to fill a contract. I'll get Misska to come to you. She's the most proficient at teleportation. Once she is there then…we'll have a better portal to go through…for all of us." She bit her lip. "Do you have anything in the carriage that we can use as a marker for her to focus on…for the teleport?"

"We have nothing but us," said Huth desperately! "The thieves stole absolutely everything that was inside the carriage… including the clothing that I was wearing at the time."

Avancha snickered. "Then I'll have her focus on those ridiculous pants that you're wearing, Huth. Where did you find anything so…frilly?"

"They're mine," said Kokee through her teeth. "He was left, as he said, with absolutely *nothing*!"

Avancha cleared her throat and coughed trying to stifle her giggling. "I'll get Misska on it right now. Hopefully the rest of us will be there before the day is over."

Twelve Owlamites were looking up through the floor of

the carriage listening in on the conversation.

Osakisha sighed. "We may need some help here as well. They're calling in their entire Clique." She shook her head. "We don't even know how many they have."

Hotherette closed her eyes. "I'm contacting the gorge right now."

Rinnboz, Raheen, Rahayn and Dahashi showed up at the slaver compound to assist in keeping track of all of the wizards that were going to be infesting the area.

Rinnboz surveyed the area. "Have any of the other new ones arrived yet?"

"Not yet," said Eela. "Apparently they did have something in the carriage that would have assisted them and since we made *it* disappear, they're having some problems."

"This is getting ridiculous," said Yatozon. "We've really stirred up a storm among these wizards. I wonder just how bad it could possibly get."

"I don't think it'll get that bad," said Ohway. "Just exactly how many *top* wizards could possibly exist?"

"True," said Na-An. "Because of what it takes to learn how to be one of the top wizards, not *everyone* could possibly be at the top. They have to learn all kinds of spells and prove their proficiency. They reach certain, what they call, plateaus, of expertise. Then and only then can they join one of these elite Cliques of High Wizards."

Vanva frowned. "Where'd you learn all of this?"

"By reading their minds," said Na-An with a smug smile.

Yoozoma chuckled. "While you've been reading the minds of the wizards and finding out some of their hierarchy, I've been reading the mind of this Thatoom. I now know the names and locations of all of his Sector Chiefs and Chiefs on this continent. I also know the names and locations of all of the other Area Chiefs on the other continents. It seems that they're very loyal to each other and they're all very interested in exactly who was this bunch of impudent fools who, not only attacked a slaver compound, but had the audacity to injure slavers and steal slaves from professional slavers. It seems that they're all gearing up to perform a massive strike against us...no matter what the cost. They have to teach the world that the slavers are to be left alone, above the law, to do their...profession." He huffed. "According to them, you don't dare defile any slaver."

Yatozon looked a little troubled. "Have you notified anyone back in the gorge about this...preparation for war?"

"I sent the information to Bikaropin and Mahanee. I hope they're giving it to Soolchakan," said Yoozoma.

Pesitenee scoffed. "Why wouldn't they give that information to Soolchakan?"

Yoozoma gave her a dull look. "He's just a little *busy*... bringing all of our deceased brothers and sisters back," said Yoozoma. "Yesterday they only got as far as Granthun. They're sleeping every night. They're doing a lot of heavy work. Would you want to be disturbed about the wizards and slavers...if you were bringing your children back?"

"It still affects all of us," said Senbower.

Yoozoma just shrugged.

The first generation quartet received the briefing about the slavers and wizards. They had just finished doing twenty-five of their children on this day so they were very tired.

Soolchakan turned to some second generation Owlamites. "Shalam, Monaha, you're going to have to rely on the expertise and wisdom of Bikaropin. He was never out of the picture so he's been living while all of this as it happened. You and everybody else may have to work with him to take care of this troubled situation. Just remember that no one outside of the Owlamite race must ever know about our place in the gorge."

Shalam and Monaha both nodded their heads in approval.

Bikaropin smiled as he looked around the room. "I'll keep everybody updated on any information that I receive…as soon as I receive it."

Soolchakan nodded. He was becoming very fond of this *delegation of authority*. It put a lot less stress on him. He especially did not need any more stress seeing as how they still had well over 2,000 Owlamites to bring back from the dead.

The first generation headed back to their bedrooms while looking over the list of those to be brought back tomorrow. Since they had already proved they could do twenty-five in one day, this list had twenty-five as well. They all took a bath, dried off and hit the pillows. This was a strange habit of any Owlamite since that firestorm weapon originally went off. Going to bed and actually sleeping on consecutive nights - totally unusual.

Twelve wizards from the Ficara Clique were now in the slaver compound. Most of them were doing what they could to refurnish (secretly) the carriage sitting in the compound.

Avancha was the leader of the Ficara Clique. She appeared to be a very old woman who was wrinkled with thin gray hair. She looked this way on purpose to deceive any enemy. She listened to all of the reports from Henteskim, Parrok, Kokee and Huth. She shook her head in gloom. "These people are just too arrogant. We've never heard of them and…they're doing things that…some of us have never dreamed of." She looked at Kokee and sighed. "We may have to bring the Clique from North Chilamte in on this."

Kokee shook her head. "You know what that means, don't you? Penbelth lives somewhere in North Chilamte. Once you inform that Clique, he'll want to get in on it."

"*That* is only one problem," scoffed Avancha. "As soon as you tell the North Chilamte Clique…of which Elathkom is a member, he'll tell his sister Elathka."

Kokee closed her eyes and groaned. "Penbelth and Elathka in the same place at the same time…competing against each other."

Avancha nodded. "Our Clique is not strong enough to stop both of them from…a very nasty face-off. Let's just hope that, for the purpose of all of us gaining knowledge, they can be somewhat civil with each other…for once."

Ohway looked at his Owlamite colleagues. "Just who are these two? Two wizards that put fear in an entire Clique. They sound dangerous."

Osakisha looked sick. "I'll inform Bikaropin."

Ohway just nodded with a concerned look on his face.

# 7

Soolchakan showed up to start the next resurrection. He was rather surprised when he saw the look on the faces of Bonarain, Kiyalee and Chyning. Before he could ask, Bikaropin came up and started scanning him with one of the medical devices from the Chokchakchok ship.

Bikaropin finished his scanning and checked the readout. He looked rather concerned. "I think that you need to stop doing this for a few days."

"Give me a *very* good reason," said Soolchakan suspiciously.

"You remember that the Teltermak said that one of their favorite target organs is that...*extra gut*...under our liver?"

Soolchakan simply nodded still looking suspicious.

"I've checked you and the others. When that text said that the stones took some *thing* away from you in order to bring someone back. That was *not* a fabrication."

Soolchakan narrowed his eyes even more.

"You and the three others of the first generation...your

*extra gut* has shrunken considerably. You need to stop for a few days and see if you…heal."

"How are you defining…heal?"

"I'll scan you tomorrow and see if that *organ* is doing any kind of self-restoration. If it is," he shrugged. "You'll be able to proceed, once the healing is fully accomplished. Until then, you have to hold off…for your own health."

Soolchakan slowly walked over to the concrete coffin. "I'm sorry Edana, but you'll have to wait. Don't know how long, but…we'll get to you as soon as we can."

Kiyalee cleared her throat. "What now? Do we just sit around…*healing*?"

Soolchakan shook his head. "No. While someone returns this coffin to Zhagool, we're going to go to that slaver compound and check on the status ourselves. I've been hearing some pretty interesting things going on there and…I'd like to see, first hand, as to what is going on and what we need to do."

The four first generation all Jumped to the slaver compound.

Bikaropin turned to Chena. "I'm sorry but you'll have to wait a little longer to see your daughter."

Chena nodded sadly. She sighed. "Better late than never." She looked at her husband, Or. "What should we do now?"

Or shrugged. "Take our daughter back to that spot in the vault on the moon and…remember that she is still number one on the list…when they start up again."

Chena sighed and looked at her husband Or, nodded and walked away sadly. Or Jumped the coffin back to Zhagool.

Soolchakan looked around at all the tents that were now in abundance in the area. He also looked over some of the new construction of houses and…cells for slaves. He heard some of the slavers planning all kinds of nasty things to do to the thugs who dared to injure a slaver…any slaver. He read minds of the wizards and was able to get the gist of their complete frustration over not being able to find out who had done these extraordinary deeds.

Osakisha interrupted Soolchakan in his mind reading. "They're so desperate that they're calling someone…who all of them say is…the ultimate wizard. They say his name with…great awe."

Soolchakan looked around. "Who? Which one is calling?"

Osakisha pointed to a trio of wizards standing close to a very elaborate carriage. "Them! They're the ones who are joining together to call him."

Being rather nosey, Soolchakan sauntered over to the trio to get into their minds and find some answers about this *Ultimate Magic Master*." He delved deep in their minds.

Bonarain, Kiyalee and Chyning joined Soolchakan in this reading. They were curious as well.

Kavluck, the leader of the South Chilamte Clique, Avancha, the leader of the Ficara Clique and Ovvtell, the leader of the North

Chilamte Clique, were all voicing some spell in unison. Each one would occasionally drop some yellow powder in the middle of a circle drawn on the ground in between them and then they would go back to their incantations, calling out to someone named Penbelth.

Soolchakan did not interrupt any of their spells. He wanted to see just exactly who this Penbelth was. If this person had three Cliques of very powerful wizards so scared of him that it took all of them together to protect themselves or call him – this was someone he wanted to find out about…as soon as possible.

A mist started forming inside the circle. It rose up in a hazy spire and started taking a humanoid shape. Someone was forming inside the circle, however, the features were not coming through clearly as far as the face was concerned. The ghostly image took on the full shape of a person and then started getting some color. The person coming in was slightly shorter than Soolchakan. He was dressed in a neon blue robe. He had a hood over his head and, Soolchakan was rather puzzled, this person was wearing a white mask that only showed two eyeholes and a long slit for the mouth.

Chyning scoffed. "Is he that ugly? He doesn't want anyone to see his face?"

Kiyalee shook her head. "It would help in anonymity. Once he takes the mask and that ostentatiously gaudy robe off, he could then walk through the streets and no one would know that it was him."

Chyning shrugged. "I guess that could be true."

Bonarain nodded. "We'll know for sure when he comes in

completely and we can read his mind."

The ghost figure spoke to the trio surrounding him. "What is so important that three of you collectively disturb my peace?" His voice did not sound distorted at all. He sounded as if he were actually standing right there.

"I am Avancha of the Grand Magic Clique of Ficara. There is some group that has desecrated a slaver compound here in southern Ficara. So far all attempts at finding out who and where they are have been totally futile. They hit one of us with a sickness spell that was devastating. They hit several of us with anti-magic spells that shut off everything including some of our most powerful protection glyphs. There have been other spells they have done that defy recognition as to how they performed them. We feel that it will take your great power, along with us, to bring these thugs to justice."

Chyning squawked. "They support the slavers and they call *us* thugs. What kind of *h'oolyach* is that?"

"I've been a little deeper in their minds," said Bonarain. "The slavers supply the wizards with slaves that are used as victims of their experiments with new spells. If the victim happens to die, they don't care because it was just a slave." She shook her head. "The slavers supply the wizards with spell fodder and the wizards supply the slavers with protection."

Kiyalee shuddered. "That is totally ghastly!"

"That is putting it mildly," muttered Soolchakan angrily. "I think we'll have to deal with both groups...in a manner that devastates both."

Bonarain nodded. "Or at least lets them know that they're not the only ones with power."

Soolchakan turned to the Owlamites who had been watching all of the proceedings unfold before his arrival. "How many of these *doovofts* are currently here?"

Hotherette responded. "We have 21 from North Chilamte, 17 from South Chilamte and 12 from Ficara. One of the people from North Chilamte has a sister named Elathka who lives on Neopaure. She might show up as well."

The ghost figure chuckled. "Some group of wizards, which you don't know about, who are making fools of all three of your Cliques. *That* is funny. I think I'll come join you and…show you how to deal with them. Remember though, when I show up, I get first grabs at any new spells. After I'm finished with them…we'll see what I give you, out of the kindness of my heart."

Soolchakan smiled. "Come on *bimyock*! It sounds as if you need to be knocked down…*hard*!"

The ghost figure held one arm out. "I suggest you stand back. I'm going to bring my own carriage and…I don't think that you want to become an involuntary part of it."

Kavluck, Avancha and Ovvtell quickly turned and walked away from the apparition.

Penbelth started shouting an incantation. Suddenly there was a huge cloud of smoke and dust coming from where the circle had been drawn. When the dust settled there was a new carriage in the area. This one was longer, wider and taller than the one brought by Kokee. It was neon blue with all kinds of fancy gold and silver trim on it.

"They sure like big fancy carriages," said Kiyalee. "Should we go inside and check this one out?"

The door on the side of the carriage opened and Penbelth stepped out. He looked around. "Tell me more about the spells… from which you haven't been able to protect yourselves. Also, I want to know anything else that you've seen or heard about these very powerful, magical thieves."

Each one of them told what had happened to them. Penbelth was very interested in the way that several of them had been teleported to different places, against their will, and while in those places they were completely powerless. No spells or gadgets had worked in those places and none of them could fathom why. He was very interested in hearing about the very short glimpse of the strangers that had appeared in the other dimension in the Quendinta Portal. Henteskim had given the best description of the strangers that had made that unusual appearance.

Penbelth chuckled. "Either you're feeding me a line of nonsense or…the Teltermak Chronicles are in error."

Henteskim frowned. "How so?"

Penbelth folded his arms across his chest. "You have described Owlam Elf. According to the Chronicles, the Owlams were all killed off. If you saw some of them then…they were able to survive in spite of the attempts of the Teltermak to kill that bunch of evil monsters."

Bonarain snarled in anger. *"We* are the evil monsters? I need to get hold of this wretched pack of lies…written by the Teltermak and…find out what all is in it. I don't like being called evil by…EVIL!"

Suddenly a loud bang came from the interior of the blue carriage. Zanashi fell to the ground under the carriage screaming in agony. Yatozon grabbed her and the two of them vanished.

Soolchakan was very concerned. **"Yatozon, where did you go**?"

**"I took Zanashi to Beasties. She is dazed but… she's no longer in pain. She looks like she may need to rest a while**."

Soolchakan watched as Penbelth ran back inside his carriage. **"Take her back to the gorge. Let her recuperate there**."

Penbelth heard the bang and ran back inside the carriage, making sure that he closed the door behind him. Inside he took his mask off and started frantically looking around at all of his treasures located inside.

Bonarain had followed him inside and chuckled as she came back out. "Those *bimyocks* in the three Cliques don't know who they're dealing with."

Kiyalee looked confused. "What do you mean?"

Bonarain looked rather smug. "These Super Magic Cliques…they're all very bigoted. They don't allow any non-Heyyah in any of the Cliques. All Elf races are not allowed because, according to the Heyyah, they cannot achieve the level of expertise that the Heyyah can obtain." She shook her head. "Total racial bigotry."

Chyning scoffed. "So?"

Bonarain wiggled her eyebrows. "Penbelth is a Zaberd Elf. He wears that stupid mask, and gloves, so that none of the Heyyah can see his aqua colored skin.

Soolchakan shook his head. "Zaberd? But…the Zaberds live on the Cifpasica continent. Penbelth lives on North Chilamte. What's he doing so far from home?"

Bonarain shrugged. "We may have to delve deeper in his mind but…he *is* a Zaberd and he *does* live in North Chilamte."

"And if these *bimyock* Cliques knew that he is not Heyyah, they'd do everything they could to kill him…because he is *not* Heyyah," said Soolchakan smugly.

Bonarain nodded with a grin.

Penbelth came out of the carriage (with the mask back on). He had a long black chain in his hands that was sparkling. "Someone was in my carriage and…tried to rob me!" He let the chain fall free except for on end that he held on to. He held that part above his head and started swinging the chain around him in a large circle.

Vanva nudged Senbower in the side. "What's that *doovoft* doing now?"

Senbower shrugged. "How should I know?" He shook his

head. "I've never seen a chain like that before."

Hotherette was standing a little too close to Penbelth. The chain passed through her as he swung it around. She yelped in pain and stumbled away from Penbelth.

Ovvtell pointed to where Hotherette was standing. "Did you see that? One of them became visible…when the chain passed through her!"

The attention of every one of the wizards was now in that area. When the chain came back around she yelped in pain again and some of the wizards started walking toward her shouting some kind of incantation.

Soolchakan clenched his teeth. "Ohway! Get her out of here!"

Ohway ran to Hotherette, grabbed her and Jumped both of them back to the gorge. As soon as they Jumped all of the wizards stopped shouting their spell and all looked very surprised and confused.

Avancha spun around looking over the total area. "How did she do that? You had her! How could she have possibly escaped? It…uh…IMPOSSIBLE!" She stopped spinning, clenched her fists at her sides and snarled. "HOW?"

"She teleported," said Penbelth. "Or…someone else got her and teleported with her. That's the only way that she could have escaped." He continued swinging the chain around.

Soolchakan was a little angry and somewhat curious about this chain. He took his red stone and shoved it down inside his shirt. "I'm going to check this thing out. No one does anything unless...I end up in *real* trouble." He walked into the area where the long chain was swinging. 'That thing has to be heavy,' he thought. 'Either that Zaberd is very strong or...some kind of magic makes the chain very much lighter than it appears.'

When the chain swung through him, Soolchakan felt a slight shock. He also felt the stone get, momentarily, rather warm. All eyes of the wizards went to Soolchakan. The wizards all started up with that same incantation. Soolchakan continued walking toward Penbelth. On the next orbit of the chain, it wrapped around Soolchakan. He felt another shock and warmth from the stone. This time, however, the stone did not cool down.

"I've got you," said Penbelth triumphantly! "I was right! You are an Owlam! How could you possibly be alive? The Teltermak killed all of you off...centuries ago."

Before he could even think of being haughty, Soolchakan blurted out the answer. "We killed the Teltermak...centuries ago. We remained hidden...so that *doovofts* like you would leave us alone."

Bonarain was a little concerned. **"Are you in trouble yet**?"

**"No, I'm not. The stone is protecting me... somehow...I think...I hope...maybe**," sent Soolchakan.

Penbelth was yanking on the chain. "Tell me where you were hiding!"

"I can't tell you. I have to show you."

"THEN SHOW ME!"

"I can't…unless I touch you."

Penbelth stopped yanking and stood frozen. "You *will* tell me! You can't resist the power of the chain. You are commanded to tell the truth by the power of the chain. Now…WHERE DO YOU HIDE?"

"I CAN'T TELL YOU. I HAVE TO SHOW YOU. I CAN'T SHOW YOU UNLESS I TOUCH YOU."

Bonarain snarled. "**Are you in trouble yet**?"

"**No, but if I touch *him*, or he touches me, he *will* be**."

Penbelth started walking towards Soolchakan while wrapping the chain up in his hands. "You will not touch me. I will touch you."

"That's fine," said Soolchakan. He fought hard to keep from smiling.

Penbelth slowly moved his left hand to Soolchakan. As soon as he touched Soolchakan – Soolchakan Jumped both of them to Beasties.

Penbelth looked around stunned. "WHAT…WHERE… HOW…?" He turned to Soolchakan. "I don't see any hiding place here! All is see is…" His gaze darted around again. "…a tropical beach."

Soolchakan did not feel any charge from the chain any more. He also did not feel any warmth from the stone. He hopped to Ghost and the chain fell to the ground. He hopped back to Beasties. "This is one of *many* places that we can hide from the likes of you." He chuckled. "One of the advantages of this place is…none of *your* spells work here."

Penbelth was looking down at the chain. "How…did you do that?"

Soolchakan shrugged. "I told you: YOUR MAGIC DOESN'T WORK HERE!" He then backhanded Penbelth. "None of your protection spells, none of your tricks or gadgets or toys work here. This place is totally devoid of your magic."

Penbelth had been momentarily knocked off balance from the slap. He regained his balance and faced Soolchakan. "If my magic doesn't work here…how could any of yours possibly work here?"

"You use coalescent. You possibly use some of the circumambient as well. None of that works here. Mine is hyperphysical. *All* of that works…*here*."

"I'll show you," he snarled. He pulled up ready to start swinging that chain again. Instead of getting the chain moving, he grunted in surprise at the effort. He looked down at the chain. "What is…how the…?" He looked up. "How did…?"

"So, the chain was made magically lighter?" He snickered. "Now that the magic is not working, it is a normal *heavy* chain." He backhanded Penbelth again.

This time the mask was knocked off of his face. He glared back at Soolchakan with his teeth clenched. "I'll show you! You think you've won? Not a chance! You may have deactivated my chain but…" He reached into his robe and pulled out a small rod. "You can't do anything about THIS!" He waved it back and forth. "*Meehava Tokashti!*" He had a confused look on his face as he stared at the rod. He started waving it again. "*Meehava Tokashti!*" He looked at Soolchakan expectantly.

Soolchakan folded his arms across his chest and sighed. "What kind of silliness is that? What are we waiting for?"

Penbelth started shaking the rod violently as he pointed one end towards Soolchakan. "*Meehava Tokashti!* "*Meehava Tokashti! Meehava Tokashti! Meehava Tokashti!*" He stopped shaking it and stood there panting while looking close to panic. "How did you do that? You couldn't possibly imprison, or shut off, the spirits of the rod." He threw it to the ground.

Soolchakan smiled. "It is this *place*. Magic…does *not* work here."

Penbelth pushed the hood off his head. He wiped some perspiration off of his forehead. He looked angrily at the rod. "Okay," he said angrily. "You can shut all magic off." He reached into his robe again. "You can't shut *this* off." He pulled out (what appeared to be) some kind of a pulse pistol.

Soolchakan immediately hopped to Spy. He took a good look at the pulse pistol. He had seen a great many technical weapons in his time. This one was different. Apparently the Zaberd, or at least this Zaberd, had not lost all of their old technology from ancient times. He was not sure how this one worked, however, he was not in the mood to find out the hard way. He knew that he could probably absorb the energy, however, this one just might be set on "full power" and that could make things rather troublesome.

Penbelth hit a button on the side of the gun. It started buzzing. "WHERE ARE YOU? COME OUT FROM... WHEREVER YOU'RE HIDING, YOU RANCID COWARD!" He looked around angrily.

Soolchakan read his mind. Penbelth knew that only Soolchakan could get both of them back to someplace that the magic would work again. He had put the gun on a low setting. He was still angry enough to jack it higher and use it as a torture device.

"You lied to me, Owlam! You said that you were going to show me your magic. You didn't. You tricked me."

Soolchakan snickered. **"No, I did not lie to you. I told you that I had to touch you in order to show you my magic. You touched me and I showed you my magic. I teleported us both to a different place in a different dimension. The fact that your magic doesn't work here, that is just fine with me. Mine still works**."

Penbelth spun around firing short bursts from the pistol.

**"That would only work if I was currently in the same dimension as you**."

Penbelth's demeanor changed from angry to confused. "How could you possibly be in a different dimension but...you're still talking to me?"

**"I'm sending mental messages. I'm not speaking**

**to you. I can see you but you can't see me. That's how this one works. Again, I've given you an example of my magic**."

Penbelth was trying to come up with some reply. Suddenly a long pink tendril wrapped around his waist, several times, and he was jerked backwards toward the beach. He grunted in surprise as he was pulled backwards. Soolchakan saw him disappear into a large gaping pink maw. The giant sand snake that had grabbed him closed that big mouth and slowly sank back down in the sand.

All that Soolchakan could think or say now was: "Oops."

The sand started shaking violently. A beam came up out of the sand and went around in a circular pattern. The sand snake came up out of the sand roaring and writhing in agony. More beams shot up in the air out from the body of the snake. The writhing was now more of a convulsion. Penbelth came out of a circular hole that he had drilled with his pulse pistol. He was covered with blood, saliva and other ichor from the damage he had caused to the snake. He sputtered for several moments as he cleared his nose and mouth of "internal debris" from the snake. He aimed the pistol at the head of the snake and fired. He moved the beam down until he had sawed the head in half. The snake was now laying there going through the last part of death quivers.

Soolchakan shook his head. 'He's a survivor,' he thought.

Penbelth finally cleared his airway and his thoughts. "WAS THAT YOUR IDEA?"

**"No, that beasty just happened to be in the area. I've never seen anyone or anything get out after being**

eaten. **Nice move. It still won't save you from this place. I'm going back home without you. You're going to have to spend the rest of your worthless life here. You'll have to learn some new occupation. Remember that magic doesn't work here. Have a nice life. Farewell and good riddance**." He picked up the fallen magical rod. He did not hear the next comment by Penbelth because he Jumped back to the slaver compound.

Bonarain saw Soolchakan come back. "Okay, so what happened?"

"Penbelth is definitely a Zaberd." He chuckled. "That should ruin the day, or life, for a whole bunch of these *bimyock,* bigoted wizards."

Bonarain was a little puzzled. "What are you gonna do? Were you planning on telling them?"

Kiyalee looked down. "What's with that stick?"

Soolchakan held it up and smiled. "It used to belong to Penbelth. Apparently it is one of those magical toys that these *bimyocks* prize so highly." He looked at the wizards. "What in the name of sanity are they doing?"

Bonarain shrugged. "They all got in that big circle and started that silly chant. From what I've been able to glean from reading a few minds...they're trying to get Penbelth back. They got that super wizard woman Elathka here from Neopaure and... since you ran off with Penbelth, they're under the assumption that it'll take all the power of all of them to defeat us. So they're trying to prove their power by getting him back."

Chyning giggled. "First, they'd have to know where he is." She got a puzzled look and turned to Soolchakan. "Uh… where is he?"

Soolchakan looked perturbed. He cleared his throat and gave them an oration of what had happened on Beasties.

Bonarain rolled her eyes. "He has a pulse pistol? GREAT!"

Soolchakan nodded. "True, he has a pulse pistol, *but*, he has no way of recharging it. Once it runs out of power…it is forever dead…until he can completely come up with an electrical and/or computer system from what he can glean from that planet."

Chyning pursed her lips. "How long should that be?"

He grunted in disgust. "How should I know? I didn't even know that the Zaberd still had technology…until he pulled that thing out."

Kiyalee smirked at him. "So what are you going to do with that stick…in the mean time?"

He shrugged. "I'm going to try it." He held it up, pointed one end at the circle of wizards and hopped the rod into Home dimension. "*Meehava Tokashti!*"

All three women looked at him and had their mouths open as if they were going to ask a question. Before any of them could voice the question, a fan shaped beam came out of the rod. Three of the closest wizards were cut completely in half, right in the middle of the rib cage, by the beam. Before Soolchakan could even think of reacting to that one, several loud pops were heard and small balls of fire shot out at five of the wizards. All five were completely engulfed in flames when they were hit by the small balls. Another fan shaped beam came out and decapitated two of the wizards.

Soolchakan finally got his senses about him, hopped the rod to dimension #45 and let go of it. He looked around in shock at the carnage that had been created in less than three mith. "That thing is…flat out NASTY!"

All of the wizards stopped their chanting. Several of the wizards were scattering, running for their lives. The three leaders of the Cliques, Kavluck, Avancha and Ovvtell were now looking more angry than shocked.

One elderly looking woman in a purple robe stretched her hands out towards where the rod had been firing from. She started a different chant.

"That's that spell they use to look into other dimensions," said Chyning.

All four of them Jumped to a spot behind the woman.

Bonarain pointed at the woman in purple. "That one is the super wizard woman that all of these *doovofts* are afraid of."

The wizards were all now over their fear. They were following Elathka as she continued chanting and walking to the spot the rod had been. Several of them were preparing some rather nasty offensive spells in preparation of what she might find.

Soolchakan decided to send out a message to all of the wizards. **"I have just reduced your numbers by eleven. Take a hint! We want to be left alone. If you want to try** to enslave us in order to obtain our spells…that is not gonna work!  Leave us alone or we're gonna take out a lot more of you."

All of the wizards stopped and froze with irritated, stunned or shocked looks on their faces.

Elathka dropped her hands to her sides. "Can we…talk?"

Kiyalee scoffed. "*Now*, they wanna talk. How tedious of them!"

"**We'll think about it**," sent Soolchakan.  He turned to his wives and the other Owlamites in the area. "Start reading some minds and see if there's any plotting against us that's going on in their minds."

All of the Owlamites that were present closed their eyes and started invading the minds of all of the wizards present.

Neffrata grunted in disgust. "**They secretly called on the Clique from Aerisau.  They're getting more worried or more desperate, or both**."

"**Both**," sent Pesitenee. "**I'm picking up on all kinds of fear**."

Soolchakan chuckled. "**Fear of the unknown.  They might just call some of the others as well**."

"We're waiting for an answer," said Elathka impatiently.

Soolchakan sighed. "**Does that mean that you're not going to send for the Clique from Aerisau?**"

Bonarain scoffed. "**They're already here**."

Soolchakan looked at her confused. "Are you sure?"

"They've all performed some kind of invisibility spell on themselves. They're standing around trying to ascertain what is going on here."

He shook his head. "Okay, let's find them and give them a nasty welcome."

"I found one," said Rinnboz. He kicked the back of a knee of the invisible Heyyah.

A man became visible as he grunted and fell to his knees. He looked around angrily and stood up.

Elathka smiled. "Welcome Zodisk of the Aerisau Clique."

Zodisk sniffed and then bowed to Elathka. "Thank you, oh magnificent one. We came in quietly. We're trying to figure out why all of these others are here. We didn't hear of any convention."

All of the other twenty-one members of the Aerisau Clique became visible.

Elathka cleared her throat and started explaining everything that had happened in this place. Several of the slavers gave their accounting as well.

Soolchakan huffed. "**You keep calling in reinforcements, yet you say that you want to talk. MAKE UP YOUR MIND! Which is it**?"

Elathka grinned showing yellow teeth. "We all wish to

learn from you.  You have some spells that…are confusing and… very profound and powerful.  Maybe we could teach you some of our spells as well."

Fevdem, the leader of the Aerisau Clique stomped his foot. "You mean that this is not an attack against…unknown foes?"

"Not anymore," said Elathka.  "We've suffered too many…"  She looked around at the corpses.  "…fatalities.  These people have proven themselves so…we would rather be at peace with them…instead of fighting a needless war that would cost too many lives."

"**Ooh, she's such a fibber**," sent Eela.  "**She wants to trick us into thinking that she's a friend, but…she's got some plans for taking us prisoner and…doing all kinds of nasty things to us**."

Soolchakan hung his head.  "Why can't anything be easy?"

"We're not cutting up fruits for a dessert," snapped Kiyalee.

Soolchakan read her mind.  He sighed again.  "**What is a bolt table**?"

Elathka's face went from a friendly smile to shock.

Eela was still deep in the mind of the super wizard.  "**It's some kind of magical table where you strap someone down and then…bolt them down.  Then you start torturing them.  Somehow they're able to keep you on the table while they're strapping and bolting.  The way they ask you the questions, after bolting you to the table, are far worse**."

Soolchakan smiled at Eela. "You realize that you sent all of that information to everyone…here and in dimension one."

Eela smiled. "They can't hide the fact that we know what the table is…and we know what they have in mind."

"They all have the same weakness," said Senbower. "We can reach up from underground, grab them by the ankles and send all of them off to some other dimension."

"Sounds like a wonderful idea," said Soolchakan. "Which one do we send them to though?"

"The brig on the Chokchakchok ship," said Kiyalee. "That one is big enough for all of these *bimyocks*."

Soolchakan nodded. "There are twenty of us and sixty-three of them. Get some more help here. That way, we can Jump all of them at the same time and none of them will have the opportunity to…defend themselves against…being moved."

Once there were enough Owlamites in the vicinity, they all grabbed a wizard and Jumped to different places on the Chokchakchok ship. That way, no two people ended up in the same place at the same time. Now, the wizards were all herded from where they were located in the huge ship, to the brig. Several of them attempted all kinds of offensive spells and protection spells and were absolutely flabbergasted when none of the spells worked. By the time the last one was brought to a holding cell, all of them were rather confused and despondent, or angry.

Soolchakan stood outside of the large holding pen. "**Each one of you start reading the mind of the one that you**

**grabbed and Jumped here. I want to know what they're thinking**." He looked directly at Bikaropin. "**You are the one who is going to collect the data from all of the mind readings and give me something if it is universal among them**."

Bikaropin nodded.

Soolchakan looked at the wizards very sternly. "Now, I'm in charge and none of you can do anything about it. By now, you know…none of your magic works here. You are going to listen! I don't understand why you're giving assistance to those wretched slavers. They do nothing and have done nothing but bring misery to untold millions over the centuries. All I wanted to do was get my daughter back from them. They had no right to keep her and I took her back."

Kavluck sneered at him. "Did you offer to buy her back or did you just take her?"

"I should *not* have to buy her," said Soolchakan disgustedly. "She was born free and they had no right to take her or sell her or keep her."

Ovvtell shook his head. "You don't understand the way of the world, do you? When a slaver gets someone…the only way you get them back is to buy them back. Where have you been living all your life…someplace under a rock?"

"I've been living on the planet Hardooth!" Soolchakan snarled. "The way I live is free. If any slaver tries to take me or any member of my family…they are the ones who are going to suffer the consequences…not me…or any family member of mine."

Avancha laughed and shook her head. "When a slaver gets someone, that person belongs to the slaver. If you want to free that someone, you have to buy them back. Haven't you been listening?"

Soolchakan looked at Bikaropin. "**Are these *bimyocks* really serious**?"

Bikaropin looked up at the ceiling. "**I was wondering when you were going to get back to me.**" He sniffed as he looked at the wizards. "**The main consensus is that the wizards support the slavers because the wizards get a lot of slaves from them and they use those unfortunate souls for their experimentation. Without some Heyyah or Elf or whatever, they can't tell if their experiment worked. If the slave ends up getting killed, they just get another slave. It is one *horrible* symbiotic relationship.**"

Soolchakan turned, giving all of the wizards the evil eye with his glare. "Seeing as how you monsters support other monsters…I will decide later what to do with you. I haven't decided yet…do I kill you or do I banish you to another place where none of your magic works? What should I do?" He grinned. "First of all, I'm going to introduce you to Penbelth…without his mask. All this time you bigots thought that only Heyyah could become powerful wizards and all this time, Penbelth…he *is* a Zaberd Elf."

"That's impossible," scoffed Elathka. "No non-Heyyah could ever achieve any of the higher plateaus of power we have achieved."

Soolchakan looked at her smugly. "I am an Owlam Elf and I have taken all of you *doovofts* prisoner! Consider *that*! Now, see if you can break out. Then try telling me who is or is not more powerful." He grinned.

Bikaropin headed to Beasties. He found Penbelth walking through the jungle shoreline screaming for his antagonist to show himself. Bikaropin quickly hopped to Spy. He walked over to Penbelth and kicked the pulse pistol out of the hand of the Zaberd. Before Penbelth could run over and retrieve the weapon, Bikaropin grabbed him and Jumped to the Chokchakchok ship.

Bikaropin looked at the sulking wizards. "**Soolchakan, I am here with the Zaberd**."

Soolchakan chuckled. "**Hold for a bit**." He sniffed as he looked over all of the wizards. "You said that it was impossible for Penbelth to be a Zaberd...or any other kind of Elf. Guess again. He is here." He smiled. "**Now**."

At that moment, Bikaropin hopped the Zaberd out of Spy.

Soolchakan pointed at him. "See? This is Penbelth. This is a Zaberd Elf. Most of you have used some kind of special spell to keep from growing old. I'd wager that he is older than any three of you...and he is still in his prime. A Zaberd normally lives around 700 years." He looked closely at Penbelth and read his mind. "This one is 446 years old."

Penbelth was shocked at how correct the "guess" was concerning his age. "How could you possibly know...how old I am?"

"It shows on your ugly face," chided Soolchakan. "This is a Zaberd Elf and he is a wizard that most of you cringe in awe when you hear his name. I am an Owlam Elf. I am more powerful than him because I have taken him…and all of you as prisoners. Do you still want to keep all non-Heyyah out of your Cliques?" He snickered. "It doesn't matter because I'm sending all of you to a place where no magic, except mine, works."

"You can't do that," snarled Ovvtell. "We won't survive. We've depended on our magic for…so long that…without it…we can't survive!"

Soolchakan shook his head. "Too bad," he said quietly. "Take this bunch of *h'oolyach* to Beasties."

After all of the wizards were gone, Bonarain stood there looking at her fingernails. "What about all of their towers? There's bound to be a bunch of magical traps in all of them. No one will be able to get in there and survive all of the traps because…I would guess that most of the traps are lethal…and in a place where, we know, magic works."

Soolchakan sighed. "A 459 cannon should take care of that problem. Fire at the towers from a distance. I doubt that any of their traps are long distance. They'd just take care of any fool who tries to get in that tower. Shoot it to pieces and any of the traps are worthless."

"Sounds good," said Chyning.

Kiyalee giggled. "All of the towers on four continents that belonged to powerful wizards. That'll be a lot of rubble."

"It'll also leave a lot of other wizards confused and curious trying to figure out what happened to these wizards," said Bonarain.

"What other wizards do…at this time, is not my concern… as long as they leave us alone," said Soolchakan. "We have a bunch of slavers to take care of."

Chyning had an evil grin. "Are we gonna send them to Beasties as well?"

Soolchakan snickered. "Which one will take care of what? Slavers and wizards all in the same area where they can't find anyone to victimize into slavery and the wizards are worthless as wizards. Puts both groups in complete turmoil. If the slavers take the wizards as slaves…to whom do they sell them?" He chuckled. "Plus, as old as most of the wizards are, and as powerless as they'll be, they're not worth much anyway."

"What a shame," said Kiyalee sarcastically.

Chyning frowned. "Are we gonna send that big high slaver muckity-muck Thatoom Showshoo to Beasties as well?"

Soolchakan contemplated for a few moments. "Yes! We're gonna send him there…after we've gleaned as much information out of his head that we can about all of the slavers all over Ficara… and remove any organs he has for procreation."

Bonarain smiled. "Demolish slavery all over this continent completely. Then we look and see what happens with the other slavers. Hopefully they'll get the message."

"Unfortunately, I doubt that they'll learn anything,"

said Soolchakan sadly. "They seem much too arrogant to learn anything."

Kiyalee grunted in disgust. "The ones that, currently remain, might think that they can expand their territories…and gain new rank."

Soolchakan sighed and shook his head.

# 8

The next day, Bikaropin tested the first quartet. He scanned each one and then shook his head. "Wow! You've all healed up completely," said Bikaropin. "It only took one day. That…extra organ is intact and back to normal…uh size, in all of you. That is wonderful…and amazing."

"So we can go back to bringing our children back," said Bonarain hopefully.

"Yes, and I'll monitor you during the whole process. It may be a situation where I have to limit you to how many you do per day. As long as I can keep track of your health as well…we'll all do fine." Bikaropin gave them a triumphant smile.

While the first generation quartet brought twenty-five more of their children back to life, the members of the fifteenth, sixteenth, seventeenth and eighteenth generations started gathering up any slavers they could find on Ficara and shuttling all of them to Beasties. They made sure that all of the slavers transferred were either castrated or spayed before sending them to the foreign dimension. They did not want the slavers procreating because they did not want any more slavers…at any level…in any dimension. They were not worried about the wizards procreating because most of them were far too old for that kind of endeavor even though they had somehow magically altered their ages, they were still too old to think about taking care of any rambunctious or highly active child now that they could no longer alter their anatomy. Then there was this strange occurrence for Kokee. Somehow, Kokee was pregnant. If she survived the pregnancy and if the child survived, this would be the only birth of any Heyyah on the Beasties planet. They decided to leave Kokee and her child alone…as far as neutering.

Bikaropin continued monitoring the first generation as they brought more Owlamites back to life. As long as they did not overwhelm themselves using too much power on each one, they could continue bringing twenty-five, per day, back from the dead. It was simply a case of doing just enough to bring them back and not any attempt at overdoing it.

Of course there was the bad news for one couple. When they brought Korint and Hypan back, they had to explain to the two of them that their daughter was not dead. She was still alive… and well…and permanently banished to be alone on a ship in #45. They were the parents of the traitor. Their son Reech would be brought back from the dead. He was not a problem. Their daughter, on the other hand, had never been killed. Nor would she ever be executed (at least not any time in the near future). She was to remain banished to a lonely existence, forever floating in that ship in #45 without any friend (or family member) coming to visit her and have any *friendly* or legal chat with her.

Soolchakan hugged Hypan. "I hear your sorrow. I can't say that I feel your pain or agony over this situation because you are her mother but…remember she is a traitor. She betrayed all of us. She is related to me as well so…I feel pain of my own as well."

"She's still my daughter," sobbed Hypan.

"That will never change," said Korint bitterly. "We raised her and…she was the one who…murdered *us*. OUR OWN DAUGHTER! I don't know how we can live with this shame…of how we failed…her and us."

Soolchakan sighed. He took a deep breath. "Korint and Hypan of the Seventh! You will listen and hear me! You will not grieve over your daughter…ever again. She is the one who must wear the disgrace, not you. She is the one who is in exile, not you. Do not feel shame or grief over this situation ever again. Prepare to meet your son Reech…when we get to him. You will never suffer over this again." He let go of Hypan. "To all Owlamites everywhere…you will not blame Korint or Hypan. You will not admonish them in any way for what their daughter did. The Traitor is the guilty one. The parents are not guilty and will not be treated as criminals for the actions of their daughter. Any child of Korint and Hypan will not be treated as criminals because of the actions of their sister." He cleared his throat and sniffed. "We don't need to speak of this again."

While Bikaropin and all the other Owlamites wanted all of their relatives brought back as soon as possible, they all realized that the first generation had to work slowly and meticulously on each resurrection. If they used too much power, they could damage that extra internal organ and have to spend more time recuperating.

Soolchakan decided that they would stop working seven days a week. He made a decision (and an ultimatum) that they were now going to rest every Initikoy. He was not the most knowledgeable in regards to any holy scriptures, however, he did remember something about the "seventh" day. That day of the week, they would rest and talk to the ones brought back. The other six days they would bring back more of their children and give most of the responsibility to the parents of those children.

Bonarain did not argue with the decision. She liked the idea of taking a day off.

Kiyalee was a little miffed over it. She wanted to get it over with as soon as possible.

Chyning did not care one way or another. She would let Soolchakan make the decisions and catch all of the flak if there was any. She was just obeying the orders of Drey Sssorg. No one could possibly argue with that. She was happy to *not* take the responsibility.


The word came back from Ficara (finally). There was only one more group of slavers to take care of on that continent. They had been on a raid to Lusaratia and the ship was on the way back to Ficara. They were going to get a rude welcome once they arrived. Their captives were going to be the ones who would be getting the riches of that group, on arrival. The captives would then be allowed to return home. The slavers would then be the neutered captives.

Each time they brought someone back who had been rather young when murdered, they were still marveling over the fact that the size of their ears (and body) appeared as if their life had not been interrupted. They were all getting ears that were the appropriate size for their age. Any that had been killed as a child came back as an adult and the parents (especially the mothers) had no problems teaching their children about anything and everything. Primarily this was because the mothers were always glad to see their children.

Even though Mahanee was very busy welcoming her children back from the dead (of whom there had been 22), she still had some duties to perform along with the rest of the other Owlamites. She had been the lead in monitoring the Wizard Cliques from the other three continents. There was noise coming from them that they were very perturbed over the disappearance of the other four Cliques. They were going to have a conference and try to find out what had happened and where they had gone.

The only reason they were suspicious about the disappearances was because all of their citadels were demolished. In the past, it seems, there had been a few accidental mass suicides because of a spell or two that went horribly awry. In each of those cases, only one tower had been damaged, not an entire collection of towers being totally flattened without any sign of dead bodies. Oh well, too late to go back and fix them. Soolchakan decided to let them all stew and fret over the mass vanishing...unless they started becoming a nuisance...which he felt might happen very soon because of their curiosity and hard headed persistence. They were known for wanting more knowledge and power...at any cost.

The day came when they resurrected Tansiki of the Seventh.

Bikaropin stood there looking around rather smugly. "Now, once again, the traitor is number 666 on the list of living Owlamites. I don't know why you allowed her to live when, at one time, there were only ten who were older than her...who were breathing. You said that if it ever dropped below twenty, she was to be executed immediately. But now, we're guaranteed that she'll be stuck in her prison for a very long time."

Soolchakan wiped some perspiration off his face. "I had hopes of bringing all of them back. Once we found that the stones were...incredibly powerful...there was hope. *That* is why I did not execute her at that time."

Bonarain took a drink of water. She looked around thoughtfully. "How many more do we have to do today?"

Bikaropin looked at the list. "We have Quihisha and Sa-Ching...why?"

She smiled. "Just wondering. There's something I want to do...and I'll take care of it after...Sa-Ching."

"So let's get to Quihisha," said Kiyalee.

Chyning scoffed. "The only errand I want to get to is take a bath and go to bed…after we get Sa-Ching done." She yawned.

Sa-Ching was finally taken care of. She was turned over to her parents, Zib and Sana.

Soolchakan turned to Bonarain. "Okay, what is so important?"

She smiled and turned to Bikaropin. "Take me to this prison ship. The one where the traitor has been exiled."

Bikaropin looked at Soolchakan frantically. He seemed just one step away from panic.

Soolchakan frowned. "Just exactly what are you planning to do there?"

Bonarain shrugged. "I don't know…maybe backhand her."

Soolchakan leaned forward scowling even more. "Why?"

Bonarain huffed. "To let her know that her plan is now totally ruined and that she never had a chance to begin with. I want to look in her eyes when she is informed that she never had the slightest chance at all."

Soolchakan sighed, looked over at Bikaropin. He grunted bitterly and nodded with his eyes closed.

Bikaropin let out a sigh of relief. He now had the blessing of the Drey Sssorg (albeit under some duress) to carry out this mission. "Okay, let's go." He took Bonarain's hand, glanced back at Soolchakan and the two of them vanished.

Kiyalee shook her head. "I don't wanna have nuthin' to do with that cruddy little *bimyock*."

Chyning sniffed. "I agree." She sighed. "Bath and beddy-by time." She vanished.

Kiyalee nodded. She vanished.

Shalam and Monaha were standing there with Soolchakan waiting to see what happened next.

Soolchakan stretched. "Is there anything important to discuss right now?"

Both men shook their heads.

"Who is first on tomorrow's list?"

Shalam looked at the list. "Gontok of the Sixth."

Soolchakan nodded. "Call me in the morning." He vanished.

Bikaropin and Bonarain were now in the control room of the prison barge.

Bonarain frowned at what she saw. "Why can't she come in here and just…fly this thing away…somewhere else?"

Bikaropin smiled. "Because she has been forbidden, by Drey Sssorg, to use any of her hopping or Jumping capabilities. She is stuck in this ship and there is nothing that she can do about it. This control bridge is attached to the main body of the ship by only four narrow legs that are just large enough to hold the two parts together. There aren't any windows in this area so she can't see it. One of the legs has the cables that run into the main ship. She can't get to the cables so…she can't trace them."

"So…she's not allowed to even try to escape even if she were to find the cables?"

"She is trapped by the word and orders of Drey Sssorg… forever if it works that way." He chuckled. "Depending on just exactly how long we are capable of living."

"What if something malfunctions in the ship?"

"We check on it regularly. We have ways of getting her to another part of the ship so we can make repairs without having to talk to her…if we have to do any repairs."

"Where is she right now?"

Bikaropin hit a few keys on the console. "She's currently in the hydroponics garden. She's eating a piece of fruit."

"Let's go to Spy. Take me there and…you can watch what happens…either from there or from here."

Bikaropin sighed. "Are you going to get yourself back to the gorge…when you're ready to go?"

"Yes."

"Okay." He took her hand. They both hopped to Spy and he Jumped them to the garden.

Bonarain circled the traitor several times before deciding what to do and how to go about it. 'Traitor,' she thought. 'That is a suitable name for her now.' She stuffed the blue stone inside her shirt in order to hide it for the first part of the conversation. The Traitor looked very disheveled, both clothing and hair. She also looked very despondent. She was not taking care of her looks, however, who was she supposed to look good for? Bonarain stood slightly behind the Traitor and hopped to #45. "Hello, *bimyock*."

Traitor yelped in surprise, dropped the fruit and fell on her back on the floor away from Bonarain. She looked up at Bonarain. She looked around, totally confused, to see if any others were there. "Uh…who…who are you?"

Bonarain smiled. "You don't recognize me at all? You don't remember any pictures of…other Owlamites?"

Traitor eyed her suspiciously. "I…don't remember… you…no."

"You were born in the year…3349…I believe."

Traitor nodded.

"I disappeared in the year 1120."

Traitor's eyes opened wide in shock. "Bonarain?"

"Very good. You're mind isn't gone…yet."

"No thanks to that wretched Soolchakan," she grumbled. She stood up. "Why're you here? Are you here to…torture me some more or…what?"

"I just came here to let you know that your plan would never have worked."

"Once I got rid of…Soolchakan and several others…yes it

would've!'"

Bonarain shook her head. "No. You never had a chance. You thought that by getting rid of Soolchakan and…all the others older than you, the power of Drey Sssorg would have been yours. Then…you control all Owlamites and…you start conquering."

"Absolutely! It would've worked…if not…for that meddling Bikaropin. He figured out that…someone was giving the Owlamites to the Teltermak. Then Soolchakan used the power…to force me to confess. If not for that…IT WOULD HAVE WORKED!"

Bonarain shook her head. "No. You never had a chance." She smiled. "Suppose that…I was the only one left who was older than you. How would you have found me?"

"I don't know," she muttered bitterly while looking off to the side.

"You would have had to have had the power…to find me at all. I was…stuck…in a place that is a magical void. No magic of any type works there. None at all, not even ours. I couldn't get out…not without help." Her cheeks flushed slightly.

Traitor noticed the embarrassment and frowned.

"Soolchakan finally remembered the place and came to investigate. He found me there and got me out. If he hadn't, I'd still be there. But…even if you had done away with Soolchakan and others, you still didn't know where I was. Kill Soolchakan and the power goes to me." She smiled. "Now, say that the power couldn't find me…because of that void…it would go to the next in line.  The next eldest Owlamite."

"That would've been ME," said Traitor adamantly!

Bonarain snickered and shook her head.  "No, it wasn't.  I have a daughter who *is* older than you."

Traitor was taken aback.  "You had two sons and they're both dead.  You didn't have any daughter."

Bonarain turned serious.  "Wrong!  The day I disappeared...I gave birth to a daughter.  She was grabbed by slavers and taken from me because I was weak from giving birth.  I was weak but...I still fought them and...killed two of them.  They trapped me inside the void and ran off with Nadiwi."

Traitor frowned.  "Who?"

"My daughter Nadiwi.  You didn't know about her...and the only way that you could have found her was if you had the power.  If the power wasn't able to find me...it would have gone to Nadiwi.  With Soolchakan being number one eldest Owlamite... my daughter Nadiwi is number 32 on the list.  She was born in the year 1120.  You are number 666 on the list.  You would have to have waited until she died...before you got the power."  She smiled.  "If you were going to enslave...no one knows how many sentient people in...over 200 dimensions, you would've needed that power to make all Owlamites obey you and enslave all those races.  Your main problem was that Nadiwi was taken by slavers and she was enslaved.  If the power had gone to her, she would have, unconsciously, used it to make all Owlamites, including you, *hate* slavery.  She would have made all surviving Owlamites come to her rescue, free her and then go on a global campaign to wipe out slavery all over this planet. Once she found out that she could go to other planets and dimensions, she would have considered pushing her campaign to all of those planets and dimensions. And you would have been one of the ones who would have been assisting her in destroying slavery because she would have used the power to make you hate slavery." She leaned forward and glared. "YOUR PLAN COULD AND WOULD *NEVER* HAVE WORKED!"

Traitor sank to her knees with total despair on her face.

"Your plan was doomed from the beginning because of what you didn't know. I've heard that…all things happen for a reason." She nodded. "My accidental exile to the void was a preventative measure…against you. Nadiwi being hidden from you was another thing that stopped you before you could even get started. Even if you had killed everyone, that you knew of, who was older than you, you might have given orders to the others, but there was no way that you could force any of them obey you. You would never have obtained the power, no matter what." She shook her head. "I just came here to let you know…your plan was absolutely devastated from the beginning." She smiled cheerfully. "We're currently bringing everyone back…because of what you found out about the stones." She pulled her stone out and showed it. "If it hadn't been for you translating that text, we would never have known that we could bring someone back with the stones. Even though you're nothing but evil, you messed up and did something positive by translating those texts from that strange ship." She took in a deep breath and let it out. She smiled. "Have a nice day." She hopped to Spy.

Traitor stood up seething with anger. Once again she spent the rest of the day walking through all of the halls of the ship, screaming herself hoarse as she shouted over and over her complete and total hatred for Soolchakan and now Bonarain. She had a few choice words for Bikaropin as well.

Bonarain shook her head. "My, my, my, my, my! Doesn't that hurt her throat?"

Bikaropin shrugged. "That's all she has left to her…is her hate. She doesn't care about the pain. This is far from the first time she has done that."

Bonarain nodded. "She did it to herself." She Jumped back to her bedroom.

Bikaropin chuckled. "Yeah, she absolutely did do it to herself." He checked several gages and maintenance schedules. Once he was satisfied that everything was okay with the ship, he Jumped to his apartment.

Mahanee reported back that all of the remaining high wizards had held a big conference. They were all determined to find out what had happened to the Cliques that had vanished in such a mysterious manner. They sent someone to each demolished tower to start doing some divining and find out what happened.

Soolchakan shook his head. "What all do we have?"

Mahanee looked at her lists. "There are eighteen in the Cifpasica Clique, twenty-one in the Lusaratia Clique and twenty-nine in the Neopaure Clique."

"They don't seem to be too picky about how many they have in their Cliques," said Chyning.

Mahanee shrugged. "All that any candidate has to do, in order to be a part of an elite Clique, is prove that they can do at least one hundred different spells. It doesn't matter if the spell is easy or complicated...just as long as they can successfully execute one hundred different spells. Once they are in the Clique, the more spells they can do, the higher their ranking in each Clique."

Kiyalee frowned. "So what was so special about those two super wizards who were completely independent of any Clique... more spells?"

"Precisely that!" Mahanee shook her head and smiled. "They were able to do virtually all of the spells ever invented. Most of the wizards had a few problems with one spell or another...or several. The two super wizards were geniuses above and beyond the intelligence of all of the Clique members. They both felt that they were being held back by less intelligent wizards so they went out on their own and they were too powerful to be stopped by any of the Cliques."

Chyning giggled. "And we spanked both of them."

Soolchakan sighed. "So we need to get some of our people to each one of the destroyed towers and stop them from figuring out what happened."

Mahanee grimaced. "Too late! The leader of the Lusaratia Clique...she already did the deed at one of the towers on Ficara. She sent messages to the other wizards about a powerful light beam that knocked the tower down and the fact that it had come from quite a distance. She's currently trying to find the point of origin of the beam."

Soolchakan huffed. "Well...INTERRUPT HER! Do... whatever you can to stop her from finding out."

Mahanee raised her eyebrows. "Even if it means sending her to Beasties?"

Soolchakan hung his head and sighed. He looked up. "Whatever it takes. We can't let them know about our technological weapons and...who it is that has that technology."

Mahanee Jumped to the location in Spy. She saw the wizard pacing around chanting some weird incantation. "Soshaka, I'm about to give you the surprise of your life." She went underground, reached up, grabbed an ankle and Jumped Soshaka to Beasties. She rose up out of the ground and hopped from Spy to Beasties. "Wizard Soshaka...you are in your new home. I hope you have fun here. One thing you'll find out is that...no magic of any type works here. You're stuck here for the rest of your life." Mahanee grinned and Jumped back to the gorge.

Soshaka looked around in shock. She attempted a few spells and found, much to her consternation that nothing was working. She heard some noises of a village near by and decided to see who was there and what was going on. Upon arrival, she recognized Kavluck and Avancha even though they were looking much older than before. Now she got an even bigger shock once she heard the explanations from them.

Mahanee now had to go back and see if someone else was divining the location of the origin of the beams at any of the other towers. Of course there was. If the leader of a Clique was using her powers to investigate the conundrum, no one in the Clique would be exempt from doing the same somewhere else. She sighed as she looked at the list and realized that there were 67 more, very powerful wizards, in the three Cliques.

The members of the Sixteenth generation were assigned to moving all of the wizards to Beasties. Now, 132 of the absolute top wizards, (who were still alive) were all banished to Beasties. No one on Hardooth, except for the Owlamites, knew what happened to them.

Now that they had been resurrected, Peldom, Baktim and Bendarik of the Third, had been assigned to keeping track of what the slavers had been doing about Ficara. They reported back to Soolchakan.

"There is still no panic at all," said Peldom.

Soolchakan sat there somewhat dismayed. "None…at all?"

"No," said Bendarik. "They've accepted that something happened and…now they're very calmly setting up others to go to Ficara and reestablish their compounds throughout the continent."

Soolchakan closed his eyes and tried to comprehend what had been said in full. "They just accept that…over 1,300 slavers just…disappeared. They just calmly start reassigning more slavers to that continent from…the other six continents?"

Baktim nodded. "Slavers from the other six continents and

from the different island chains as well. They have some committee that…is looking into the disappearance. This committee is investigating but…there doesn't seem to be any sense of urgency, panic or desperation."

Peldom shrugged. "Apparently, mass arrests have occurred in the past. They just accept it as part of the way of their life. Arrests happen. Someone gets a little tired of some of their citizenry being taken from them. They do some mass arrests of slavers to stop it and the rest of the citizenry is placated into believing that the problem has been solved. None of them will have to worry about slavers…for a while. Once the slavers find out who, what, where, and when, they strike with a vengeance to teach everyone the lesson that they are still there. They also go all out to free any of their slaver friends from any prison…even the Turgon Wall." He chuckled. "Fortunately, no one has ever been rescued from the Wall…except for one strange situation in the long past."

Soolchakan nodded. "That means that they're trying to determine what happened to the groups on Ficara. They're putting them back in place…so they have contacts on the continent…until they can find out where their unholy brethren are…incarcerated."

Kiyalee scoffed. "Then, they'll try to get them out."

Chyning giggled. "Without the help of any powerful wizards, they won't have much of a chance to do that."

Mahanee was at this meeting. She stood up and cleared her throat to get attention. "There are a few…so far…who are trying to make new Cliques…on the different continents. These are wizards who hadn't yet met the minimum requirements to join an established Clique. So far…there are only three new Cliques… who have a membership of one. They're on Ficara, Lusaratia and North Chilamte."

Bonarain closed her eyes. "And it just gets deeper and deeper and deeper." She hung her head.

Soolchakan gave her a nasty look. "Hey, you had a few thousand year break in between all of this. I don't wanna hear any complaints about it."

"Some break," said Bonarain sardonically.

Kiyalee stood up. "Let's get back to what we're supposed to be doing. Right now, there is no crisis. The slavers don't know what happened, the wizards have been considerably weakened and aren't much of a threat right now." She looked over at the concrete casket. "Tene-Or of the Eleventh is inside that thing, waiting to start breathing again. He's the first one for today, so… let's get to that."

"I agree," said Chyning.

Soolchakan looked back at Peldom. "If you want to put someone in charge of hindering the new setup of slaver compounds…give that to Nadiwi. I'm sure that she won't mind giving the slavers a bunch of really nasty headaches."

Bonarain smiled. "We have some important things to do today…possibly including the welcoming of a new baby. Dirmnena could be calling at any time. Her water could break and we would have a new Owlamite to welcome to the world."

Kiyalee grinned. "Boy or girl?"

Bonarain returned the big grin. "She named *him* Tozzer."

Kiyalee smiled as she prepared for the resurrection.

Peldom returned to Soolchakan. "Was that a good idea… putting Nadiwi in charge of handling slavers?"

Soolchakan frowned. "Why?"

Baktim cleared his throat. "Mass murder."

Soolchakan was shocked. "How many…or do you know?"

Bendarik scoffed. "So far, the count stands…somewhere around 1,400."

Bonarain groaned. "Pull her off of it. Yes, I agree, the slavers should not be allowed to run rampant, but…this kind of thing just might get them to gear up and…cause all kinds of trouble."

Kiyalee scoffed. "Really," she said sarcastically? "Why would they want to do that sort of thing?"

Soolchakan shook his head. "No! The whole thing was to…sterilize them and banish them to Beasties. What has she been doing with them?"

Peldom scoffed. "Oh, she has been sending them to dimension 10. The problem is that they're floating in space. They're not on the planet."

Soolchakan's shoulders sagged and he shook his head. "Nadiwi, STOP! Stop killing the slavers and come to me now."

Nadiwi Jumped in dragging a Heyyah man who looked like he had been run over by large stampeding herd beasts. She had bloodstains all over her clothing. His breathing was shallow and rasping. She smiled cheerfully. "What did you need?"

Soolchakan sighed. "The entire purpose of banishing the slavers to Beasties is to make them suffer. Sterilize them and they realize that there will not be another generation. Banish them to Beasties and they have no one to enslave other than themselves and the now non-magical wizards. If you kill them - they don't suffer."

She looked off to the side sulking. "They don't deserve to live."

"I agree," said Bonarain. "The whole point of this is to let them live…without hope. Their livelihood is gone. Their fortunes are gone. They have nothing to look forward to because there won't be another generation of them…especially on that other planet. They live in utter futility. They have to start from scratch in building a new community and it is all for nothing because there will be no *next* generation. The best part is that most of them don't even know how it happened. They just know that they're stuck there and they have nothing to look for as far as any advancement of life, fortune, family or anything."

Nadiwi pondered for a while. She frowned. "So…killing them…is more merciful."

"Right," said Kiyalee. "We have no reason to be merciful

to that lot."

Nadiwi turned to Baktim. "You take this thing to Beasties then." She smiled. "I'm finished with it."

Baktim looked at the brutalized man. "Will he live?"

Bendarik scoffed. "Who cares? Just make sure that he *is* sterilized and then…off to Beasties."

Soolchakan rolled his eyes. "Shalam…who is next on the list?"

Shalam looked at the list. "That would be Drak of the Seventh."

Soolchakan nodded. "Okay, go get to him."

Monaha looked at his list. "I can hardly wait until we get to Tala of the Seventh."

Chyning frowned. "Why…what is so special about her?"

Monaha grinned. "She is the last of the victims of the traitor. After that…they're all victims of the third war with the Teltermak."

Kiyalee shook her head. "They're all victims of the Teltermak."

"Yes," said Bendarik. "But the fact that *all* of the victims of the traitor will be breathing before this day is over…the defeat of the traitor is totally complete."

"There is *some* satisfaction in that fact," said Soolchakan dryly.

The slavers were now starting to become a little more of a nuisance. They wanted an investigation as to how so many of their brethren had disappeared without a trace. They were, at first, willing to accept the fact that they could not find out anything due to the equally mystifying disappearance of all of the wizards, however, they were now getting rather upset. They could no longer just accept the fact that a many of their number had disappeared. Now it was beyond epidemic and that was not acceptable. The fact that now, some of them had been found brutally beaten to death, instead of being incarcerated, was getting rather upsetting as well. They needed to get vengeance, however, they needed the assistance of the most powerful wizards to find out who they were after. Those wizards were gone as well. The less powerful wizards were not that much help because they usually had to get at least four together in order to get any good search accomplished.

Soolchakan looked at the report. "So they're getting upset? SO WHAT! How many lives have those *doovofts* ruined over the centuries?"

"Obviously, multi-millions," said Bonarain. "Possibly even…multi-billions."

"We're a little busy with our own right now," said Kiyalee.

"We can always hit them just as hard as we hit the wizards," said Chyning. "Once we've finished with this grand task…we'll have all kinds of time for fun."

Soolchakan gave Chyning a nasty glare. "Fun," he grunted. "It won't be fun. It'll be more killing. That is *not* fun."

"No, but it can still be satisfying if we're removing a scourge from this planet," said Chyning with a smile.

Soolchakan turned to Shalam. "Who is next on the list?"

"Emera of the Sixth," said Shalam.

"Let's get to work on her," said Bonarain.


"Here's a bit of a celebration," said Shalam. "The next one is Minnar of the Sixth. She is officially number 1,000 on the list from the eldest to the youngest."

Bonarain looked off to the side. "So Poolkiy and Noela are here, once again, to welcome a daughter back to the living."

"Along with her husband Soolkan," said Shalam.

"She is not going to get anywhere as long as we stand here just babbling about it," said Soolchakan. "We need to start the process on her."

The First quartet leaned over the body of Minnar and allowed the stones to perform their magic.

After finishing with Minnar, they were informed that Pahensa of the Seventeenth had just broken her water. They delayed bringing number 1001 back to the living by just a little while as they went and welcomed Soolalee of the Eighteenth into the world.

Soolchakan held the newborn in his arms and once again repeated the order using the power of Drey Sssorg. "Child, this is Soolchakan of the First. I welcome you into the world and give you the order that under no circumstances will you ever betray any Owlamite to any cause. You will remain loyal to the Owlamite race that you were born into and never stray from that." Soolalee started crying.

Bonarain huffed. "Look at that! You scared her." She took the baby from Soolchakan and tried to calm the newborn girl.

"Better to scare her now, when she won't remember it, than to allow her to become another murdering traitor later on," said Kiyalee bitterly.

Chyning smiled. "She won't remember being scared, but like all Owlamites, she will obey the order." She nodded. "I agree that we don't need another traitor." She chuckled. "If we have to frighten a few of our own children in order to stop treason…" She shrugged. "…so be it."

After each of the women of the First generation had done their oohs and ahs over the new infant, Soolchakan gave them each a bit of a patronizing look. "Shall we get on to Hesano of the Eighth? She is only the sixth one today and including her, we still have twenty to bring back, today."

"Onward and forward," said Kiyalee. She vanished.

Chyning huffed. "Hey! Aren't we supposed to go there in a certain order?"

Soolchakan shrugged. "So she took this one out of turn. As long as she doesn't make it a habit…we'll be okay." He vanished.

Bonarain took one more look at the baby girl, Soolalee.

She sniffled with joy as she did a ten count. She vanished.

Chyning took another look at the baby. "This is the advantage of going last. I get to enjoy seeing a baby longer than any of the other three." She kissed the forehead of the infant, wiggled her eyebrows at the mother and then vanished.

Mikondor and Pahensa smiled as they joyfully stared at their new daughter.

Mikondor kissed Pahensa. "Good job. Beautiful child." He kissed her again.

Pahensa sighed and relaxed a little. "My little one, your greatest adventures are just beginning."

While looking down at the body Kiyalee frowned. "How many more new babies are we expecting this year?"

"Five," said Shalam.

Bonarain looked over at her son and chuckled. "You're keeping track of how many women are currently pregnant?"

He shrugged. "I know that you see it as important to welcome each new baby to the world. So...yes, I keep track of that information for you."

Soolchakan chuckled as he took his position over Hesano. "Ladies? Let's get to this one. Remember that there are still nineteen more...today."

They took their positions.

The First quartet watched as Queeyana of the Eighth sat up looking rather startled and confused as she started breathing once again. Her mother, Yeema of the Seventh, was there to give her the explanation of what had happened.

"Where do we stand now," asked Soolchakan?

Shalam smiled. "She was the last one for today. Tomorrow we start on Xamshim of the Thirteenth."

Bonarain walked over to Bikaropin with a strange look in her eyes. Bikaropin looked a little nervous as she approached him.

Bonarain stopped in front of him with her hands clasped behind her back. "As I recall...originally, we were having problems doing twenty-five per day...at the beginning. Why are we able to do twenty-five...now...without problems?"

Bikaropin was relieved that it was an inquiry and not some accusation. He smiled. "Because you're getting used to it...and you're not going all out on each one. Before, you were using too much...of yourselves. Now, you bring them back without straining yourselves." He shrugged. "It comes down to being practiced at it. The more often you do it, the better you are at doing it." He shrugged. "The only difference between an amateur and a professional...the professional has done *it* more often."

"That sounds reasonable...and familiar," said Kiyalee.

Chyning sighed. "What sounds reasonable right now...is a bath and then to bed." She vanished.

Soolchakan shook his head. "She is always the first to the bathtub. I'm so grateful for the amount of rain we get here in the gorge. If it wasn't for all of that rain…she'd never get all of the bathing done that she wants."

Kiyalee blew a raspberry at him. "We could always use one of the ships in dimension 45 if we want." She snickered. "Probably get a lot cleaner as well." She vanished.

Bonarain looked around. "Tomorrow." She vanished.

Soolchakan just smiled and then vanished.

Shalam looked at Monaha. "Let's go get Xamshim in place for tomorrow.

Monaha grunted. "With all of the trimmings, frills, pomp and circumstances." He stretched. "All of this has been very satisfying. I wonder what we'll do after we finish with all of them."

"Live!"

Monaha chuckled and nodded his head.

Shalam nodded and the two of them vanished, leaving Yeema there to give all of the explanations to a wide-eyed and bewildered Queeyana.

# 9

The work to bring all of the children back continued. It almost seemed to be routine. All they needed to know was: Which one is next? And: Is this the last one of the day?

They finished bringing Dowgom of the Eleventh back to life. Soolchakan sat down and watched with a smile as the explanations to Dowgom were quickly given to him by his parents, Gamen and Denosasha. He tilted his head back. "Which one is next?"

Shalam chuckled. "Don't you know the significance of this one?"

Soolchakan looked up puzzled. Bonarain, Kiyalee and Chyning were all equally confused.

Shalam smiled. "Dowgom is number 2,000 on the list of eldest to youngest. We're getting closer and closer to the end but...I thought that you might want to stop and reflect for a while on this."

Bonarain sighed. "How many are still to be done today?"

Now it was Shalam's turn to look confused. "Uhm... seven...why?"

Kiyalee snarled. "The only thing that we're worried about is getting all of them back. Their numbers on the list are…rather unimportant at this time. If you want to enjoy the moment then you go right ahead and enjoy it. We'd rather get on to the next one." She smiled. "Who is it?"

Chyning put her arm around his shoulder. "Shalam, don't be discouraged. We know that everyone is enjoying each new victory but…until we're done…we can't just sit here and… reflect…on all of them. We'll have time for reflection when we're finished."

Shalam smiled weakly. "Udakami of the Thirteenth is next."

Bonarain smiled. "Thank you."

Kiyalee and Chyning both sighed as the body was brought in.

Soolchakan smiled at Shalam and prepared for the task.


Osakisha came in. Denjen of the Fourteenth had just been brought back and was getting an earful of happenings and history from his parents. Osakisha tried to walk around everyone on her way to Shalam.

She got close to Shalam. "**Is this the last one of the day**?"

Shalam just nodded.

Osakisha turned to Soolchakan. "I thought you might be

interested in the fact that the Magic Cliques are being reestablished. The ones on Aerisau, Ficara, Lusaratia, Neopaure and North Chilamte all have one member. The one on Cifpasica has two. No one has met the requirements on South Chilamte yet."

Bonarain scoffed. "Seven wizards…so far."

"Seven *top* wizards, on six continents," said Kiyalee flatly.

Chyning yawned. "Should we be scared?"

"No," said Osakisha. "I just thought you wanted to be kept informed."

Soolchakan smiled. "Yes, my Dear, we do wish to be kept informed. Right now we're just a little tired from all of the tasks of the day."

Chyning snickered. "When we get tired…well…we sometimes get sarcastic."

Kiyalee huffed. "Sometimes?"

Bonarain stretched. "Any reports on how we're doing with the slavers?"

Osakisha shrugged. "Nadiwi is in charge of that. From what I understand…she has been sterilizing them…without any anesthetics."

Soolchakan scratched his chin. "They're slavers. Who cares how badly they get hurt…or how much pain they feel?"

Osakisha nodded. "Talk to her anyway. She'll be the one taking care of numbers."

"Right," said Bonarain. She closed her eyes. "**Nadiwi, my Dear, this is your mother. What are you doing right now**?"

Nadiwi looked up from the table. "**A castration...why**?"

Bonarain winced. "**We were wondering if you could tell us how things are going with the task of getting rid of slavers.**"

"**So far, we've sterilized and transported 6,857 of the monsters to Beasties**."

"**How many continents have been cleaned off**?"

Nadiwi snarled. "**None! Just as soon as we clear an area, the monsters move back in. They breed faster than insects.**"

Soolchakan had been eavesdropping. "Over 6,800 and not one lousy continent is clear of that vermin?" He hung his head. "We may need some assistance in this matter. All this time, over 6,800 and...it seems we have practically nothing to show for it."

Kiyalee shook her head. "6,800 *is* 6,800. There are 6,800 less since this campaign was started."

Soolchakan nodded. "That is a very positive note, however, we still may need help." He sighed. "A lot of help."

Bikaropin went to Soolchakan. "The ones that were brought back...are rather squeamish about any form of...procreation."

Soolchakan gave him a furtive glance. "Why…do you think this is happening?"

Bikaropin shrugged. "They're scared. They don't know what might happen."

Soolchakan huffed. "I am *not* going to order anyone to… have babies."

"You don't have to order anything. All you have to do is set an example."

Soolchakan frowned.

"Nadiwi was the last child of Bonarain in 1120. Hamar was the last child of Kiyalee in 1430. Molkan was the last child of Chyning in 1437. There are sixteen members of the second generation. If you and your three wives were to start…" He cleared his throat. "…something. Others would, or should… follow."

"Are you suggesting that I *order* my wives to…start *that* ball rolling…by dropping their pants?"

Bikaropin shook his head. "Not orders…just strong suggestions…at least this one time."

Soolchakan looked off in thought. "I'll think about it," he said calmly. He was wondering if he should do this thing. It went against what he had been living by since they discovered that they could procreate. He had made several rules and now…

The First Quartet finished the last one of the day. They

were headed for their bedrooms to recover.  Tomorrow was to be the day of rest so it was equally satisfying that they would have more time to rest before the next session.  Kiyalee and Chyning had Jumped to their bedrooms already.

Soolchakan turned and looked at Bonarain. **"Before you go, I need to talk to you**."

She frowned back at him.  **"Since we're talking mentally, we don't even need to be in the same room. Can't I go to my room and…we'll discuss it mentally**?"

He raised his eyebrows. **"I want to discuss this…face to face.  I feel that it is much more appropriate**."

She rolled her eyes. **"Okay!  What's so flaming important**?"

**"The ones who never died…are still procreating. The ones who have spent several thousand years in the grave aren't doing a thing**."

She scoffed. **"I can't do anything about that!**"

**"You can set an example**."  With that, he dabbed the back of his neck and striped her forehead.

She grunted in surprise and disgust.  She looked back at the parents who were educating their newly resurrected child.  She did not want to make a scene in front of them. **"Why did you do that you *worm*?  You said that it was up to the woman to decide when she wanted to….**"

**"As I said:  We need to be the example**."

She groaned as she grabbed her crotch to try to stop some of the burning.  Her hands did not help.  "**I was never dead!  I was…TRAPPED…on that island.  How am I making an example to the ones who've been resurrected**?"

"**You can be the example for Nadiwi.**"

"**HOW**?"

"**For several thousand years, she was a sex slave. She has no idea what a loving relationship is.  You will be gestating and…you can teach her that if she wants to have a normal relationship with a man…it is *not* a problem.**"

"**This could've been done in a much better…or different way…you rodent!**"

He shrugged.  "**I've already got it started.  What are *you* going to do now**?"

She grabbed hold of his arm with a look of desperation (and a little anger).  "**Jump us to your bedroom…if you want to complete this.**"

"**Why my bedroom?  Normally you three have all wanted to copulate in your own bedrooms.**"

She clenched her teeth.  "**If we're gonna befoul any sheets with our sweat tonight…YOUR sheets, not mine.**"

He shrugged.  "**Okay.**"  He Jumped them to his bedroom. "Why couldn't you do the Jumping?"

She had a bit of a wild look in her eyes.  "It has been

over 4,300 years since…I got slapped with your goo! I…can't concentrate…on *anything*!" With that she took some of her mucus from the back of her neck and angrily smacked his face. "Now… are you ready?"

He opened and closed his eyes several times. "It has been…quite some time for me as well. Remember that…Kiyalee and Chyning…were taken…only a few hundred years after you disappeared. You disappeared in 1120, Molkan was born in 1437."

She snarled as she removed her shirt. "Let's get to this! You started it so…I don't wanna hear any complaints."

He smiled weakly as he started removing his clothing.

Bonarain woke up and yawned. She blinked a few times and was confused at what she was seeing. Then she remembered that she was not in her bedroom. She turned to her right and saw Soolchakan looking at her while scratching his shoulder.

"Good morning," he said.

She huffed and looked back up at the ceiling. "After what you pulled, how could it possibly be a good morning?"

"We don't have to get up today. Shagorn of the Fifth will wait until tomorrow."

"We don't have to go to Shagorn until tomorrow," she said in a nasally demeaning manner. She huffed again. "Are you gonna do the same to Kiyalee and Chyning?" She looked back at him. "Are you gonna break your promise to them as well?"

He growled. He figured that he would hate himself later on. Right now he just felt guilty about doing it. He cleared his throat. "You, Bonarain, will remember this coupling as your idea. You will only remember that. You know that we had sex, however, you, from this day forth, will remember it as you being the one who initiated it. You will not speak to Kiyalee or Chyning about it unless you are talking about it being your idea." He was wrong. He hated himself now for doing it. He looked back at her.

Bonarain smiled at him. "So now I'm going to have a fourth child." She frowned. "I remember that…before I got trapped…Kiyalee and Chyning each had two children." She raised her eyebrows and looked at him sideways. "How many do they have…now?"

He smiled back. "Kiyalee has seven. Chyning has six."

She looked back at the ceiling. "I wonder if I should try catching up to them."

"*That* is entirely up to you." He smiled at her while feeling like such a rancid hypocrite. He grimaced and flushed in agony over the way he was fabricating this mess.

She stretched. "Now is the time to clean your sheets and… for both of us to take a bath."

"Yes, it is," he said quietly.

She sat up and Jumped to her bedroom.

He got up and looked in a mirror. "Rodent!"

Six days later, they finished bringing Mokwo of the Eleventh back from the dead. Soolchakan took Kiyalee by the hand and Jumped her to his bedroom. She looked a little surprised.

"This is your idea Kiyalee. You are the one initiating this act." With that he striped her forehead with his mucus.

She stood there looking a little startled for a moment and moaned. With a somewhat startled look on her face, she touched the back of her neck and then striped his forehead.

The next morning he felt rotten…again.


Six days later, they finished bringing Kinshum of the Seventh back from the dead. Soolchakan took Chyning by the hand and Jumped her to his bedroom. She looked a little surprised.

"This is your idea Chyning. You are the one initiating this act." With that he striped her forehead with his mucus.

She stood there looking a little startled for a moment. She touched the back of her neck and then striped his forehead.

The next morning he, again, felt rotten. He tried to concentrate on the positive aspect that there were, now, only 235 left on the list to be brought back. Even that did not help much at all.


Once the rest of the Owlamite nation heard that all three,

Bonarain, Kiyalee and Chyning were pregnant, the ones who had been brought back started looking at each other with hope. They were all jubilant over the fact that all were being brought back and since Kiyalee and Chyning were pregnant, that meant that there should be nothing physically wrong with any of the others. After all, they were Owlamites and they could repair anything…in the womb…couldn't they?

Nadiwi walked up to Loov looking rather distressed. She was not sure what to say or how to say it. Loov looked at her expectantly while he waited for her to say…or do something. She stood in front of him nervously looking around, fluttering her hands a little, licking her lips, clearing her throat and just generally looking upset.

Loov sighed impatiently. "Can I help you with something?"

Her demeanor changed to concern. "I…don't know…how to…uh…I'm not sure if I…It's hard to…"

"It'll be even more difficult to understand you if you don't finish at least one single sentence."

She swallowed hard. "I don't know how to ask."

He shrugged. "You open your mouth and communicate." He smiled. **"Of course as an Owlamite, you always have the choice of mentally sending a message."**

She hung her head. "I don't know how to say it…orally or mentally."

He shook his head impatiently. "Maybe you should go somewhere and contemplate for a while. Clear your head and... decide what you want to say...and how."

She huffed. "Oh...*h'oolyach*!" She reached up, moistened her fingertip with her mucus and rubbed it on his left cheek.

Loov instantly bent over. "OH! These are the wrong pants to be wearing right now! They're too tight for..." While still bent over, he looked up clenching his teeth. "Why didn't you give me some warning?"

She looked a little apologetic. "I...just wasn't sure...what to do or say."

He grabbed her arm and Jumped them both to his bedroom. He unfastened his pants and was able to relax...a little. He touched the back of his neck and then striped her forehead.

Nadiwi gasped with her eyes wide open and grabbed her crotch. "No one...ever told me...it would be like...*this*!" Her breathing was very rapid as she grabbed her crotch.

"Well it is," he panted through clenched teeth. "Now, get undressed and...the bed is right over there."


Nadiwi woke up. She found herself curled up at the foot of the bed. She had been forced to be in this position by her masters whenever they had used her and then gone to sleep. She was to wait at the foot of the bed until they were ready to go again. She felt rather disgusted that she had gone to that position on her own from habit. She saw that Loov was still asleep. She slowly crawled up next to him and got under the blanket. She stared at him for quite a while before he started stirring from his slumber.

Loov woke up and sat up. He turned to Nadiwi. "Good morning. Are you able to communicate a little easier today?" He scratched his left shoulder looking a little perturbed.

She shrugged. "It was never like that…with any of those Heyyah. I don't understand why…I couldn't control myself… last night. I didn't want to stop. With those Heyyah…I didn't or couldn't care less. They were…*boring*! They got on top of me and…they'd grunt and sweat and…make stupid faces. There was no…" Her brow furrowed as she looked for the right word.

Loov smiled. "Burning desire?"

She flushed. "Yeah, I guess that's as good a term as any. They wanted me to tell them how much fun it was and how good it felt. They got mad at me if I acted like I didn't like, or care, what was going on." She looked away disgusted. "Some of them slapped or punched me…for their weird kind of fun."

He lay back down and scratched his stomach. "You *are* an Owlamite. The only time that an Owlamite can enjoy…or usually even participate in copulation is…after coming in contact with the neck mucus of another Owlamite…of the opposite sex."

She frowned again. "Why?"

He shrugged. "That is the way that we're made. We're possibly made that way so that…our people remain pure. We don't mix with any other races. I can't get excited with any female other than an Owlamite female. You, being a female Owlamite, cannot get excited, or even ovulate, unless it is with an Owlamite male. Again, neither can get excited until you come in contact with the neck mucus of the other sex. With any other race…we're completely sterile…or totally uninterested."

She looked confused. "Uh…what do you mean…ovulate?"

He was the one who was confused now, and a little concerned. "Didn't your mother ever explain…any of that to you?"

She chuckled nervously. "Not…all of it…I guess." She swallowed. "Can you tell me…about it?"

He groaned. "You, are a female. I can't tell you all of the workings or feelings of the female body. I think that…it'd be best if you discussed this particular issue with either your mother or talk to my other two wives - Sona and Zhontam."

"What do you mean…other?"

He smiled. "Sona and Zhontam are two of my wives. By choosing me…the way you did, you became my third wife. Now, the four of us are a complete family. You, being my third wife, should move in here to apartment 2-22 with the rest of us."

"Why should I move in here?"

"Because you are now going to have a baby, by me, and…"

"WHAT?!" She was in total shock.

He was taken aback by her reaction. He stammered a little, regained his composure and smiled. "You and I have…mated. You are now pregnant and…you're going to have a baby."

She looked horrified. "HOW? WHAT? WHY?"

He groaned. "Go talk to your mother…or Sona or Zhontam. I can't explain it completely. Since they're all females…with experience at getting pregnant and giving birth…they can explain it a lot better than I can. I don't even know where to start."

She looked around still mystified. "I'm definitely gonna do that."

"I think you should take a bath first. Copulation is a very sweaty activity."

She smiled weakly, got out of the bed and headed for the bathroom.

Loov closed his eyes. 'I hope she doesn't spend too much time in there,' he thought.

Nadiwi sat in the bathtub for quite some time before really cleaning herself off. She finally decided that she should talk to her mother about this confusing situation. She finished bathing, dried off and went back to the bedroom. "I'm going to take my clothing and…head back to…my mother's bedroom and…talk to her."

Loov smiled. "That sounds like a good idea. I'll help you when you get ready to move in here."

She smiled weakly and Jumped to Bonarain's bedroom.


After getting dressed, Nadiwi closed her eyes. "**Momma Bonarain, this is Nadiwi. Where are you**?"

Bonarain came back. **"We're here to bring Opary of the Tenth back. We're with her parent's…Porok and Flanda. What did you need**?"

**"I've got some…questions for you**?"

Bonarain groaned. "I'm getting some…inquiry from Nadiwi. She sounds rather frantic." She shrugged. "Can we hold on for a little while I find out what is so important?"

Soolchakan sighed. "Opary has been waiting since 4856 ATUT. I guess she can wait a little longer." He nodded. "Go see what she wants. We can rest in the meantime."

Bonarain got ready to Jump, then hesitated. **"Nadiwi dear…where are you**?"

**"In your bedroom**."

Bonarain smiled. **"You mean *our* bedroom**?"

Nadiwi sighed. **"Not for much longer**."

Bonarain was now a little confused by that statement. She decided to Jump to the bathroom because she was not sure exactly where Nadiwi was in the bedroom. She hurried to the bedroom and saw Nadiwi sitting on the bed.

"What is so important, my child?"

Nadiwi looked up rather concerned. "I've been… wondering about all this…about the stuff on the back of my neck. You told me that…it can drive…*any* man wild." She sighed. "I decided to try it…and…according to what I was told…I could only…be with a man of my generation…the second generation."

Bonarain ran a quick roll call through her head. The only men that she could mate with would be either Loov, Jotsoom or Molkan. Shalam and Monaha were absolutely off limits. She was getting a little anxious with anticipation.

Nadiwi looked off to the side. "Anyway...I got with Loov and...I put some of my mucus on his face." She cleared her throat. "He did the same...to me...and...the next thing I know...I was..." She looked up rather concerned. "I was having sex...and *enjoying* it...for the first time in my life."

Bonarain was now relieved to hear that it was Loov. "That is one of the oddities of our race. The only time that any of us can enjoy sex...is...with one of our own race...after coming in contact with their neck mucus."

Nadiwi nodded. "Okay, I can believe that." She shook her head. "It was never like that...with any of those Heyyah. It was always...so boring...and disgusting." She looked at Bonarain without moving her head, just her eyes. She looked very concerned. "He said that...now...I'm going to have a baby. I had sex...thousands of times with the Heyyah...but...I never got pregnant. How can it possibly happen...now?"

Bonarain smiled as she went to her daughter to comfort her. She sat down next to her and hugged her. "That is another oddity of our race. The only time that an Owlamite woman can get pregnant is by an Owlamite man. We just cannot breed...with any other race. We are...forced...by things unknown to us as to how or why...to be a pure species. Some of the other Elf races have successfully crossed with other species. We...cannot...or at least…have not."

Nadiwi placed her hand on her stomach. "How…will I know…if I really am…going to have a baby?"

Bonarain hugged her daughter close again. "You won't be able to see it for at least four or five days."

Nadiwi frowned.

"We'll talk about it in four or five days and I'll show you how to see your baby."

Now Nadiwi looked totally bewildered…and a little horrified.

"During that time, you need to move into Loov's apartment…uh…which one is it?"

"2-22."

Bonarain kissed her daughter on her forehead. "I have to get back to Opary. You go ahead and do your moving and like I said…we'll talk about it in five or six days." She gave her daughter one last smile, kissed her forehead and then Jumped back to Opary.

Nadiwi sat there for a little while longer trying to grasp the full situation.

Bonarain walked back in. The body of Opary was ready for them to start.

Soolchakan cleared his throat. He looked at Bonarain expectantly. "What was so important?"

Bonarain grinned. "She coupled with Loov. She's going to move in with him now."

Kiyalee stood there wide-eyed. "Loov…and Nadiwi?" She grinned. "That's a start for someone other than our generation. I hope that some of the other resurrected children can start… coupling and…get more Owlamites in this world."

Soolchakan sat there looking a little red-faced guilty. "For the moment…let's get to Opary."

Nadiwi sat there feeling a little lost and confused. "**Loov… this is Nadiwi. Can you hear me**?"

Loov was still drying himself off from his bath. "**Yes, I can. What did you need**?"

She sighed. "**I guess I need help…moving…to your apartment**."

He shrugged as he thought to himself. "**Where are you**?"

"**In my mother's bedroom**."

He grunted in exasperation and clenched his eyes shut. "**Your mother's bedroom…in *which* apartment**?"

"**12-562**."

"**I just finished bathing. I'll be there as soon as I get dressed**."

Bonarain informed the others that she would be fashionably late in getting to the next resurrection. Rassiv and Ponon would have to wait a little while before welcoming their daughter Tangchi back to the world of the living. She joined Nadiwi in apartment 2-22. The two of them were sitting in the new bedroom of Nadiwi.

Bonarain hugged Nadiwi. "Now, daughter, I'm going to send some imagery to you. I want you to see it carefully and learn it." She closed her eyes and started sending.

Nadiwi closed her eyes and frowned as she was receiving this new information. She moved her head around as she was digesting the unfamiliar images. "Okay, I got it. Now what?"

"Now, you start using it yourself. Use it *on* yourself."

She looked confused. "And do…what?"

"Start looking into your own body, using the imagery."

"Okay, so I'm…" She opened her eyes and gasped. "WHAT WAS THAT?"

"That was your stomach, dear. Uh…wrong organ. What you saw was some food being digested. Yes, it appears very disgusting at this juncture. You're supposed to be trying to see inside your womb."

Nadiwi cleared her throat and swallowed nervously. She closed her eyes again and started the process all over.

Bonarain was going with her. "No, dear, the other way… that's right. Now down a little. A little more. Okay, that's the outside of your womb. Now we need to go inside and…*there it is*! Do you see that little dark spot?"

"I do…uh…what is it?"

"That, my *pregnant* daughter, is a zygote. That is what is going to form itself into a new Owlamite baby."

Nadiwi was a little overwhelmed. She lost all of her concentration on the imagery and the inside of her womb. She was sitting there wide-eyed and stunned. "Is it...a...boy or girl?"

"Don't worry about that right now. You'll be able to see things a lot more clearly over the next few months. Right now, it is just in the beginning stage." She smiled as she kissed her daughter on the forehead. "Right now, just practice the imagery so you can see your baby anytime you want. I'm going down the hall. We have an appointment with Tangchi of the Tenth. Her parents, Rassiv and Ponon, are getting impatient." She smiled and vanished.

Nadiwi started looking at every part of her anatomy using this new information. She was amazed at how she could see each organ and what was going on inside her body.

Bonarain walked in and joined the others. "Kiyalee, Nadiwi is definitely pregnant. She and Loov are probably having a little girl."

Chyning frowned. "Are you sure that it *is* a girl? Seems a little early to be able to tell what the child is."

Bonarain looked thoughtful and then grinned. "I'm... uh...pretty sure."

Kiyalee smiled. "And we will always be there to help her...and Loov...in getting used to this new life."

"Okay," said Soolchakan impatiently. "Can we get to Tangchi? She's only the first of twenty-five for today."

Shalam held his hand up. "Tangchi is the first of twelve."

Soolchakan was a little miffed and confused. "*Why* are we only doing twelve today?"

Chyning started laughing. "All this time...all of you have been griping at me to read something. The one time I do read something - *none of you did*." She turned off to the side laughing and holding her sides.

Bonarain was getting upset as well. "What is going on?"

Bikaropin shook his head. "What Chyning is trying to tell you...none of you have been counting. She has. The reason that you're only doing twelve today...is because that is *all* that is left. Today you do the *last* twelve...and you're *done* with this...quest!"

Soolchakan was now a little stunned. "We're...done... and...hopefully we won't have to ever do this again."

"Amen to that," said Kiyalee.

Bonarain pursed her lips. "These last twelve...they were all...just little children when they were..."

"Yes," said Bikaropin. "They ranged in ages two through eight."

"So we have some very anxious mothers," said Chyning. "Come on! Let's do it!"

They performed the ceremony on Tangchi. Then Instee,

then Tondome, then Shellbyno, then Pelemini, then Yenpasha, then Sherdoz, then Bellphya, then Penaten, then Yindall, then Unanhee, then finally Qualkipiy.

Gremet and Kaluka tearfully welcomed their daughter Qualkipiy and started educating her about all that had transpired while she was laying in her coffin.

"It almost seems anticlimactic," said Kiyalee looking rather lost. "We've been doing this...for so long that...almost 2,900 of them done...including me and Chyning...and...now... we can get back to normal living...whatever that is."

Chyning scoffed. "Exactly *what*...do you consider normal...around here?"

Bonarain smiled. "Welcoming new babies to the world."

Bikaropin shook his head. "We also still have a few problems with some of those wizards, who are still trying to find out what happened to the ones who disappeared."

"Don't forget those *h'oolyach* slavers," said Inorim.

Bikaropin looked at his first wife. "Yes, we do still have that pestilence."

Monaha grunted in disgust. "I'm still amazed at how many of those things exist. "We've sent over 11,000 of those things to Beasties. When we look around...it seems like we still haven't made a dent in their numbers."

Soolchakan smiled. "Now that we're finished with the resurrections...we can devote a lot more time to...ridding the world of that *h'oolyach*. Let's go make a dent. A *big* dent!" He shook his head. "I never realized that it was this big a problem... until now."

In early 5476 ATUT, all three of the first generation women were late in their pregnancies. They still were there to greet Pronthor of the Twenty-Second. He was the first of his generation to be born.

Two days later, Bonarain gave birth to her new daughter Sonotana. Seven days after that, Kiyalee produced a new son, Piykroom. Seven days after that, Chyning had a new daughter, Nondaza.

Shortly after all of that, Nadiwi was staring down at a little girl in her arms. She was now the mother of Monanya of the Third. She looked in wonder and awe at the new life that had been created inside her womb. This little child who had been regularly beating on her bladder while wiggling inside her. A child that she had looked at daily using the imagery her mother taught her. She looked up at her parents with awe in her eyes. "I don't believe this. This...baby...grew...*inside* me!"

"There are plenty of women here who can help you," said Soolchakan with a smile.

"All of them are ready and eager to assist...including me," said Bonarain.

"Even your husband," said Kiyalee with a smirk.

Loov stood there chuckling and nodding.

"No," said Nadiwi still looking confused. "Over the... centuries...I've held probably thousands of babies in my arms. This one! This is the first one that...I really want to hold." Tears formed in her eyes and she hugged the baby closer. "This one is... *mine*! I'm not...taking care of some screaming, smelly Heyyah brat. I'm holding and am going to take care of...*my baby*!" She looked up at Loov, smiling through quivering lips, who smiled back at her.

Bonarain handed her baby Sonotana to Soolchakan. She walked over and hugged Nadiwi. "Yes, that one is yours. Reflect on and cherish this moment forever."

Altogether, there were 146 new additions to the Owlamite population in the year 5476. It was a very good year for the Owlamite population growth. They still had the problem of getting rid of slavers and keeping an eye on all of the wizards of the new Cliques.

A few days later, the first quartet was sitting in their lunch room having a meal while feeding their newborns.

Bonarain smiled as she wiped the face of her new daughter. "I'm so glad that I decided to have another baby."

Soolchakan choked on his fruit juice. He sputtered as the juice came squirting out of his nose as well. He coughed and hacked loudly as he tried to clear his air passage and nose.

Kiyalee and Chyning were both beating on his back while holding their newborns.

He tried to wave the two women away as he hacked, gasped, gagged and sputtered.

Bonarain huffed. "If you want to say something while you're eating, you know that you can mentally send it. You don't have to try to talk and eat at the same time."

Soolchakan finally got to a rasping breathing instead of constant coughing. "I didn't try to say anything. I just... swallowed wrong. You've done it before, so...no I'm not perfect. I admit that." He loudly cleared his throat several times.

Kiyalee snickered. "Yeah! You're also old enough that you should know what goes where."

He snarled at her through some more hacking.


Bikaropin came to Soolchakan smiling.

"I'm glad that you talked your wives into procreating. We've had so many babies born this year and...there are several hundred women who are...in different stages of gestation."

Soolchakan snarled. "From this day forth, you will forget that you ever gave me that suggestion! You will accept that the women have decided to procreate and it was not from any suggestion of mine or yours."

Bikaropin stood there looking rather confused.

Soolchakan raised his eyebrows. "Did you need...or want something?"

Bikaropin looked around confused. "I…thought I had… something to say to you but…for some reason it…uh…just slipped my mind." He cleared his throat while thinking. He frowned as he looked up at the ceiling in contemplation. "What was it? It seemed…important."

Soolchakan shrugged. "If you think of it later, you can always come back and tell me about it, especially if it is something important." He gave a wan smile.

Bikaropin nodded. He scratched his head looking confused. He vanished.

Soolchakan sat there growling to himself. "*H'oolyach!*" He huffed. "Now, I've got the problem of remembering who I lied *to* and about *what*." He snarled in disgust again.

5477 had been showing signs of being an even better year. By the end of 5477, 460 new Owlamites had been added to the population. A total count of 8,218 Owlamites, including that *one* that was exiled to dimension #45. The year 5478 began with numerous other women in different stages of gestation. The population count was definitely improving.

# 10

Nadiwi was having a difficult time taking care of her child while still trying to ravage any and every slaver she could find. Some of them had very young babies as well, however, she remembered that those were Heyyah children...not Owlamite...or any child of hers. They were children of slavers who would grow up to become the next generation of slavers. She had personally seen that happen too many times to ignore the fact that they were still just babies.

She did not mind the agonized screaming of any of the slavers. Any whimper from Monanya and Nadiwi dropped everything she was doing to take care of her precious little one. She was losing interest in demolishing slavers. She was finding out that love did really exist. Love was what she felt for her daughter. Love was what she was getting from her parents. Love was what she was getting from Loov. Love was real and it was not some sweaty physical act, it was a powerful emotion...and it was an incredibly huge and wonderful distraction from the hatred she had for slavers.

Soolchakan was looking at all of the mounting information

on all of the slavers. They were being located, sterilized and then Jumped to Beasties. He felt rather overwhelmed because of the number that had been moved so far and yet they were still getting leads on all seven continents of even more.

Bonarain was looking at all of the statistics as well. "You said that we probably needed some help, I agree!"

He shook his head. "I never dreamed that…there could possibly be so many. People who are slavers and other parasites who want to be slavers, as well as people who want slaves." He scoffed. "Is there really that big a demand for, what they call, disposable people?"

She shrugged. "We are talking about something that goes on throughout the entire globe. Anyone can be in a situation where they want some kind of power over…just about anything or anyone else."

He scoffed. "True! It still mystifies me how…so many people can make enough money to make it worthwhile…for all of them."

"From what I'm seeing, they don't battle among each other. They have a strict set of rules that they follow – or else." She sighed. "One thing I see about it is that the only way that they can be assured they are not sold into slavery is to become slavers themselves. Then and only then are their families immune to that nastiness. Become part of the problem before you suffer from the problem. Plus, the more slavers we send off to Beasties, the more new recruits the higher ups seem to find."

He clenched his teeth. "The slavers are just one problem.

Those lousy wizards like to use slaves as...experimental lab rodents. They like to test their spells on those poor souls. If they kill one, they just buy another one and start testing on that one as well." He hung his head. "They get a discount on their slaves, by assisting the slavers. Or they get the ones that would bring the least amount of money in the auctions." He grunted in disgust. "We don't just have a case of destroying the slavers – we have to dry up the market for slaves...in order to put all of the slavers permanently out of business."

Kiyalee had come in and was listening to the conversation. "How? How do we make it so that no one even wants a slave?"

Bonarain nodded. "That is a problem. There are several countries that have outlawed any form of slavery. They're the ones that are being hit the hardest for fresh slaves by and for the slavers."

"And the slavers always seem to know how to avoid any of the military of those countries...in order to obtain...merchandise," said Kiyalee. "Maybe that is one of the ways the wizards assist the slavers...and why they get a discount. Hide the slavers and their...merchandise...from any enemies."

"One of the main sources of protection and purchasing seems to be the wizards," said Soolchakan. "I wonder if there is any way that we can convince them to stop protecting and purchasing."

"Maybe we should try talking to them," said Kiyalee with a shrug.

Soolchakan sat there brooding for a few moments.

"Bikaropin, this is Soolchakan.  Can you hear me?"

Bikaropin looked up from the information that he was putting together.  **"This is Bikaropin.  What did you need?"**

**"How many of those wretched wizards are out there...in those covens, at this time?"**

**"Currently, there are 28."**

**"Which one is the most powerful...or at least the best at what he or she does?"**

Bikaropin checked his notes on the wizards.  **"The one that seems to be making the biggest noise...is a man named Wyhoshton.  He lives in Tabrow."**

**"I'm not interested in the one with the biggest mouth.  I want to know which one is the most powerful."**

Bikaropin chuckled.  **"That is Wyhoshton.  He was the fourth wizard to join the clique on North Chilamte. In less than two months after joining, he became the leader because of the number of spells he is able to perform...plus he is still learning even more."**

Soolchakan sat there nodding with his eyes closed.  **"Okay. Thank you."**

Kiyalee frowned.  "Why did you want the most powerful one?"

He sighed.  "Start at the top.  You make that one buckle and, the rest are just a little frightened of trying to fight on."

Bonarain cleared her throat. "So why are you looking so despondent?"

He glanced at her with a disgusted look on his face. "That *bimyock* lives in Tabrow. I get a little tired of going into a northern country that has a short summer and a blistering cold, *long* winter." He looked up at the ceiling. "Even in the summer it always seems cold in a place like that. After all this time, I am very comfortable in a tropical environment,"

Bonarain huffed. "We had some cold winters in the city of Owlam as well."

"Not like the ones as far north as Tabrow. Remember that Tabrow is almost as far north as the Turgon Wall...just on the eastern side of the continent instead of the west."

Bonarain giggled. "You've become too accustomed to the constantly warm climate here in the gorge. You're getting spoiled."

Soolchakan just scowled back. "I already said that."

"So take a coat with you," said Kiyalee with a caustic smile.


Soolchakan headed to Tabrow with Shalam, Monaha and Bikaropin. They found that it was cooler, at this time, however it was not cold.

Soolchakan looked around the main square of the capital city of Yiyji. "Where does this wizard live?"

Bikaropin checked his map. "Since he is the lead wizard of the coven, the whole bunch had to move to his home in some small town north of here."

Shalam looked surprised. "He doesn't live in the capital city?"

Bikaropin chuckled. "It seems that many of the elite of the capital constantly want favors. He moved up north to be away from them so that he could be left alone to research his spells. That way, it became inconvenient to them to come by every day, asking for or demanding favors. They have to go through all of the undignified act of going to him to beg for favors. He wants to learn as many new spells as possible. His main desire is to become even better than the legendary Penbelth."

Monaha snickered. "Does he know that Penbelth is a Zaberd Elf?"

Bikaropin shook his head. "Don't know. Should we shock him by telling him?"

"That is irrelevant," said Soolchakan. "All we're trying to do is to find out what his attitude is about slavery. If he has the right attitude, we use him. If he has the wrong attitude...he may end up in dimension 45...with Penbelth." He sighed. "Do you have any idea where this town is...or are we going to have to walk?"

"We'll be able to Jump," said Bikaropin. "I got the information from Voord."

Shalam frowned. "From...what?"

Bikaropin smiled. "Voord is one of the members of the North Chilamte Clique. I found out that they're testing a new wizard today for membership. Since they're testing him for membership, all of the current members have to be there. That means that all six will be in that private tower belonging to Wyhoshton." He looked at Soolchakan. "Yes, I've been there. I can Jump us there. Of course we do need to be in Spy when we Jump."

Soolchakan nodded. "Fine! Let's go to Spy...and get where we need to be."

The four of them hopped to Spy and Bikaropin Jumped all of them to a spot near the main entrance of a rather tall stone tower on top of a hill. It looked to be at least eight floors high. It was located north of a small village. The town consisted of numerous stone structures.

Shalam frowned. "I don't see any wooden buildings. I wonder why."

Bikaropin looked down the hill at the town. "From what I understand, during the dead of winter, there are some pretty strong winds that come whipping out of the north. Most wooden buildings can't stand up to that wind and the weight of a lot of snow on top of the roof." He chuckled. "If you take a good close look at all of the houses - you won't find a single one with any windows on the north wall. Plus, those very high pointed roofs make it hard for snow to collect...without falling off. That way, the roof doesn't collapse under the weight of the snow."

Monaha looked up at the tower. "What is all that noise...

coming from inside?"

Soolchakan shrugged. "Let's go in and find out."

Since they were in Spy, there was no need to knock on the door. They saw no one in the main room. They all heaved a sigh and headed for the stairs. Second, third, fourth and fifth floors were all empty of any intelligent life. On the sixth floor, they found nineteen people, ten men and nine women, dressed in rags. They were all wearing iron collars.

Soolchakan growled. "This does not look good. I wonder how many of these unfortunate people are enslaved by this Wyhoshton."

Shalam looked confused. "Why wouldn't they all belong to him?"

"Because there is a meeting going on right now," said Monaha. "If all six of the current members are present…some of those people could belong to the others. They don't necessarily all have to be the property of Wyhoshton."

Shalam nodded. "I see what you mean."

They continued up to the seventh floor. They came up and found themselves on the south wall. The entire seventh floor was one large room. There were four men and two women seated on rather ornate chairs against the west wall. One obese man was standing in the middle of the room looking at the six seated ones. He was panting and perspiring profusely.

Bikaropin pointed to one of the seated men who was dressed in a maroon robe. "That one is Wyhoshton. The man in black is Shoyoll. The man in green is Voord. The woman is yellow in Twaya. The woman in scarlet is Nanhimpa. The man in dark blue is Toroom. The fat one in brown…is the initiate – Hovong."

Twaya looked at a list in her lap. "So far, Hovong, you have successfully executed ninety-eight spells. You still need two more to obtain membership."

Hovong smiled as he wiped perspiration off of his bald head. "Yes, Great Mage Twaya. I have five more that I can choose from…in order to show the minimum one hundred spells." He took a deep breath and blew it out. "For my next one…I wonder if I could obtain a slave from one of you." He shrugged with a smile. "Preferably…an expendable one."

Wyhoshton snarled at him. "If you wanted an expendable slave, you should have brought one of your own with you. I don't want to throw any of mine away for some extravagant showing by you."

Shoyoll leaned forward. "You're not required to dazzle any of us. The requirement is prove that you can execute a minimum of one hundred spells successfully. So far, all of the spells that I've seen, I'm capable of doing them myself. If you were here to dazzle us, you've only managed to bore me with things that I already know. Now, if you have five to choose from, go ahead and do two of them that don't require any of us to give up one of our slaves just for your edification."

Shalam shook his head. "Absolutely not sounding good. Those slaves might be property of all six of these *bimyocks*."

"I'm painfully aware of that," sighed Soolchakan.

Bikaropin headed back down the stairs. "I'll see if I can find anything in their minds...as to which one belongs to which wizard."

Hovong went to a large binder that was on a podium near him. He opened it and ran his fingers down a page. He nodded. "This one will do nicely." He closed his eyes and prepared to continue his initiation.

Bikaropin came back up the stairs. "That lot on the sixth floor is only a portion of the slaves. There're more out in the stables. These *bimyocks* have others who tend their carriages and equines. Those stay with the animals. The ones downstairs are all domestics or..." He cleared his throat. "...sex slaves."

"Wonderful," said Soolchakan flatly. "We may end up sending this entire Clique to Beasties...today." He growled in frustration. "Shalam, Monaha, why don't you go into that town and...scout around? See if there are any...respectable persons there, who don't believe in abusing others."

At that moment, Hovong made a ball of light appear in the air. He moved the ball about as if it were something solid. He started to perform several ways of moving it towards the six judges.

"Enough of that," grunted Shoyoll impatiently. "That makes ninety-nine. Move on to number one hundred. I'm getting hungry...and even more bored."

"Get ready to punch that *bimyock*," said Soolchakan.

Bikaropin was confused. "Which *bimyock*?"

"The initiate."

Bikaropin followed Soolchakan and nodded.

Hovong was looking in his book again. He stroked his chin, wiped some sweat from his forehead and nodded. "That will do."

Soolchakan grabbed Hovong and hopped him to Spy. "Clobber him now!"

Both Soolchakan and Bikaropin punched and kicked the very surprised Hovong. It was not long before that fat man was laying on the floor unconscious.

Bikaropin smiled. "What now?"

"Castrate him and send him to Beasties."

Bikaropin nodded.

The six judges were all looking a little startled.

"You already showed us the Invisibility Spell," said Nanhimpa.

"He didn't answer," said Toroom. "Do you think he... Teleported...somewhere?"

"If he did, he'd better come back quickly," said Wyhoshton in a mocking manner. "He left his private ledger." He chuckled. "No one leaves that sort of thing for others to play with."

Bikaropin stood in front of the six judges. "Are we going

to do the same to them?"

"Yes, we are," said Soolchakan. "They believe in slavery and, the nonchalant way they talked about an *expendable* slave was…" He snarled. "…revolting!" He looked back at Hovong. "Are you just about finished with him?"

"Yes," said Bikaropin. He held up two testicles. "What should I do with these?"

"Throw them into dimension 2 and throw that Hovong into Beasties."

Voord looked at his colleagues. "How long should we wait for him to come back?"

"Good question," said Wyhoshton. "Teleportation is one that can be…sometimes, very unpredictable."

At that moment, Soolchakan touched Toroom and hopped him into Spy. Before the shocked Toroom could utter one syllable, Bikaropin coldcocked the mage. The rest of the mages in the room were rather startled at the disappearance of their colleague. They started doing all kinds of cantrips and spells to determine where he had gone. Meanwhile, Bikaropin sterilized Toroom and the new eunuch was Jumped to Beasties.

Bikaropin looked at the other five. "Which one is next?"

"Let's not be bigots. We grabbed two of the men, now it's time for one of the women to disappear." Soolchakan grabbed Nanhimpa and hopped her to Spy. She was then given the "anti-ovarian alteration" before being Jumped to Beasties.

Wyhoshton stood up. "HOVONG, STOP THIS NOW! YOU'VE PROVEN YOURSELF WITH ONE HUNDRED SPELLS! Enough is enough. Show yourself and bring the others back with you."

At that moment Voord vanished into Spy. The remaining mages started setting up all kinds of protection spells in order to keep from being grabbed (by what they thought was Hovong) and pulled out to who knows where. The protection spells did not help them at all. They all ended up in Beasties in a very short time – minus any and all genitals.

Soolchakan sighed. "Now, we go through this entire tower and find all unfortunate souls who were enslaved. Once we remove the iron collars, they should all get the message that they're totally free."

"Hopefully they also have some kind of intestinal fortitude to be able to function as free people. Some of the ones who were *really* broken just don't have…any kind of mentality for freedom."

Soolchakan groaned. "We may have to give them some kind of mental boost."

Bikaropin nodded. "A swift kick in the cerebellum."

"I'm going upstairs and see what that *bimyock* has hidden up there."

Bikaropin chuckled. "Let me know if you need any help."

Soolchakan went upstairs while Bikaropin went down. He found one very large room that had to be the laboratory. There were things hanging from the walls that he could not even guess what they were or what they were for. He would have to have guidance from Wyhoshton or some other wizard and he doubted that he would get any cooperation from any of them. There were four tables covered with different sized bowls, cups and bottles. On the north side of the big room there was a small stove near a table and cupboard. He walked to the cupboard and opened it up. There were several different types of food in there. Why not? If you had something up here, you would not need to go downstairs in order to get something to eat. There was already something palatable up here.

He was startled when he heard a snort coming from behind a large chest. He cautiously walked around in order to get a good look – from a safe distance. Laying asleep on the floor was what appeared to be an extremely pale and skinny Heyyah. He or she was laying on his or her left side. Soolchakan was looking at the head of the person and the shoulders appeared to be nothing but skin and bone. The thin, stringy hair was light brown. Soolchakan crept closer. He tried to read the mind to see if there was anything there. He could not pick up any form of an intelligent thought or dream. He scratched his head and sighed. He walked over and nudged the person lightly.

The Heyyah woke up with a start, looked around until Soolchakan was spotted. The Heyyah scrambled away on all fours making some kind of strange sound from the mouth as it rapidly crawled. Now, Soolchakan could see, from the total nakedness, it was a woman. She was absolutely nothing but skin and bone – and totally insane. She got to the wall, turned around and sat there looking at Soolchakan through wild eyes. Again he tried to read her mind since she was now awake. There was nothing in there other than random scattered unintelligible thoughts and fear. Apparently Wyhoshten had been experimenting on her and that was what drove her out of her mind. Since she was still alive he had continued some of his diabolical experiments on her.

"You're better off dead," whispered Soolchakan. He hopped to Spy. He walked over to her. "Whoever you are...or were...I'm so sorry." He reached down, touched her and hopped her to dimension #2. In the void of space, she was dead instantly. He sighed and shook his head. "Again, whoever you were...my deepest apologies...but...you are no longer in pain and can no longer be abused."

He continued his tour of the lab. He came up to a rather ornate shadow box that was sitting on the floor and was taller than he. He looked at the compartments and was totally dumbfounded. Some of them had tiny little creatures that were moving around in them. He looked closer at one of the people (?). The tiny man glared back at him angrily.

"*Let me out of here,*" shouted the tiny man.

Soolchakan was rather taken aback by this. "Uh...how?"

"*Break the rotten spell!*"

Soolchakan looked around rather confused. He looked back at the tiny man. "How?"

"*Just smash the box! Don't worry about me.*"

Soolchakan found a mortar and pestle on one of the tables. He shrugged and threw the mortar. The mortar hit the shadow box and it sounded as if glass had just shattered even though it seemed to be made entirely of wood. A very tall Heyyah man came out of the box as the debris fell to the floor. Now that he was out of the box, his clothing was more apparent and it looked like a very expensive tan robe.

The man had a very angry and insane look in his eyes. "Where is that...thing? That...Wyhoshton!"

"Uh...why?"

"I'm gonna to kill him...if it's the last thing I do."

Soolchakan shrugged. "Too late, he's already dead." 'Might as well be,' he thought. 'He's banished to Beasties without any magical capability.'

The angry look froze on the man's face for several moments. It slowly changed to confusion, then finally a dead pan look. "I wish that it had been me who killed him."

Soolchakan smiled and clasped his hands together. "I didn't know that anyone was standing in line." He frowned. "Who are you and...what is this...of being miniaturized inside a compartment of a shadow box?"

The man calmed and took a deep breath. "I am Unjer. I was trapped inside that magical trinket. I was trapped in it by...someone else. That fiend gave the shadow box to someone else. It has passed between the hands of at least six people until Wyhoshton got it. That thing had promised to let me out...but never kept his word."

Soolchakan nodded thoughtfully. "So...how long were

you in there?"

Unjer opened his mouth to say something and then stopped himself. He looked thoughtful and then a little startled. "I've been in there since…uh…what year is this?"

"The Fall Equinox was four days ago. So it is now the fourth day of Statichy in the year 5478."

Unjer was now looking rather sick. "I've been…trapped… in that thing…since…" He sank to his knees. He moved his lips slightly as he was doing some mental calculations. "474 *years*!" He now sat down on the floor. "I was trapped in that thing in the month of Lergan, 5004." He leaned his head back. "So you're telling me that I'm now 474 years older…without aging a day while I was stranded inside that infernal thing."

"Quite possible," said Soolchakan. "So, being Heyyah, everyone that you knew is…probably long dead."

"I'd been promised a wife. I'm thirty years old. She was seventeen." He sighed. "I doubt she waited." He looked up. "Are we still in…Varnast?"

Soolchakan shook his head. "No, we're currently in Tabrow."

"No wonder I feel a chill." He rubbed his arms as if to make an attempt at some warming of his body.

"As long as you have no argument with me, I have no reason to have an argument with you. I will let you go in peace."

Unjer chuckled. "Where?"

Soolchakan shrugged. "Varnast."

"It won't be the same."

"Nothing ever is. Change is constantly occurring."

Soolchakan felt that the man seemed sincere, however, he decided to read that mind anyway. After a few moments he felt sick. Unjer was scheming on ways to go back to Varnast and regain his power as a political figure. The man had hoarded a fortune away in a hidden cavern. If the wealth was still there, Unjer would be able to buy his way back into power – as well as restocking any new home with a minimum of twenty slaves. Most of those slaves would be attractive women...that he could sexually abuse at his whim.

Soolchakan shoved his will on the man and got the precise location of the cavern. He kept the man frozen long enough to sterilize him and then Jump him to Beasties. He headed to the stairs mumbling. "I should've left him in that flaming box." He looked over at the shadow box and noticed that none of the other tiny figures that had been moving in those compartments were in there any more. He had no idea where they were. He was almost afraid to even attempt finding out where they were. The only thing he could surmise was that Unjer came out here, because that was the one he had been communicating with, when he shattered that...thing.

Bikaropin was heading up the stairs. "What did you say?"

Soolchakan just shook his head. "I was just thinking out loud. What did you find?"

"There's a dungeon under the tower. There are forty-five prisoners in the cells. It seems that Wyhoshton kept a large supply of slaves to experiment on."

Soolchakan groaned. "Go back to the gorge. Get some more help. A lot of help. The *ex*-slaves of Wyhoshton and the others need to get home. We're talking over sixty slaves. It may take a little time to get them all home."

Bikaropin nodded. "Anything else?"

"Yes, see if you can find out where the other wizards lived. I doubt very seriously that all of them lived in this tower. They have carriages here so, they had to come from somewhere."

"Okay. Uh…what's on the top floor?"

"The main laboratory where he mixed…who knows what."

Bikaropin scoffed. "Why not?" He sighed. "I'll go get help now." He vanished.

Soolchakan continued wondering about all of the other tiny people in those compartments. Only one had come out. All the others…what happened to them? He might never know…or understand. Maybe it *was* a case where the only one rescued was the one he had been talking to at the time and the others…(?).

Soolchakan departed the tower and headed down the hill. **"Shalam, Monaha, did you find anything in the village?"**

Shalam responded. **"Yes, we found something very interesting**."

**"Such as?"**

**"Where are you right now?"**

**"Coming toward the village, why?"**

At that moment Monaha appeared in front of him – with a big grin on his face. "Hop to Spy and I'll Jump us both there."

Soolchakan frowned, shrugged, and hopped. Monaha took his arm and Jumped them to a room above a tavern. Shalam was sitting there staring at a young Heyyah man who was sitting in a chair in a stupor.

Monaha hopped to Home dimension. Soolchakan followed.

Shalam grinned. "Father, I would like you to meet Prince Zebyuro Progerom. He's originally from Oosam."

Soolchakan took a closer look at the rather unkempt man. "If he's a Prince from Oosam, he is a *long* way from home. He also seems to have forgotten any kind of entourage. Usually, someone of royalty has a bunch of boot-lickers and bodyguards surrounding them."

Shalam snickered. "Usually! This one has a very interesting story to tell. The reason why he has no entourage is just part of the story."

Soolchakan sat down on a chair. "I have a feeling that it'll be a rather long story."

Shalam nodded. "We picked his mind and found out that he was born to the royal family of Oosam. As a young boy, he was kidnapped from Oosam, taken to the city of Malantroi in Agrosha and sold into slavery. He was the sex slave of the top military leader in Malantroi. He got tired of being a sex slave, especially to a man, he murdered his…" He cleared his throat. "…master, ended up lying his way out of the situation and got out of Agrosha. He's been wandering around, for about a year, looking for someone who can assist him in finding the kidnappers and getting him back to his rightful place in Oosam…where he plans on waging war against all slavers and slavery."

Monaha chuckled. "You said that we would probably need a lot of help in battling slavery. Who better than a member of a royal family?" He grinned. "Especially someone from a country that seems to be a major victim of slavers."

Soolchakan nodded. "Yes, especially from a land where slavery is outlawed. That could be very good." He tried to think for a moment. "What's the capital city of Oosam?"

"That would be Saditelo," said Shalam. "It's located in Lower Oosam."

Soolchakan pursed his lips as he thought. "Get someone to Saditelo and find out the current political structure. Find out if this Zebyuro is related to the current monarch. If he isn't, we need to get all of the specifics we can find and then act on that."

Shalam frowned. "What if he is related?"

Soolchakan groaned. "If he is related, we'll act on that information as well. First, find out which one applies…then we'll do what needs to be done."

The next month had a lot of activity. The women with very young children had to take care of all of those mundane activities of watching the monitors that were watching outer space (even though no one had seen any activity in centuries). Bikaropin had a group of men who were working at getting all of the freed slaves back to their homes. Another group of men, headed by Shalam, doing reconnaissance in Oosam to determine if Zebyuro actually was a true Prince of Oosam.

Soolchakan did not feel like reading all of the information that was piling up. "What are in the reports?"

"No new sightings of any enemies from outer space," said Bonarain.

"All of the one-seat fighters, that we have stored in dimension #45 are all ready for action," said Kiyalee. "We've had to do a little training on some of the ones who've just come of age to be allowed to fly the things and participate in battle. All of the training is going well."

"Every form of life that has been in the area above our dwellings in the gorge has been scared away because they think the entire area is haunted, on both sides of the gorge," said Chyning. "We haven't had to scare anyone off in some time now."

"There are still three of the freed slaves who have no idea where they came from or how to live as a free person," said Bikaropin. "We've turned them over to a group in North Paselter who are devout anti-slavery people. Those people are training them how to cope with freedom."

Shalam sighed as he looked at his report. "Several years ago, this Zebyuro Progerom was the rightful heir to the throne of Upper and Lower Oosam. He has a sister named Sanyee Progerom. So far we've been unable to locate her. If we want the assistance from the Kingdom of Oosam, then...we may have to use some...or maybe a lot of our magic in order to influence the current Monarch to assist in any form of global abolishment of slavery."

Soolchakan listened to all of it. "This current Monarch in Oosam – is this person aware of the history of Zebyuro?"

Shalam nodded. "Yes. He is not related to Zebyuro at all. When Zebyuro and Sanyee disappeared, the Queen went missing as well. The King that had been on the throne was found assassinated. Nothing was ever solved in any investigation as to what happened to any of the other members of the royal family."

"Until now," muttered Soolchakan. "It could present quite a problem if we try to convince the current King to accept Zebyuro."

"Nevertheless, that is something we'll have to consider," said Shalam.

Soolchakan frowned. "Where is the Prince...at this time?"

"He is currently being given, what he thinks, is a tour of some vast vaults, filled with riches that he is having a problem accepting," said Monaha. "He has been told that we're willing to utilize just about all of it in order to globally end the slave trade."

Soolchakan now looked confused. "What he...thinks?

What do you mean by that?"

"We're planting all kinds of things in his mind," said Monaha. "Those riches exist, but, we're not going to show him where they actually are located."

"So, you're not twisting his mind, you're just dazzling him with riches," said Soolchakan.

"Exactly," replied Monaha.

Soolchakan looked around at all those present. "Shall we send a group to Oosam and start doing some convincing? Convince the current King, whatever his name is, that he should cooperate with us?"

"His name is Fonzen Mardanian," said Monaha.

Kiyalee was a little anxious. "If he wants to remain on the throne, how are we supposed to convince him to accept Zebyuro?"

Bonarain smiled. "Oosam is located on two different continents. We have to convince both of them to work together. One will be in Upper Oosam on Ficara and the other will be in Lower Oosam on Lusaratia. They will have to agree between the two of them which one has the final word."

Soolchakan sighed. "So, let's get Zebyuro, and our contingency to Oosam, and get started with some negotiations."

# 11

Soolchakan led the contingency to Oosam. He wanted to see exactly what they were facing without any second-hand information. He had three men from the third generation working directly with him: Peldom, Baktim and Bendarik.

The current King Fonzen Mardanian was not anti-slavery. He did not care what happened, as far as slavery raids in his kingdom. He knew that slavery was illegal in Oosam, however, he could not convince enough of the Provincial Barons to accept any change – even though he was the King. He did not want any kind of civil war, so he kept his mouth shut. The slavers were able to grab entire villages without any fear of reprisal from the throne. King Fonzen would simply tell the Barons that he did not know where to attack in order to stop the grabbing of citizens. He did, secretly, get a message to the slavers that they had better not overdo it…if they wanted to be able to continue with their trade.

After nine days of reconnaissance, Soolchakan decided to face the King directly. He decided to do it in a very unorthodox manner. Protocol was thrown out the window.

Soolchakan stood there smiling. "Peldom and Baktim, you will follow behind me. One on each side. Bendarik, you will stay in Spy…with a bottle of water."

Bendarik closed his eyes and had his mouth hanging open. "What am I going to do with a bottle of water?"

Soolchakan turned to him looking very calm. "You will hand it to me when I ask for it." He gave a very insincere smile.

Bendarik looked to Peldom and Baktim for some kind of help. Both just shrugged.

"All right, my children, let's enter the throne room!" Soolchakan led them to the entrance. "Peldom and Baktim, we now go to Home dimension."

Several guards, servants and a few elitists who were near the door were all startled at the sudden appearance of the trio.

The throne room was one of those huge, very long rooms with twelve columns on each side of the main aisle. Four guards were standing with two-handed swords around each column. There were numerous large colorful tapestries lining each of the side walls along with a few ostentatious and huge paintings. At the far end of the room was the throne. Fifteen steps led up to the throne where the King was lounging. There was a smaller throne to the right of the King. A woman who was dressed in a very garish voluminous dress was sitting on that throne with a worried look on her face. There were four women surrounding the Queen. On each side of the throne there were lines of guards standing at attention with pikes. One guard lined up on each step.

The entire room was crowded, on both sides, with all kinds of people dressed (or over-dressed) in all kinds of expensive and showy clothing. They all looked at Soolchakan with some disdain.

"**Let's go forward**," sent Soolchakan.

A man with a very large staff walked directly in front of them. He held out his left hand. "STOP! You have not introduced yourselves and…you have not been announced."

"Then announce me," said Soolchakan patronizingly.

"I don't know who you are," the man spat back.

Soolchakan looked over his right shoulder at Baktim. "We're dealing with a complete ignoramus." He looked back at the defiant Heyyah. "Who are you?"

"I am the Master at Arms! No one enters the throne room until I announce them."

Soolchakan rolled his eyes and grunted in disgust. He sniffed. He got right in the face of the Heyyah. "I am Drey Sssorg Soolchakan."

The Master at Arms sniffed back. "From where and why are you here?"

"I came here from Tabrow. I'm not originally from there, but I come here representing Prince Zebyuro Progerom."

Several jaws, within hearing distance, dropped.

Soolchakan sent a mental message. "**Monaha, get that Prince here to the throne room…quickly**."

Monaha came back. "**Do you want him in Spy or Home**?"

"HERE!"

**"Okay, I'm here with the Prince...in Spy.**"

The Master at Arms turned around. He bounced the end of his big staff on the floor three times. All talking ceased at the sound of his staff bouncing off of the floor. His loud voice now echoed throughout the quiet room. "My King Fonzen Mardanian. I announce...Drey Sssorg Soolchakan, most recently from Tabrow. He is here representing the long missing Prince Zebyuro Progerom."

Fonzen was sitting nonchalantly listening until he heard the name of Zebyuro. Suddenly his nonchalance changed to shock and confusion. He sat up and leaned forward on the throne as this strange trio started walking forward.

Peldom snorted. **"Do you think this room is big enough?"**

Baktim bit his lip to keep from laughing. **"Or long enough?"**

**"They've got to have plenty of room for all of the butt-kissers, guards and servants,**" sent Soolchakan.

As they took the long walk, they heard a lot of murmuring on each side of them. They ignored all of it and continued on.

As they neared the steps, King Fonzen held up his right hand. "That's far enough." He dropped his hand. "You say that you represent Prince Zebyuro. No one has seen him, his mother or his sister...in many years."

Soolchakan opened his mouth to start speaking. Before he could say anything the King got an angry look.

"Why aren't you kneeling," Fonzen snarled through his teeth?

Soolchakan raised his eyebrows. "I don't *kneel* to anyone. When does one King kneel for another?"

Fonzen chuckled. "Are you claiming to be a King?"

"I am the Drey Sssorg. In an ancient tongue or ours, that means *Voice of Power*. I have the power…and that makes me equal to any King."

Fonzen looked disgusted. "I know of no such title or power."

Soolchakan sighed. "**Bendarik, hand me the bottle**." He stretched his left arm out and hopped only his arm to Spy. Bendarik handed him the bottle. He hopped his left arm back to Home, pulled the stopper and took a drink. He replaced the stopper, stretched his left arm out and hopped it to Spy. "**Take the bottle**." Bendarik took the bottle. Soolchakan hopped his arm back to Home.

Fonzen tried, unsuccessfully, to hide his surprise at the stunt he had just witnessed.

"That, King Fonzen, is just one of the many powers that I have. Another power that I have - I…do…not…kneel…to… anyone, save the Great Maker."

Fonzen leaned back in the throne. He looked to his right.

He gave a swift motion with his right hand. He looked to the left and gave a similar wave with his left hand. All thirty of the pike men lowered their points of their pikes and aimed them at Soolchakan. They started walking forward menacingly.

"**Hop to Ghost**." He looked around as the thirty guards surrounded the trio with all of the points aimed at them. "**Let's go up the stairs and show this *bimyock* another power**."

The trio started forward up the steps. The guards started jabbing at them with the points of their pikes. After the first jabs, some of them were too startled to move. The ones who did still move were waving their long pole arms helplessly through the trio. Several clangs were heard as the steel points were banging against each other with nothing affecting the trio of Owlamites. Several of the guards followed the progression of the trio, still attempting to stick the points into the Owlamites. They reached the top of the stairs where Fonzen was fearfully attempting to push himself through the back of the throne.

Fonzen put his hands up as the points of the pikes came dangerously close to him. "GET THOSE THINGS OUT OF MY FACE!"

The guards stopped and raised the pikes back up, all looking rather apprehensive.

Fonzen was trying to keep from panicking. "Very impressive! Is this another one of your powers…wizardry?"

"You could say that," said Soolchakan flatly.

"Is this how you represent Zebyuro…with tricks?"

Soolchakan smiled. "Whatever it takes to get your undivided attention."

Fonzen looked over at his Queen. She was sitting there frozen in fear...other than trying to push herself through the back of her throne. Her handmaidens were equally terrified and doing some ducking and dodging behind her throne.

"All right...Drey Sssorg! You'll get my undivided attention! But, you have to prove that you really have Zebyuro with you!"

"Fair enough," chuckled Soolchakan. He crossed his arms. He gave Fonzen a stern look. He glared at the guards to his left and then the ones to his right. "Call off your mutts!"

Fonzen looked rather miffed. "GUARDS! BACK TO YOUR POSTS!"

All of the guards went back to their places on the stairs.

Soolchakan looked around. **"Monaha, are you here with Zebyuro?"**

**"Of course I am. Do you want him now?"**

**"Show yourself...with him."**

Fonzen suddenly had a look of shock on his face. Monaha had hopped to Home, with Zebyuro, while walking up the steps to the throne. When they got to the landing with the throne, Zebyuro gave a quick simple nod.

"The resemblance is striking," said Fonzen in a shaky voice. "I must remember that...it was over ten years ago that I last saw the…Prince. How can I be sure that you haven't brought some man who…is a look-alike or some other kind of pretender?"

Zebyuro looked over at one of the guards. "Commander Brelling! Do you recognize me?"

The leader of the guards had been staring with wonder on his face. He cleared his throat nervously. "As his Majesty stated – the resemblance is most striking. You could be the Prince Zebyuro, but…seeing as how it has been so long – other proof needs to be required…and shown."

Zebyuro chuckled. "My father told me of an escape hatch here in the throne room." He leaned forward towards Fonzen. "Are you aware of it?"

Fonzen swallowed hard. "Uh…escape…hatch? No! I know of no such thing."

Zebyuro walked up to the throne. He reached out. He did some fiddling with something under the bottom of the right armrest on the throne. Fonzen had pulled his arm away from the armrest as if it were something filthy. He watched as Zebyuro was moving something on the underside. A loud clank was heard and suddenly the seat and part of the floor fell out from under the King.

All that was heard was an exclamation of: "WHAT DUH!" from the King and then a loud *whump* as he landed below on a large mattress (along with several pillows). A cloud of dust came up from the opening and they could hear Fonzen coughing and sputtering below.

Zebyuro looked down through the orifice. "That is the

escape hatch, Your Majesty. It appears that...since you didn't know of it, the area has not been cleaned in some time."

Everyone up top, including the Queen, was waving the irritating flying dust away from their faces.

'That should prove something,' thought Soolchakan. **"Baktim, please go down there and get him back up**."

Baktim vanished and was back almost immediately with Fonzen. Fonzen was coughing while wiping dust and cobwebs off of his face.

Soolchakan stood there still with a calm demeanor. **"Bendarik, the water please**." He hopped his left arm to Spy and took the water from Bendarik and held the bottle up for Fonzen. "Would Your Majesty, you like to clean your throat...and face?"

Fonzen took the bottle, removed the stopper and took a long drink. He poured some of the water in his hand and used it to clean some of the dust off his face. He cleared his throat, in a rather loud manner, several times. He looked back down at the hanging seat. "How do you get it back up?"

Zebyuro reached behind the throne and pulled on a lever. The seat came back up. Zebyuro pulled on it again and a loud bang was heard. Fonzen pushed down on the seat to make sure that it was sturdy. He walked behind the throne and looked at the lever.

"I've often wondered what that thing was there for. I've even pulled it several times. Why didn't the seat fall before?"

Zebyuro smiled. "The lever on the back is for bringing the seat, and the part of the floor that is attached to the escape hatch, back up. If the seat is not down – nothing happens. Only the knob on the underside of the armrest can make the seat fall."

Fonzen nodded and cleared his throat. "As much as I hate to admit it…it seems that in order for you to have performed that… stunt, you had to have been here in the throne room…before." He dusted himself off a little more. "Before I can accept you as the son of King Tooron and Queen Amrona, I require…one more piece of proof."

"How to gain entrance into the private vault of the Prince," said Zebyuro flatly.

Fonzen was completely shocked by the statement. "How did you…?" He cleared his throat again. "Yes, that's the test. More and more I'm believing that you *are* Prince Zebyuro. You know too much about…this palace to have not been here before." He looked at the throne. "Especially about an escape hatch…that I wasn't aware of." He turned and walked to the edge of the stairs. "NO MORE APPOINTMENTS OR MEETINGS! I AND THE QUEEN WILL RETIRE FOR THE DAY!" He looked back. "Let us go and open the vault. See what childhood treasures you placed in there."

Zebyuro sighed and smiled. "Unfortunately I was only a boy of 10. I did not have a *great* treasure. I simply had favorite toys." He chuckled. "But there is that chest that my father had placed in there. He made me promise to not open it…until after he was gone."

Fonzen led the procession. His Queen Niska left for her chambers. Zebyuro, along with the Owlamites followed Fonzen.

The guards walked along on both sides. As they proceeded through one of the hallways, the guards, one by one, broke ranks and went to a rack. They placed the long pikes in a rack and each pulled a spear off of the rack. Now that they were in a different part of the palace, the ceilings were not quite so high. The long pikes would have been more of a hindrance in these areas.

Fonzen stopped. Everyone stopped with him. He turned and faced Zebyuro with a smug smile and clasped his arms behind his back. "You…lead the way…to your childhood vault."

Zebyuro smiled and bowed his head slightly. "Of course… Your Majesty." He started forward.

The procession fell in line on Zebyuro. They arrived at a point where there was a cross hallway. Zebyuro never hesitated. He turned to the left.

Soolchakan did a little mind reading on Fonzen. The King was realizing that the claim of this young man was gaining more credibility with every step. The King was wondering how he could get out of this mess without a lot of bloodshed – primarily his own. Soolchakan smiled as he considered things. He wondered how he could negotiate a peace between these two and stop any form of bloodshed.

Zebyuro arrived at a set of double doors. He took a deep breath let it out and then sniffed. He wiped a tear off his cheek. "It has been a long time. I hoped but…I wondered if I would ever see this room again."

Fonzen gave a quick signal. Two guards opened the doors for Zebyuro. The Prince walked forward slowly. He stopped and looked around. Now there were more tears flowing down his cheeks.

Soolchakan looked around and noticed that the room was immaculate. It seemed that it was just way too clean. It was way too clean to have been ignored for over a decade.

A door came open on the other side of the room. A rather short and very pudgy woman came through looking very upset.

"I thought that Your Majesty said that you would leave this room alone until..." Her eyes and mouth were suddenly open wide with shock. She brought her hands up to her mouth and slowly started walking towards Zebyuro. She held out her arms as she moved as quickly as her heavy little body could manage. "MY PRINCE! YOU'VE COME BACK! After all these years it is…so good…" She reached him and fell to her knees hugging his legs. She was laughing and crying at the same time.

Tears were now flowing freely down the cheeks of Zebyuro as he lovingly rubbed the head and shoulders of his childhood nanny.

Fonzen turned to Soolchakan. "That is one woman I knew could not be fooled by a fraud. The woman who wet-nursed him, changed his diapers, bathed him, dressed him and watched him grow." He shook his head. "More and more I'm believing that this is truly the long lost Prince Zebyuro." He sighed. "Now… what to do about…his right to the throne and the fact that I am already crowned and sitting on the throne."

"I suggest that we talk to your High Council and...I have a few ideas of my own," said Soolchakan with a warm smile. "A way we can all benefit...peacefully."

Fonzen nodded and cleared his throat. "Any suggestion that is peaceful and acceptable to all, is very welcome." He cleared his throat again. "Uh...*Prince* Zebyuro...the vault...if you don't mind."

Zebyuro wiped the tears off his face. He pulled a kerchief out of his sleeve and blew his nose. The nanny backed away a little. She could not stop a silent laugh because she was so pleased to see her charge once again. She kept one hand on his sleeve as she walked with him, just to reassure herself that he was really back from...wherever. The other hand was persistently wiping away her tears as she sniffled and continued giggling with joy.

He walked over to a tapestry on the wall. "It is still a beautiful piece of work," he said while still sniffing. "I was too young to really appreciate how beautiful it is. Now..." He nodded. He reached to the left of the tapestry and pulled a thick cord. The tapestry was raised up revealing a metal door. There were several hundred raised nodules on the door from top to bottom. Zebyuro stood there counting from the left side on the bottom row. He got to a certain point and then moved up. He got to one specific nodule and pushed on it. He then counted up from that one. He pushed on another nodule. He counted to the right of that one and pushed another nodule. A clank was heard. He counted up four more and pushed hard. The door released and opened slightly. He turned around and looked at Fonzen. "Any more questions, Your Majesty?"

Fonzen shook his head. "If you're a fraud, you're a very good one. I can't think of anything else that might trip you up." He nodded. "It seems that I must accept that you are the long lost Prince Zebyuro." He sighed. "Who else could have known the combination to the vault?"

Zebyuro sat there despondently looking at the floor. "So it is true. The same day that I was kidnapped, my mother and sister were kidnapped as well." He looked up angrily. "And my father was assassinated."

Fonzen nodded. "I'm afraid so." He cleared his throat. "Your nannies were poisoned. There were several physicians who said that they shouldn't have survived, however, they did. One of the physicians stated that the amount of the poison was too little. If it had been administered to you and your sister, the two of you would have definitely died. The amount was insufficient to kill an adult, according to that one physician. Another physician stated that the two women were just too obstinate to die. They wanted to see the return of the two royal children."

"What was the poison that was used?"

Fonzen grunted, shrugged and shook his head. "I cannot pronounce it."

"Was my father poisoned as well?"

Fonzen hung his head. "No, he was stabbed to death."

Zebyuro shook his head. "Were there no clues to what happened?"

"The best investigators in the constabulary, they wore themselves out looking for anything that would give them any clue. They found nothing constructive or convincing."

Soolchakan sat there reading the mind of Fonzen. He could find no guile in anything that was being said. Whatever did happen, Fonzen was not part of the plot. The only problem that he could think of was convincing Fonzen to become a complete anti-slavery King.

Zebyuro looked at Soolchakan. "Where should I start... looking for my sister and mother?"

Soolchakan shrugged. "You were taken to Agrosha. Specifically Malantroi. I would say that harbor town is as good a place as any to start. The trail may be ten years old but..." He looked up thoughtfully. "...who knows?"

Fonzen cleared his throat. "I know that it saddens you to find out what happened to your family, however, at this time, we still have a few affairs of state to discuss."

Zebyuro nodded. "Like who goes where for what reason."

Bikaropin stood up. "Majesties, may I make a few suggestions?"

Fonzen gave him a side glance. "As long as it is relevant and constructive, yes."

Bikaropin nodded. "Relevant and constructive... absolutely! Now, King Fonzen, I understand that you are originally from Upper Oosam...is that correct?"

Fonzen nodded.

"Now, Oosam is a Kingdom that is wholly unique. It is the only Kingdom that is located on two separate continents. No other Kingdom can make a claim like that."

One of the Barons of the High Council interrupted. "Ciscaumen is not all on one land mass."

Bikaropin smiled. "Yes, Baron Sonoll, however, Ciscaumen is located on three rather large *islands*. Not one single part of Ciscaumen is on any continent. Oosam can claim to be on two continents and own several coastal islands as well. If you take the total land mass of the three parts of Ciscaumen, it does not equal the land mass of either Upper or Lower Oosam."

Sonoll looked rather embarrassed. "Uh, yes, that is quite correct." He cleared his throat and smiled nervously. "Please continue."

Bikaropin smiled again. "From what I understand, there are a few problems in getting messages from Upper to Lower and Lower to Upper in a timely manner. There are also a few problems with the fact that Upper is ruled from Lower. The Barons of Upper Oosam feel somewhat left out of any high decisions that are being made. Now, since King Fonzen was born in Upper Oosam, it might be expedient to make a capital city in Upper Oosam as well. Since King Fonzen is originally from Upper Oosam, he could move to that capital and be with the Barons of Upper Oosam. Prince Zebyuro could take control in the capital city here in Lower Oosam and the Barons here would not feel left out either. My suggestion would be that you decree an unbreakable pact that would keep the two parts of Oosam remaining as one Kingdom. This would halt any form of a revolution or bad blood between a Baron of Upper and one of Lower causing some…unnecessary civil war between the two parts."

Fonzen nodded. "So if there is an argument between two Barons, both I and Prince Zebyuro would be a part of solving the problem…as peacefully as possible."

"Absolutely," said Bikaropin with a smile.

Fonzen looked up in thought. "I wonder where I would put this capital city."

"I know that I would move the capital of Lower Oosam," said Zebyuro.

Fonzen raised his eyebrows. "Oh really, why?"

Zebyuro shook his head. "There is too much pain for me in this palace. I was kidnapped from here, my sister and mother were kidnapped as well. My father was murdered here." He sighed. "Too much pain. I would prefer a coastal city. I think that the harbor city of Semoron would be a better location. That way, any dispatches that I have to send to, or receive from King Fonzen… would only require a ship. It would not need some runner who has to have a collection of equines waiting lined up between the coast and this city of Saditelo."

"That is an excellent idea," said Fonzen nodding. "I would place the capital of Upper Oosam on the coast…for the same reason. That way, both capitals are as close together as possible and that would cut down on the time that dispatches are sent and received." He nodded. "Very excellent idea." He thought for a few moments. "It sounds as if the, very large, harbor city of Mardan would be the ideal place for the capital of Upper Oosam. That way, both capitals are as close as they can possibly be to each other…and somewhat centrally located between the two parts."

One of the Barons groaned. "I am sorry, Your Majesty, but…I have no desire to move to Upper Oosam. I would like to stay here."

"And so you should, Baron Diymosh," said Fonzen merrily. "Prince Zebyuro will need a High Council here. Why shouldn't you be on that council? I know that Baron Sonoll has had complaints about coming here to Lower Oosam for such council meetings. If he were to go with me to Upper Oosam, he would be a lot closer to home and still maintain his status. Baron Diymosh, you would maintain your status as well."

Zebyuro looked over at the military member of the Council. "What about him? What would we do about the High Military Commander? Which Council would he be advising?"

Fonzen frowned. "That is a good question." He turned to the Commander. "What do you advise on this matter, Commander Vooshk?"

Vooshk stroked his very neatly manicured gray beard. "One thing that I have always told my field commanders is… observe what is in front of you and act on that. Don't wait to send a message and ask what to do. By the time the answer comes back, you may have already been defeated because of indecision. My suggestion is: Have one High Military Commander in Upper

Oosam and one High Military Commander in Lower Oosam. It is not as if I were demanding equal status with the crown. To have a Commander equal to my rank in Lower Oosam is acceptable. As a matter of fact, I suggest that Field Commander Voseses Teeveel be given that office."

Fonzen frowned. "By that suggestion...I take it that you wish to be the High Commander in Upper Oosam, while Teeveel is the High Commander in Lower Oosam."

Vooshk smiled. "Majesty, you are from Upper Oosam, as am I. Prince Zebyuro is from Lower Oosam, so is Commander Teeveel. Both of us would be much closer to our original homes."

"Excellent," said Fonzen jubilantly. "We'll draw up the agreement and proceed with the plans as soon as possible."

Bikaropin looked at Soolchakan. **"I can't believe that this is going so well. They're all going for it.**"

Soolchakan gave him a side glance. **"It is going well because I am forcing a few minds to accept it...whether they like it or not.**"

Bikaropin smiled. **"And they're all being that cordial about it**?"

**"No! With two of them, they're accepting it because of blackmail. Either they accept, with a smile, or I expose certain secrets about them.**" Soolchakan grinned.

Bikaropin now had a look of concern on his face. **"How certain are you that they'll keep their part of the bargain**?"

"I've already given them a dose of what I can do mentally. They're terrified of me...and you. I told them that they will never know when I'm watching them or will expose them. They'll accept the proposal...or get beheaded for treason."

Bikaropin shook his head. "Not very polite...but effective."

"I am Drey Sssorg. I'm not here for nice. I don't have to be nice. They have to be nice. I'm being forcefully expedient." He smiled.

"Good point." Bikaropin had to fight to keep from laughing.

"One problem that I see," said Fonzen. "This is going to be rather expensive. Setting up two new capital cities...is not cheap."

Bikaropin smiled. "As long as you assist us in destroying the slavery industry on a global basis, we will supply you with plenty of financial assistance."

Monaha looked horrified. "Where are we going to find that much money?"

Bikaropin gave Monaha a stare. "Bri."

Soolchakan nodded. "Yes there is a huge amount of gold on the planet Bri. We can take all we want from there and that way, we're not stealing from anyone."

"My thoughts exactly," sent Bikaropin.

"**We need to get that project started quickly**," sent Monaha.

Soolchakan looked off to the side. "**Bendarik?  Go back to the gorge.  Get some help.  Go to Bri and bring back a fortune in gold**."

Bendarik looked a little worried. "**How much gold**?"

Soolchakan pondered. "**We have seven council members and a King.  Bring enough to make all eight jaws drop...but don't get stupid**."

Bendarik sighed. "**On my way**."


Bendarik was the one Jumping the armada of ships to the planet Bri. Several of the members of this mission were still baffled as to why they were going to give an inordinate amount of gold to some Heyyah. Yes, they did agree with Soolchakan and especially Nadiwi that slavery must be abolished globally, however, giving all that gold to one nation still seemed extravagant. Nevertheless, Soolchakan had ordered it so they were going to comply.

After gathering 50 fenshon of gold ore (which would be just over 150 tons) from the huge vein on Bri, they headed back with the cargo.

Chylid looked back at all of the raw ore on his ship. "**Where are we supposed to dump all of this gold**?"

Bendarik sighed. "**In the royal coffers of Lower Oosam in Saditelo**."

"**You could buy a kingdom with this mess**," sent Too-Oram.

"**I think *that* is the idea**," sent Gorchon. "**The more we give them, the more they owe us. When you supply money to someone, you have some influence and control.   The more money you give...the more you control**."

"**That much makes sense**," sent Chylid.

Bendarik snarled to himself. "**Everybody shut up and Jump to Saditelo.  We get rid of all of this ore there. Then we can go home and play with our children**."

"**That's the best suggestion I've heard all day**," sent Gorchon. "**Just say when, so we can get this over with**."

On one side of the large room, King Fonzen and his High Council members:  Baron Canthon Sonoll, Baron Sloomon Tay, Baron Vossok Whaymoth and the High Military Commander Nennok Vooshk. On the other side of the room was Prince Zebyuro and his High Council members:  Baron Panporik Diymosh, Baron Elvik Twan, Baron Sevon Jujuvik and the newly appointed High Military Commander Voseses Teeveel.

All ten men were standing there gawking with open mouths and wide eyes.

Fonzen turned to Soolchakan.  "Drey Sssorg, all of... this..."  He pointed at the massive piles or ore spread throughout the large room. "All of this is...gold?"

"It is raw ore, Your Majesty," said Soolchakan calmly. "If you don't believe me, get your best metallurgists in the city and they'll confirm it."

Fonzen turned to Sloomon Tay. "Baron, where are our best...in metallurgy?"

Sloomon looked back at Fonzen. "Majesty, that would be in that very smelly section, on the north side of the city where the majority of the blacksmiths do their business. There are many there who work with copper, silver and gold."

Fonzen nodded as he again scanned the entire pile of ore. "Get an entire garrison of guards dispatched there. Bring back every single one of them that deals in precious metals. I want this stuff...processed and turned into coin...or jewelry...or just bars... at the earliest possible moment."

"At once, Your Majesty," said Vooshk. "He almost ran out of the room to inform the garrison Commander."

Fonzen again turned to Soolchakan. "Drey Sssorg, why...all of this...for us? Why would...how could...you be so generous?"

"Majesty, you can see from this amount, that we are determined to end slavery all over the world," said Soolchakan. "We cannot do it by ourselves. We've tried, but so far we've only made a slight dent in that horrid business."

Fonzen nodded. "Once our goldsmiths get here and... confirm that this is what you say it is – onward and forward to the total damnation and annihilation of any and all slavery business. We've been plagued by those parasites for far too long. We've lost too many Oosam citizens, in both Upper and Lower Oosam." He shook his head. "Drey Sssorg, we are in your debt…" He looked back at the pile of ore. "…in more ways than one…and we will live up to the promise to bring the final end to that global scourge."

'Thanks a lot…you greedy hypocrite,' thought Soolchakan. He smiled and bowed his head slightly.

Once the goldsmiths were brought into the great vault and saw the ore, they were all skeptical – at first. Once they had examined the ore and found that it was a mammoth collection of the largest gold nuggets that any of them had ever seen, they were convinced. One was so convinced, he wet his pants. He, of course, had to change his pants before they started processing the ore.

It took 58 days, with all of the smelting pots going, day and night, to get all of the gold processed. They had to get 40 carpenters working on chests that were large and strong enough to hold all of the gold coins.

Fonzen sat there looking at all of the chests. "How should we divide this great wealth?"

Zebyuro chuckled. "Your Majesty, I would suggest that we divide it evenly. If we don't…I'm sure that the Drey Sssorg would have something nasty to say to us…or do to us."

Fonzen just nodded silently for a few moments. "I quite agree, Prince. I do not want that Elf angry at me. Even though we haven't seen him since the smelting started, I'm sure he is aware of our progress."

"Yes, Your Majesty," said Zebyuro. "He said that he would come back to discuss the plans with us. Plans on how we start this campaign against slavers…may they all rot in the lowest level of the 666 punishments!"

Fonzen sighed. "I think that it is more of a situation where…we are assisting, greatly, in continuing their quest, to end slavery…globally."

Zebyuro simply smiled.

# 12

"Diversion," said Bikaropin. "That is one of the most effective tactics in war. Divert the attention of the enemy in one direction while you're bringing in your power and attacking from another."

The two High Military Commanders looked at each other and nodded.

Vooshk spoke first. "I agree that diversion is an excellent tactic. The problem here is that we don't know, yet, who needs to be distracted or in what direction or for how long."

"The city High Council is the main group that needs to be distracted," said Zebyuro. "You have eight civilian and eight military on this Council. If you can put them in some kind of quandary, the population is not that important. The city guard does what the military leader commands. The constabulary obeys the civilian leader."

Teeveel shook his head. "No, before we decide on what kind of diversion we're going to attempt on this city, we need more intelligence data. We need to know the population as well. How many people are we dealing with? How many military? How many constables? How many people are there who are in some kind of reserve military in case of an attack from hostile forces? Sixteen on the High Council is just not enough information."

Zebyuro smiled. "Once a year they have a full census taken. We get to them right after the census is taken and..." He grinned. "...they will supply us with every name, age and occupation of every citizen in the city. Free or slave, rich or poor, male or female, we'll know them all."

"That's very good to know," said Vooshk. "I still want to see...a few more things before we commit to anything. I don't think that we'll be able to launch this attack this year. I don't know if we'll have enough information next year as well. For something like this we just...have to be patient regarding what we get and figure out how we're going to use it."

"Very patient," said Teeveel. "The distance that we have to travel from here to Agrosha makes a supply line...very long and thin. It could be easily broken...and all of our work is for nothing."

Soolchakan sighed. "Full reconnaissance on the city and all inhabitants." He sniffed. "I think that we should take Prince Zebyuro there, disguised, and do a little bit of walking around. He knows the place better than anyone here and can give us a full tour. Maybe we can watch the results of a census. We can then possibly plan on hitting them the next year, after getting all kinds of useful information."

Zebyuro hung his head. "I hate that city and I hate the thought of going back."

Soolchakan smiled. "Don't worry. We protected you this

far. I'm not in the mood for any kind of failure now. Besides that, this time you're going there to pick the town to pieces and get as much information as possible for an invasion that they will not be able to withstand."

"It also has to be an invasion that we can execute in a very short time," said Teeveel. "I don't think that the King of Agrosha will take too kindly to having one of his major harbor cities invaded. We have to get in and out quickly…unless you can think of some diplomatic way of informing His Majesty that this was necessary. Otherwise, we have to leave no clues behind us as to who performed the great deed…or misdeed, as it were."

Zebyuro hung his head. "So much to plan. I didn't know that it could be so involved. My father tried to tell me some of these things but…I was just too young to understand them at that time." He hung his head. "I was also too busy enjoying myself with all kinds of…childish, personal indulgences."


Shalam, Monaha, Loov, Jotsoom and Molkan of the Second Generation escorted Zebyuro back to Malantroi. The Prince was not happy with this particular job. He had finally been convinced that it was necessary. The first few days he had his jaws clenched very tight. The Owlamites hopped him to Spy dimension and now he was not so upset. He now knew that he could walk through walls and not be seen or recognized by any of the citizens of the city that he hated so much. He was amazed, amused and frightened.

Soolchakan had been worried about showing the Spy

dimension to any non-Owlamite, however, since Zebyuro had already been there, it was nothing new to that Heyyah. Soolchakan was wondering if he could somehow make Zebyuro forget his escapades in the other dimension. He wondered if the threat of death would make Zebyuro keep his mouth shut if they did not figure out some way to wipe his memory. There was still time to contemplate before any final decision was etched in granite.

The sixth day the spy group was observing and taking notes, Zebyuro stopped, gasped and pointed with his mouth wide open in shock. He could not get any words out because he was so surprised.

Shalam tried to see exactly which one of the people in the very crowded marketplace was the one being pointed at by Zebyuro.

Loov started reading the mind of Zebyuro. Maybe his mind was working better than his mouth. He had little luck because the thoughts were so confused that it was difficult to pick out which one was the current lucid thought.

Finally, Zebyuro shook his head and got a conscious thought. "That woman! That woman with the big wide, light purple dress! That's my mother! Queen Amrona!"

Shalam turned back to him. "If that one is your mother, why is she *not* a slave? She looks like she is doing rather well for herself. If she were kidnapped and sold into slavery…I don't think she'd be dressed so fine."

Monaha shook his head. "If she is your mother, then there seems to be more to the plot that killed your father and put you into slavery…and still has your sister missing from the picture."

"Best thing we can do is get her when she is getting ready to go to bed," said Jotsoom. "We get her when she is tired and we start delving deep in her mind."

Zebyuro was puzzled. "How will that help?"

Jotsoom kept staring at the woman. "She is free and very finely dressed. If she is your mother, then there is a horrible possibility that she was part of the plot that got you kidnapped and your father murdered."

"That's ridiculous," spat Zebyuro! "I refuse to believe any nonsense like that about my mother."

Monaha intervened. "First of all, wait until we can get into her mind to find out everything. If she is not your mother, just someone who closely resembles her, then this is nothing but a fantastic coincidence. If she is your mother then we need to find out a lot more about her and if she did have something to do with your abduction and the abduction of your sister…and the assassination of your father."

Zebyuro still looked rather upset. "So what do we do in the meantime?"

"We follow her," said Loov with a shrug.

"Yes," said Jotsoom. "We follow her to her home, wait until bedtime and then once we have her in some private area, we dig deep in her mind."

Zebyuro looked a little despondent. "Right now, I could

use something to eat. Problem is I can't touch anything while we're in this…invisible status."

"Hold on," said Shalam. He walked over to a fruit vendor. There was a row of fruits on the table where the man could keep track of his goods. Shalam waited until the man looked away from his table. As quickly as he could, he picked up one of the pieces of fruit and dropped a coin in the same spot. He walked back to Zebyuro. "Here you are, Your Majesty. Enjoy."

The fruit vendor looked back at the table and almost instantly noticed the missing piece of fruit. He angrily reached over and picked the coin up. The anger quickly left his face and turned to surprise. He looked around rather confused, wondering who had taken the piece of fruit and why had they paid ten times what it was worth? He shrugged, grinned as he stared at the coin and dropped it in his pocket. He then continued glancing around suspiciously.

Zebyuro took the fruit. "How do you do that?"

Shalam smiled. "Practice, practice, practice."

Zebyuro shook his head. "Incredible." He bit into the fruit.

The group followed the woman for the rest of the day. Every time she did anything, Zebyuro was even more convinced that this woman absolutely was Queen Amrona. Her walk, her mannerisms, her voice – all of it pointed directly to his mother.

The woman finally finished her shopping. She had four young women who were dressed in clothing that was not as fine as the "Queen" was wearing. They were all so thin, they appeared undernourished. When they finally arrived at her home, the Queen went to her bedchambers to change her clothing and the four women went to the kitchen to put things away. Molkan went with the quartet. He read their minds.

Molkan came back to join the group. "The four women are slaves. They have it in their minds that they are the property of the Lady Aboreema Keldigin. They've seen this woman do some rather nasty things to others who displease her." He gave Zebyuro a stern look. "Are you still positive that this *is* your mother?"

Zebyuro almost looked desperate. "Yes! It *is* her! Everything that I've seen tells me that this is my mother. I don't know who this…Aboreema Keldigin is, but…that woman has to be Queen Amrona."

Jotsoom looked around the main room. He suddenly spied a small painting, on the wall, that was lost in the middle of at least twenty others. "**There might be some truth to what the Prince is saying**."

Shalam frowned. "**What makes you so sure of that**?"

"**Over on the south wall. Look at the paintings. Two from the left and three from the top**."

Loov saw it first. He grabbed Zebyuro by his arm and dragged him over to the paintings. He pointed directly at the one in question.

Zebyuro was rather miffed at being dragged. Once he saw the painting, his eyes lit up. "I TOLD YOU! That woman IS the

Queen Amrona!"

Loov nodded. "And the boy in front of the elder man – is that a very young Prince Zebyuro?"

"Absolutely!" Zebyuro pointed at a young girl. "That one is my sister, the Princess Sanyee. The older man is my father – King Tooron."

Loov nodded again. "And the elder woman is the woman that we've been following for most of the day." He turned back to his fellow Owlamites. "This is getting *very* interesting."

Monaha nodded. "Yes, very!"

Shalam cocked his head. "I think that…Soolchakan should be informed of this piece of information…now. This has created a brand new jigsaw puzzle."

"Or a few thousand more parts," said Loov.

Shalam licked his lips. "**Keep watching the woman. I'm going to get Soolchakan**." He vanished.

Zebyuro looked around rather confused. "Where did… uh…Shalam go?"

"Don't worry," said Monaha. "He'll be back shortly."

Soolchakan and Shalam walked in the room.

Soolchakan looked riled. "What is all of this?"

Loov pointed at the small painting. Soolchakan walked over and perused it carefully.

Soolchakan looked at Zebyuro. "This is…your family…at a better time?"

Zebyuro nodded with a triumphant grin.

Soolchakan looked back at the painting. "Has anyone seen the girl?"

"No," said Jotsoom. "The girl in the painting has light brown hair. The four slave women in this house – two with flaxen hair, two with very dark hair."

Soolchakan nodded. "Then we'd better keep a very close watch on this woman." He looked around the room. "Where is she?"

"She's in her bedchamber, changing clothes," said Loov.

"Good!" Soolchakan looked around at his five sons. "Someone get in there and don't lose sight of her."

Zebyuro headed for the bedchambers. Shalam and Monaha chuckled at each other and followed Zebyuro.

Aboreema was sitting on a small stool. She was wearing a minimum amount of underwear as one of the four slave women was brushing her hair.

"That birthmark on her shoulder," said Zebyuro excitedly. "I remember it. She would wear some gown that had her shoulders completely exposed and…that birthmark, just at the neck…more proof of who she is."

Shalam mentally sent the information to Soolchakan.

"**This is getting more interesting with each tick of the clock**," sent Soolchakan.

Zebyuro rushed out to confront Soolchakan. "Why don't you do that…mind reading stuff now? Knock her out, knock the slaves out and…dig in!?"

"Patience, Your Majesty," said Soolchakan calmly. "We don't want anyone to know that we were here. If we do something to upset her routine, then she will know that something is amiss. Let them all do their daily rituals. Then when they bed down…we start the digging then." He smiled. He held his arms out. "Look around, explore, see if there's anything else that you recognize. We'll keep a good eye on her."

Aboreema came out wearing a robe, followed by the slave. She went to the dining room and sat down at the table. She looked somewhat irate. "MITHINA! I'M IN THE DINING ROOM, WHERE'S MY SUPPER?"

One of the women came out looking rather terrified. "I'm sorry, mistress but…the bird isn't quite ready yet."

Aboreema raised a small whip. "WHY IS IT TAKING SO LONG?"

Mithina fell to her knees and covered her head with her arms. "I'm sorry, mistress, but, I can't change how long it takes to properly cook the bird."

Aboreema growled. "Well…somebody bring me something! I'm starving." She put the whip down on the table and caressed it.

Mithina ran back to the kitchen. One of the other women came out with a small platter full of steaming vegetables. Another woman came out with a carafe of wine.

Molkan shook his head. "Isn't she a joy to be around," he said sarcastically?

The others all chuckled.

The cooked bird was brought out later. Aboreema nibbled at everything until she was satisfied. She got up from the table. "Time for my massage and then the four of you can eat." She headed to her bedchamber.

Soolchakan did not move his head to look at anyone else in the room. "Loov, go get Bonarain and bring her here. Jotsoom, go get Kiyalee and bring her here. Molkan, go get Chyning and bring her here. Before you bring them here, tell them everything that you know about this...Aboreema...so far."

The three men vanished. Shortly after that they came back with the three women in tow.

Once all of them were there Bonarain stood there with her arms folded across her chest. "Okay, what's going on? Why are all of us here?"

Soolchakan grinned. "This is beyond interesting. It is getting mysterious. We are going to use all four stones together. We are going to dig *deep*, very deep, into that mind and find out anything and everything we can about this...strange woman. She was a Queen, now she's not. She lived in a palace with her family, now she is living in luxury while her son was sold into slavery.

The daughter is still unaccounted for. I want to know *everything* about this woman that we can possibly discover."

Bonarain nodded.

Kiyalee blew her breath out in a huff.

Chyning was looking around for some goodies to steal with a lascivious grin on her face. "She has a nice collection."

"No," said Soolchakan. "We don't want her to miss anything…yet. We may be back later and then…you may indulge yourself."

Chyning wrinkled her nose at Soolchakan. She then looked around the room with nothing but greed on her face.

They waited for Aboreema to fall asleep. She was laying on her stomach. The four slaves were massaging the shoulders, arms and legs of their mistress.

Mithina looked over at one of the other women. "Faffy, is she asleep?"

Faffy looked closely at the face of Aboreema. She stood up and sighed in relief. "Yes," she whispered. She got an evil grin on her face. She turned her backside to Aboreema, pulled her pants down and farted in the woman's face.

All four stood up straight and stretched. They all four gave their mistress an obscene gesture and quietly crept out of the room.

Soolchakan smiled. "Loov, Jotsoom, make sure they don't come back before we're finished."

Loov and Jotsoom left the room.

The First quartet surrounded the sleeping woman. Their stones all started glowing. They held the stones up and the four joined. The room was filled with golden light as the stones were working their magic. Gold rays started going from the joined stones to the head of Aboreema. The quartet stood there silently with their heads lowered as they probed through the mind of woman.

Zebyuro nudged Shalam. "How long is this gonna take?"

Shalam shrugged. "As long as it takes to get what they want…or need."

Zebyuro sighed impatiently. "You people are capable of… some very strange and curious things."

After a while, Zebyuro was asleep. The mind probe continued on through the night. Shalam looked out the window and saw the first sign of dawn.

"Morning is here," said Shalam.

Soolchakan raised his head. The four stones released from each other and it was dark in the room.

Bonarain shook her head. "Can you believe it?"

"This *bimyock* is a real piece of work," said Chyning.

Kiyalee stretched. "So what do we do now?"

"We go back to Saditelo and tell everyone what we found out," said Soolchakan. "We get all of the higher ups from Oosam together so we only have to tell this story *once*."

Bonarain nodded. "I agree."

The meeting in Saditelo was called to order. Fonzen and his Council were a little upset over the fact that they still had to meet in Saditelo and not in Mardan. Zebyuro and his Council were upset over the fact that they still had to meet in Saditelo and not Semoron.

Soolchakan was getting a little irate over the petty squabbling of these self-serving bureaucrats. "Until you establish a suitable place in either Mardan or Semoron, this is still the place to meet. It'll take a while to erect the appropriate buildings. Do either of you have a place more suitable than this that is established in either Mardan or Semoron? NO! Remember who supplied you with all that gold. I still have some say in this because of that and until you've accomplished the full task of moving the capitals to Mardan and Semoron, it still remains in Saditelo. Any questions?"

There were several who were staring at the floor, or ceiling, or the top of their shoes or…at nothing in particular. Several others were glaring at Soolchakan with clenched teeth and tight lips in an attempt at looking patient.

Soolchakan smiled at them cordially. "Good! Now, we have uncovered something that might bring a new tactic into play in this situation."

Commander Vooshk scoffed. "What could possibly make a military invasion any easier?"

Soolchakan stared at Vooshk and cleared his throat. "What if I were to inform you, that we have a reliable source, which confirms that the harbor city of Malantroi is the refuge for a... Monarch assassin?"

Fonzen looked as if he had been slapped. "That...would give us...a considerable diplomatic and political advantage. We could inform King Suntram that...we're going after that assassin. Is it the assassin that murdered King Tooron?"

"We're absolutely certain that she is," said Soolchakan happily. "You knew her as Queen Amrona. We've now found out that she is a professional assassin named Aboreema Keldigin. She lives in luxury in Malantroi, with several slaves of her own." He leaned forward. "Three of which, we can prove, were abducted from Oosam." He leaned back. "They were free citizens of Oosam originally. Slavers abducted them, put them in irons, took them to Malantroi and sold them into slavery."

"That's even more diplomatic weaponry in our favor," said Baron Whaymoth. "A refuge for a Monarch assassin and free citizens of our country now held in involuntary bondage."

Fonzen sat there puzzled. "If she was the Queen then... why did she suddenly assassinate the King and steal away with the two children?"

Soolchakan sighed. "Her job was to do everything that she could to get King Tooron to cease any and all actions against slavers. The slavers wanted to be able to attack any place in either Upper or Lower Oosam and take whom they wanted, what they wanted, when they wanted, how, where and why. Tooron refused to budge on the slavery issue. The assassin slept in bed with him doing what she could for over ten years to try to make him change his mind, even giving birth to two children. After all that time, when he would not change, she gave up, killed him, stole the children and escaped...and sold at least one of them into slavery. We still don't know where the girl is, however, all indications are that she was sold into slavery as well."

Commander Teeveel shook his head. "So we have a lot of governmental *stuff* and *laws* in our favor. That still doesn't give us any idea about how to invade without suffering all kinds of unnecessary casualties."

"Maritime law gives us a way," said Bikaropin with a grin.

Fonzen scoffed. "How could we possibly use maritime law to our advantage in this situation?"

"I've been checking on some of the maritime laws that are accepted throughout the world," said Bikaropin. "One of them states that if a shipwrecked sailor, somehow manages to get into a harbor town or city, that city is obligated to take care of the sailor. Feeding, clothing and billeting, until the home country can compensate the host city...after repatriation."

"Yes, I'm aware of that law," said Vooshk shaking his head angrily. "How does that help us?"

"What if..." Bikaropin grinned. "...instead of just one sailor or one ship...an entire armada were to enter that harbor?"

Vooshk looked at Bikaropin incredulously. "Just sail the entire invasion force into the harbor? You actually think that they'd be welcomed with open arms?"

"They would...if the ships appear crippled. They would if the survivors aboard the ships state that all officers and navigators were washed overboard, or died, during a massive storm at sea. We make the ships appear to have been in some tremendous storm." Bikaropin looked victorious. "We have...oh say twenty-five or twenty-six ships, all appearing to be damaged, with somewhere between 1900 and 2000 rather haggard looking crewmembers on board. The more damaged the ships appear to be and the more haggard the crews, the more believable their story and the city of Malantroi will have to accept them as shipwrecked. They'll be obligated to billet, feed and clothe all of those personnel. They'll be so overwhelmed at the prospect of the cost, until such time that they can be compensated, that they won't be looking at these personnel as an invasion force, but helpless, shipwrecked sailors... who are going to cost them a fortune."

Teeveel huffed. "Where are they coming from and where are they going...and why?"

Bikaropin contemplated. "Obviously they're coming from Oosam. It would be those great big merchant vessels that are built here in Lower Oosam."

Teeveel still looked apprehensive. "So where are they going and why?"

"They're going to...oh say, Tabrow," said Zebyuro. "Tabrow is the place where I first met the Drey Sssorg. Agrosha is, somewhat, between Oosam and Tabrow."

Teeveel nodded. "Fine, fine. Now, again, why? What

would such a big armada be all sailing together on such a long voyage?"

"Training," said Bonarain. "The country of Tabrow has purchased a few dozen of those large merchant ships from Oosam. You have all those sailors on board so that they can get used to seeing how those great big ships handle at sea. They'll be in training all the way from Oosam to Tabrow and…on the way they encounter that tremendous storm. The first harbor that the remaining crippled armada is able to find is…Malantroi."

Vooshk leaned back in his chair. "You people have evil minds. I pray to the Great Maker that I never have to go to war against you."

Fonzen gasped. "HOLD ON!" He stood up. "Are you saying that you want us to severely damage…several of the ships that we so proudly build…and make them look like crippled messes…on *purpose*?" He stood there glaring angrily.

"You won't damage them," said Soolchakan calmly. "The ships will *appear* to be crippled or damaged."

Fonzen still looked a little upset. He closed his eyes and shook his head. "How?"

Soolchakan stood up. He touched the conference table. The portion he was touching disappeared. He walked forward and another portion disappeared. Bikaropin made a portion disappear. He walked to his left and made another portion disappear. Bonarain, Kiyalee and Chyning all took chunks out of the table. Chyning made another trail in the table.

"Now," said Soolchakan. "The table appears to be damaged. There appears to be several parts of it missing. They're not missing, they're just invisible…and untouchable." He went back to his seat. He stretched out his hands and the parts that he had made disappear were now back in their place.

Bonarain, Kiyalee, Chyning and Bikaropin all did the same thing.

Soolchakan smiled. "The table appeared to be damaged, now it does not appear to be damaged. We can make *parts* of ships disappear. We can hide supplies in the invisible parts of the ships. We can create many illusions of this type. We could have forty ships embark on this invasion mission. Only twenty go limping into the Malantroi harbor. The other twenty would be waiting, out of sight, off shore, until dark. After dark, when the Malantroi High Council has been put into complete panic over having to take care of almost two thousand shipwrecked sailors…then…the next day, after that census has been taken, the invaders start taking prisoners. We catch them all in their beds."

"All except the night watch," said Teeveel.

"*We* can take care of a lot of that," said Soolchakan. "In this way, I predict that we could take the entire city…with very few, if any, casualties…on our side."

Bonarain cleared her throat. "Just before the attack, we could dispatch a message to King Suntram of Agrosha that…we are going in there to retrieve the illegally enslaved citizens of Oosam and that we are also going in there to arrest the Monarch assassin who murdered King Tooron." She smiled. "No King, in his right mind, would impede us from catching an assassin who has had the *nerve* to kill a *King*...and then hide in *his* country. That King just might be labeled as a co-conspirator in the assassination... which could lead to war...or an embargo...that right now, Agrosha cannot afford."

Fonzen sat there with eyes forward looking at no one. "We wait until their next census. We get a look at those figures and find out what we're dealing with. The next year, just after their census is taken...we strike."

Vooshk nodded. "That gives us plenty of time to look over the plan and get all of the wrinkles out of it."

Teeveel smiled. "I heartily agree."

Soolchakan nodded. "So, we strike just after the census of 5480 ATUT."

Zebyuro stood up with an angry look. "Is there any way that we can find out where the Princess Sanyee is?"

"She's probably still in Malantroi...we hope," said Soolchakan. "We found out that both of you were sold into slavery after Aboreema arrived back there."

Zebyuro looked around adamantly. "I want her out of there. I want her rescued at the...earliest possible date. I want her out of there, NOW!"

Soolchakan hung his head for a moment. He looked up. "We'll see what we can do to find her. We'll rescue her...at the earliest possible opportunity...unless it fouls the invasion plan." He saw an angry look from Zebyuro. "WE CAN'T AFFORD

TO MESS UP THIS PLAN BY RESCUING ONE PERSON! No matter who that person is. If she can be pulled out of there, without much ado and without altering any of the invasion plans…" He stood up and spoke forcefully. "…I vow that we'll get her out of there…safely."

Zebyuro sat down staring at the table emotionless. "Thank you, Drey Sssorg."

Soolchakan bowed his head. "You're welcome, Your Majesty."

Chyning scowled at Soolchakan. **"We're gonna have to go through every house in that *chokwad* town! How long do you think that'll take**?"

**"The more people we get in there, the less time it'll take**," sent Bonarain.

Kiyalee huffed. **"How do we recognize her**?"

Soolchakan smiled. **"Anyone who sees a woman that resembles her, just start reading her mind and see if the names Tooron, Amrona, Zebyuro and Sanyee sound familiar to her**."

Chyning huffed. **"*H'oolyach*!**"

Every available male Owlamite (over 90 years old) was dispatched to the duty of finding the Princess Sanyee. Many of the women were either pregnant or taking care of very small children. Soolchakan did not like the idea of being sexist, however, leaving their very young children was something that many mothers did not (and some would not) want to do. Having a group of very young children in the middle of a reconnaissance mission could be a little disturbing. The children might distract the observer by wanting to do some unnecessary sight-seeing.

They started at the waterfront and worked their way up the winding roads of the town. It was not the bustling metropolis that most of them thought it would be, however, it was not a tiny hamlet town either.

On the third day of looking, Konchoo of the Eighth called out. "**I think I've got her**."

"**Where are you**," sent Ah-Aro of the Fifth?

Konchoo shook his head. "**I'm in her home**."

"**Fat lot of good that does us**," sent Reebuck of the Seventh. "**Is there any way that you can give us a better clue**?"

"**It looks like the home belongs to some wealthy merchant. I'll go up on the roof and...start waving my cape**," sent Konchoo.

All the Owlamite men headed up to the roofs of the buildings.

"**I see him**," sent Falchon of the Eleventh. "**He's in district four**."

All of the men checked their map of Malantroi.

Konchoo was getting tired. "**Can I stop waving this**

thing?"

"**Yes**," sent Soolchakan. "**Falchon said that he saw you. Go back in the house and try to ascertain if she really is Sanyee. Also, try to find out all you can about the home owner. The rest of you, stay where you are just in case this is not Sanyee. I don't want any of you having to retrace your steps and start over again. This has been a big enough, time consuming, fiasco.**"

Soolchakan had become somewhat familiar with the town so he was able to Jump to a certain large plaza in District 4. He looked around the plaza and growled in frustration. He was in the right district, however, he did not know which house he was supposed to be invading.

"**Falchon, this is Soolchakan. Go back up to a roof and wave your cape so I can see where you are.**" He Jumped to the top of a building adjacent to the plaza and looked for Falchon. Once he spotted Falchon, he Jumped to that roof. "Okay, where are we going?"

Falchon stopped waving the cape and stood there panting a little. "I Jumped to the roof that Konchoo was waving from. We're here. All we need to do is go downstairs and start questioning... that woman."

This merchant was very wealthy. He was also very fat. Right now, he was also very, very drunk. The woman in question was standing behind the huge overstuffed chair that, somehow, held all of the fat of the rotund merchant. She was holding a large pitcher of wine. Every time he held his cup out, she would fill it.

He was so drunk that he had to grab the cup with both hands in order to properly aim it at his mouth. He would slurp it down, sit there for a moment, belch and then hold the cup out for more wine.

Soolchakan watched the man take three more cups of wine. 'Did I ever get, or look, that stupid, when I was drunk,' he thought? He groaned.

The merchant giggled. He looked over his right shoulder at the woman. In a whiny voice he tried to speak. "Imisha… Imi…Imishisha…howood yoo lich to plezher me?" He giggled again.

The woman grimaced. She looked as if she were going to gag. She spoke hesitatingly. "If…the master…wishes."

He giggled again. "I wishit!"

Now she visibly gagged, put one hand over her mouth and looked really nauseous.

"I'm *not* going to be audience to that," said Soolchakan. He walked over to the fat man. He saw that the woman was looking away and gagging while trying to keep from throwing up. He hopped his right foot into Home dimension and clobbered the fat Heyyah. It took two kicks to knock the drunkard unconscious.

"Thank you," said Konchoo.

"I agree," said Falchon.

The woman slowly came around to a place in front of the merchant looking even more nauseous. She bent over and noticed that he was unconscious. "Master," she whispered? She very carefully watched for a few moments to see if there was any reaction. When she saw none, she stood up tall, placed her hands over her heart, looked heavenward and whispered: "Oh, thank you." She let out a sigh of relief, went back to the pitcher of wine and took it back to the kitchen.

In the kitchen, Soolchakan took hold of the mind of the woman. She sank to the floor with a dull look on her face. The large silver pitcher hit the floor and fell over spilling all of the contents.

Soolchakan growled. "Go out there and make sure that fat boy doesn't wake up."

Falchon and Konchoo both headed back to the den.

Soolchakan went deep in her mind. The names were familiar to her. Here she was, renamed Imichia. He closed his eyes and sighed. "**Konchoo did indeed find the Princess. We can get her out of here and not hurt the plan. We've found her so the search is over. You men can all go back about your business**."

Konchoo stood there looking at the merchant. "**What do we do with the, oh so, bloated drunkard? Won't he be a little upset if she's gone**?"

Soolchakan sighed. "**I've often heard of drunkards choking to death on their own vomit. I think that'll be appropriate for him. Chyning, if you want some goodies to…steal…come to the house of this merchant. He has some rather nice looking goodies**." He shook his head. "She'll probably clean the whole *chokwad* place out." He shrugged. "So what!"

Konchoo snickered. "If she doesn't, I'm sure that others will."

Chyning popped in and started looking around with nothing but greed in her eyes. She giggled several times as she walked along and perused all of the expensive baubles and goodies in the room. "This is going to be a very nice haul." She giggled again.

Soolchakan just sighed and rolled his eyes in disgust. 'What are you training your children to become,' he thought?

# 13

Sanyee woke up in a private room on a ship. She looked around bewildered and suspicious as she got up out of the bunk. She looked down at herself and was rather surprised to see that she was wearing a full length nightgown. Her master would never have allowed her to wear anything near that amount of modest clothing. He had always wanted to keep her as scantily clad as possible...if she had been allowed to wear anything at all.

She sniffed. There was an aroma in the air. She had never smelled anything like it in her life. Considering all of the food that she had been forced to prepare for her oh-so-rotund master and how little she had been able to eat, she was confused by this smell. It was pleasant, however, it was totally unfamiliar.

She crept over to the door of the room. There was light coming from under the door. She listened at the door and heard nothing. She took several deep breaths and opened the door.

She was looking into a small room. Sitting at a table were two of those Elf people, with enormous ears, she had heard about all of her life. They were both women. They each had a large mug in one hand and a spoon in the other. They were both staring at her.

One of them smiled. "Good morning, Princess Sanyee. My name is Osakisha of the Fifteenth."

The other one swallowed something she had been chewing on. "Good morning, Princess Sanyee. My name is Hotherette of the Fifteenth."

Sanyee smiled weakly as she nodded. Then she felt a mental jolt. She looked back and forth at the two in shock. "You called me…by my real name! You didn't call me…that other name."

Osakisha shrugged. "Do you want us to call you by the other name?"

Sanyee waved her hands at the two Elf women. "No, no, no, no! The fact that you know my real name…is wonderful… and a little confusing." She placed her hand over her mouth as she tried to keep from weeping for joy. She cleared her throat. "And my title." She looked around. "Uh…where…am I?"

Hotherette answered. "We're aboard one of our ships. We're heading to Lower Oosam. Your brother asked us to find you and bring you back."

"So we are," said Osakisha merrily.

Sanyee smiled nervously again. Her thoughts were equally nervous. "Thank you."

Hotherette frowned. "Is that your stomach making all of those noises?"

Sanyee placed her hands over her stomach. "Yes, it is.

I…I'm very hungry."

Osakisha got up. "Would you like some kwatha?"

Sanyee was taken aback slightly. "I…never heard of… what did you call it?"

"Kwatha," said Hotherette. "It's one of our favorites."

Sanyee figured that this kwatha was the odor that she was smelling. She had never heard of it, however, it sounded better than any of that nasty gruel she had been forced to choke down in Malantroi. "Sounds interesting. Yes…I'll try some, thank you."

Osakisha walked over to a small stove. There was a large pot on the stove. Osakisha picked up a ladle and used it to fill another mug with the thick broth. She brought the mug, with a spoon to the table and held a chair for Sanyee.

Sanyee sat down. She took the spoon and started spooning the broth as if it were a soup dish.

"Oh no," said Hotherette. "The first thing you want to do is find the big lumps of the kwatha tuber in the broth." She spooned through hers for a few moments and then came up with a lump, covered with creamy white gravy, sitting on the spoon. "You eat the lumps first – then you drink the broth from the mug after you can't find any more lumps." She smiled.

Sanyee shrugged. She started spooning through the thick broth. She decided that if her hosts had a traditional way of eating this dish…why not try it? She felt as if there were something trapped between the inner part of the mug and the spoon. She pulled it up out of the broth.

"Oh, that's a nice one," said Osakisha with a big friendly grin. "Go ahead and eat it," she encouraged.

Sanyee shrugged. She opened wide and took the lump in her mouth. She started chewing. The taste was unlike anything she had ever eaten. It was not the best tasting thing she had eaten, however, it most definitely was not the worst. The taste was so totally unique. She could not compare it to anything else she had ever eaten. The good thing was that it was *not* gruel. She watched the two Elf women continue spooning through their broth as they pulled large and small lumps out. She shrugged and followed along. She was too hungry to argue.

Sanyee looked at Osakisha. "You said that my brother commissioned you to find me?"

"Yes, he did."

"Why did it take so long for him to look for me?"

Hotherette hung her head.

Osakisha sighed. "Because, unfortunately, until a little while ago, he was held as a slave in Malantroi as well."

Sanyee's jaw dropped.

"Once he obtained his freedom, he made his way back to Oosam and…our Drey Sssorg met him and…had us look for you."

Sanyee frowned. "Uh…Drey…what?"

"Drey Sssorg," said Hotherette. "You could say that the Drey Sssorg, Soolchakan is equivalent to a King."

Sanyee was puzzled. "Then why don't you call him a King?"

"Because that word does not exist in our native dialect," said Osakisha.

Sanyee did not feel like arguing the point. She just accepted it as she spooned for another lump. "What about my mother and father? Why weren't they looking for me?"

Both Osakisha and Hotherette hung their heads. Now Sanyee was very suspicious and concerned.

Osakisha sighed and looked back up. "Your father...was assassinated...on the same day that you were abducted and taken off to Agrosha."

Sanyee was now more upset. "And my mother?"

"She...*is*...the assassin," said Hotherette grimly. "She is also the one who took you and your brother to Agrosha and sold both of you into slavery."

Now Sanyee was staring in horror at Hotherette.

"We have very reliable evidence to back this up," said Hotherette rather softly. "This is a delicate situation for you, but... we are *very* sure of what we're saying."

There was a knock on the door. Both Osakisha and Hotherette closed their eyes. They opened their eyes and the door came open.

"I see that our guest is awake," said the woman who entered the room. "Good morning, Princess Sanyee, I'm Nadiwi of the Second." She looked down at a small child standing next to her. "This is my daughter Monanya."

Sanyee sniffed. "I'm sorry if I don't receive you properly. I've just been informed that...my father is dead and...my mother is a murdering traitor."

"Yes, I know," said Nadiwi softly. "All of that, hitting you at one time, can leave some very bitter thoughts in your mind. I can feel some of your pain."

Sanyee was a little irritated at that. "How could you possibly know what pain I'm going through or what I've been through?"

Nadiwi looked stern. "Because I was held a sex slave as well. I was passed around between over a thousand men in that time. I was stolen from my parents as a baby. They finally found me...after...a long time. They've taught me the difference between the mere sex act and true love."

Sanyee felt a little guilty now. "The...child. Is she from...?"

"She is from my husband," said Nadiwi with a smile. "I'm proud to say that none of those Heyyah men could ever do the full deed."

"So that's very good then," said Sanyee.

"Yes, very good," said Nadiwi. "Go ahead and finish your kwatha and then we'll tell you all of the plans for arresting the traitorous assassin and also rescuing all of the citizens of Oosam that are held in bondage in Malantroi."

Sanyee ate another lump. "What about...my Master, Mumfooth?"

Nadiwi looked somewhat disgusted. "Mumfooth? Was that the name of that big fat drunken blob?" She giggled. "You won't have to worry about him again...ever."

Sanyee sighed in relief and started spooning for another lump of kwatha as a tear of joy rolled down her right cheek.

They let the new life of freedom sink in the mind of Sanyee on the long voyage back to Oosam. They did not really want to take all of the time to be on that voyage, however, there had to be some kind of reality for Sanyee and time to absorb all of this new information.

When they finally arrived in Semoron, they saw the construction of the new palace was well under way. There were numerous people who worked in construction who could not figure out how the Owlamites were able to move the huge blocks of stone into place without winches and a great deal of manpower. They did not complain. They were happy to receive the assistance, however they were mystified – and rather awed... and a little terrified.

Sanyee was taken to a special set of chambers where her childhood nanny was currently living. That woman had been very irate about having to move out of the palace in Saditelo. She was sure that the lost Sanyee would be back any day, just like Zebyuro had suddenly appeared. When Sanyee met her nanny, after all that time separated, the two of them fell into each other's arms, giggling and weeping for quite a while before anyone else could get reacquainted with the lost Princess.

Zebyuro stood by patiently waiting for the embrace and crying to end between Sanyee and nanny. He remembered the meeting with his nanny. Several times he had to wipe tears from his eyes as well, however the smile never left his face.

Zebyuro sat there staring despondently at nothing in particular. "She is right," he said sadly. "No one will want her."

"You wanted her," said Soolchakan. "You wanted to get her out of that situation. We got her out. Do you want us to take her back?"

"No, Drey Sssorg. That would be even worse. She is a Princess, but, for over ten years she was the sex toy for some curmudgeon in Agrosha. Any member of royalty who wants to arrange a marriage for…the usual political reasons…they wouldn't have her for anything in the world. No self-respecting Prince, or King, would have her."

"Is she upset over being rescued?"

"No, she is very glad to know that she'll never have to be taken back to that monster or that anyone will ever abuse her again." He sighed. "But, I and her nanny are the only ones who care for her…at all." He shrugged. "Of course, my nanny is fond of her as well."

Soolchakan chuckled. "Invite her to be in on all of the final plans for the invasion of Malantroi. Don't you think that the idea of getting back at the monster who sold both of you into slavery might do something to cheer her up?"

Zebyuro scoffed. "That is one of the things that is upsetting her as well." He slammed his fist on the table. "OUR OWN MOTHER! That woman will stoop to...any level to...perform some nasty deed." He shook his head. "That garbage is in our blood."

"Doesn't mean that you have to become that kind of person."

"And I won't!"

"Good." Soolchakan stood up. "Why don't we go see if there is any new X-factor that we may have to look at? That should get your mind off of your personal problems for a while."

Zebyuro yawned. "I can't think of anything that we haven't covered at least ten times." He shook his head. "That...Teeveel...he is such a pessimist."

"No," said Soolchakan adamantly! "What he is doing is bringing up issues that we haven't thought of yet. He is being a realist when he does that. Someone like that can be a great deal of help when it comes to all of the fine planning that's necessary. Don't, for one heartbeat think that he's trying to sink your boat. He's trying to make sure that when those invasion troops go into Malantroi...they go in with every angle and advantage of surprise on their side."

Zebyuro nodded. "There's still so much I have to learn." He chuckled. "I see why a King or a Prince has need of advisors."

He turned to Soolchakan. "They do what they can to insure success."

"Exactly."

Zebyuro stood up. "Okay, let's go see what part of the plan he'll destroy, just so we can build it back up, today."


Vooshk and Teeveel were both doing everything they could to question the plans. They came up with all kinds of contingencies where something could go wrong. They were ecstatic over the idea of sending in ships that were disguised as damaged. This had never been done before and it would definitely take the citizens of Malantroi by surprise. The fact that they had some diplomatic leverage over the King of Agrosha was something they never expected. They tried every way they could to come up with a way that it would not work. Each negative was met with new positive plans, or change in plans.

The fact that Malantroi was the refuge for a Monarch assassin was priceless. The fact that the same person had also kidnapped two other members of a royal family and sold them into slavery added more fuel to that diplomatic fire.

Thousands of the slaves in Malantroi were Oosam citizens. They had been abducted by the slavers and used to purchase supplies in Malantroi instead of spending money.

Everything was working in their favor. The initial invasion force was going to be rather small. They might get the local slaves on their side and that would aid immensely in capturing all of the citizens of Malantroi, hopefully with as few casualties as possible.

The alleged shipwrecked sailors would go into the harbor after the census was finalized and given to the High Council. The morning before they were to strike, the rest of the invasion force would arrive on shore, east and west of Malantroi (they did not have to worry about north because the rugged mountains had no passes for anyone to travel through). They would cut off all communication with the town, from every direction and then pull into the town with enough chains for all of the free citizens to be free no more.

The only X-factor left was the people enslaved in Malantroi. How many of them had become loyal to their masters? Hopefully very few. More hopefully – none.

Soolchakan had to show the people of Oosam just how they were going to disguise the ships. At first the citizens were shocked and horrified at how the ships looked. They had to keep reminding themselves that this was an illusion and that the ships had suffered no actual damage. They were going to need all of them completely intact for the return from the invasion.

The building of the palaces at Mardan and Semoron proceeded slowly. The Owlamites had to give more assistance than they had initially intended. Then they found out that the construction workers were getting lazy and hoping that the Owlamites would do all of the work. The Owlamites left the construction sites, informing Fonzen and Zebyuro of what was going on.

Soolchakan hated being the bearer of bad news about the construction, however, when the two sovereigns found out about the lackadaisical attitude of the construction workers, a few "personnel" with lashes showed up. Very quickly the construction was getting back on schedule, mainly with personnel from Oosam. It is amazing how the crack of a whip can motivate someone.

Senbower came back from a drop off in Beasties. He went to Soolchakan. He was rather puzzled.

Soolchakan had just welcomed another new Owlamite baby to the world. Like all of the new babies, he had to hold the newborn in his arms. Each time he would utter a command to them. "Remember little child that you are an Owlamite. You will never betray us. You will remember this for the rest of your life." He would then give the child back to the mother.

Senbower walked up. "I'm confused about something that happened in Beasties."

Soolchakan frowned. "Are those monsters coming up with a way for their spells to start working there?"

Senbower chuckled. "Oh, no! They're still heartbroken over the fact that none of their spells work. No, this is a situation that we haven't seen there before." He cleared his throat. "There was this unusual Heyyah named Unjer. He has been there for...I don't know how long. He's been there a while. Anyway, he suddenly came across one of the ex-wizards and...screamed his name. He then proceeded to bludgeon that ex-wizard Wyhoshton to death." He scratched the side of his head as if he was thinking.

"Then he started screaming about you. He said that if he ever saw you again, he would beat you to death as well...for some fabrication that you...passed on to him."

Soolchakan closed his eyes and hung his head. "Oh yes." He looked up. "Don't worry about it." He shook his head. "That one is...a long complicated story. At first I informed this Unjer that Wyhoshton was dead. Then that stupid Heyyah started thinking about how he was going to go back to his homeland and...restore his home...including the staffing of an entire group of slaves." He chuckled. "Initially, I was going to let him go home, but, when he started thinking about a house full of slaves that had to bow and kneel and give all kinds of sexual favors...I chucked him into Beasties. I forgot what I told him about Wyhoshton." He sighed. "Nothing I can do about that now." He licked his lips. "Wyhoshton was a pompous fool and Unjer is a very vindictive Heyyah. Either way, Beasties is a good place for both of them... dead or alive."

"There are still a few that are a little upset about what happened. They're wondering if that...Unjer is going to go off again."

Soolchakan snickered. "Only if he sees me again. Don't worry. I'll stay away from Beasties as long as he is still alive. The main target of his wrath is now dead and I'm just a secondary target...if I show up there." He stretched. "Right now, we both have to get back to some duties."

Senbower nodded. He Jumped back to Peegruch to collect another pair of captured slavers and take them to Beasties.

Soolchakan headed back to Semoron to see if there were any new discussions about the plans for the invasion of Malantroi.

# 14

The day that Soolchakan was dreading finally arrived. The day that the Oosam armada weighed anchor and started the long, long, *long* journey to the city of Malantroi in Agrosha. All of the Owlamites could easily Jump to Agrosha, however, that could give a few things away they did not wish to reveal to outsiders. No, they were going to have to ride the ships all the way on that long and boring trip to Agrosha from Oosam.

They had a total of seventy-five of the giant merchant ships that the Shipwrights of Oosam were famous for building. No one could make a ship larger or sturdier. For a fleet of these ships to be damaged by some super storm at sea was going to be a good diversion for the people of Malantroi.

The plan was for thirty-two of the ships to be disguised as damaged and then have those ships limp into the Malantroi harbor with exactly 1,977 men aboard the wreckages. Zebyuro had suggested they should have an even 2,000. Teeveel had stepped on that idea because if they had an even, round number like that, someone could get rather suspicious. A number that appeared random would be believable. The ones who were chosen to be the shipwrecked sailors each had a disguise of rags they had wadded up in a corner, or slept on, in order to make it appear they had really been through a real nasty mess. All the rest of the personnel were to be wearing a brown uniform that had been designed and manufactured just for this excursion.

Bonarain was visiting Soolchakan in his cabin on the ship. She brought four-year-old Sonotana with her so that Soolchakan could have some time with his daughter.

Bonarain shook her head. "Why didn't you tell them that you'd meet them there in Agrosha?"

"That would have been the simpler way of doing it," he said. "It would also make them wonder just how we got there so quickly." He looked up. "They'd want to use our ship to assist in moving all of the prisoners to Oosam. How would we explain the absence of a ship? How would we explain why we didn't have one or wouldn't or couldn't render any transportation assistance?"

Bonarain shook her head and chuckled. "You are getting smarter."

He snickered. "Thank you for the compliment, but, I still feel rather inadequate in some areas. That is why…I depend on you and Bikaropin so much."

Bonarain raised her eyebrows. "You mean…you don't also depend on Kiyalee and Chyning?"

He smiled. "They're friendly and…fun to be around, but, Kiyalee is devoted to her trucks and other mechanical or electrical devices and…Chyning still hasn't completely grown up. She is devoted to obtaining as much valuable possessions as possible."

Bonarain looked up in thought. "You're right. They do still seem to be living in a world of their own." She sighed. "Their children still come to me and ask a few questions that... they should be putting to their own mothers."

They heard someone in the hall walking towards the cabin. They both did a little mind-reading on whoever was coming that way. It was Zebyuro coming to invite Soolchakan to lunch.

Soolchakan smiled at Bonarain. "Better take Sonotana and scram. I don't want to have to explain how the two of you got on board."

Bonarain smiled. She picked Sonotana up and hopped to Spy. Sonotana was a little upset over her game being interrupted, however, Bonarain was able to convince her (mentally) that fussing was not going to get her anything positive. Plus the fact that Daddy has some very boring business to discuss with another man.

Soolchakan graciously accepted the invitation to lunch. He looked back at the chair that Bonarain had been sitting in before the hop. He knew that she was still there with Sonotana. He let out a small snarl (with a smile on his face). Bonarain chuckled and Jumped the two of them back to the gorge.


Zebyuro looked up from his plate. "I don't remember the other ships I've been on being this...turbulent."

Soolchakan smiled. "We have been catching a lot of very favorable winds. That does add a little to the rocking of the ship.

We're moving a lot faster than we thought we'd be going. We'll make it to Malantroi in plenty of time."

"Yeah, the Fleet Commander has said that we're already three days ahead of schedule." He shook his head. "I don't understand how he knows precisely where we are."

"Years of studying and steering by the stars," said Soolchakan with a smile. "Just like Vooshk and Teeveel have been studying military strategy and tactics for years."

Zebyuro smiled and shook his head. "I'm so glad you taught me the difference between pessimism and careful planning."

"Like I said, they were showing flaws in the plan that needed to be corrected."

"And every time they found a flaw, we found a solution."

"Just like we were supposed to do. All this time and now… not even those two can come up with a negative. They advised wisely."

"Seventy-five ships in the fleet. Thirty-two will be disguised, and…" He snickered. "…limp into Malantroi Bay. One Command ship – twenty-one ships go east, twenty-one go west. Those forty-two ships land all of their troops and we cut off all travelers in or out of Malantroi to the east and west. The mountains to the north cut off any escape in that direction. We have them in the bay. The day after the census books are completed, we get the books and…" He had an evil grin. "…we strike! Catch them in the morning just before the city wakes up and…we have them – *all of them* - in our clutches before they even realize what happened." He frowned. "Do we have any numbers yet?"

Soolchakan simply shook his head. "I sent Dolchon, Choyatim, Za-Urik and Sontor ahead to see if they could get a hint at the numbers. Za-Urik and Sontor are supposed to meet us outside of the bay to give us that information. Dolchon will head east while Choyatim goes west. They'll be informing all of those forces regarding the numbers."

"I'd like to know now," said Zebyuro in a sulking manner.

"One thing that you're going to have to learn, especially in the position that you're in, is *patience*! Don't ever let anyone know if you have any weaknesses. If you do, they'll exploit your weaknesses to get anything and everything that they want from you."

Zebyuro nodded. "I guess that I will learn that…in time."

"You're on the throne in Lower Oosam! You don't have time to learn it – you must exercise it…*now*!"

Zebyuro sat up straight doing everything he could to look regal. He would have pulled it off completely if not for the fact that his jaws were clenched tight. "You are correct. We must maintain…at all times."

Soolchakan smiled. "A little more practice and you'll get really good at it."


Night was falling. Soolchakan and Bikaropin were standing on the bridge of the ship looking up at the stars.

"This is so boring," said Bikaropin. "We could have been there…a long time ago if we didn't have to ride on these big, slow, lumbering ships."

"Then we'd be giving away the knowledge of all kinds of capabilities. Then Fonzen and Zebyuro would be demanding all kinds of favors. No! We've given them far too much about us already. No, we do what I just told Zebyuro. We learn patience."

Bikaropin chuckled. "We don't have to be patient. We are Owlamites. We can go anywhere we want to go and at any time."

Soolchakan chuckled back. "They don't know that. I don't want them to know that…ever. We did give away a few secrets to Zebyuro, but, that mind wipe on him covers that. I don't want to have to perform a mass mind wipe on all of these Oosam citizens."

Bikaropin sniffed and sighed. "I know." He looked back over the railing at the rest of the fleet. "Still…two of us on each ship…seems excessive."

Soolchakan shook his head. "They all feel safer with two of us on each ship…for some silly reason. I guess that, with all we've done, in front of them, so far, they think that we can even control the weather and…many other divine things."

"Maybe we should Jump the whole fleet to the Doolood planet. Let them sail around there for a while and then Jump them to the mouth of the harbor at Malantroi."

Soolchakan rolled his eyes and groaned. "If you're going to make a suggestion, make one that is a constructive idea. The constellations and all other star patterns would be too different.

They'd know that *we* did something silly. Not to mention the fact that the high alkaline, high saline water of Doolood…would probably eat the entire bottom out of all of these ships."

Bikaropin laughed. "Good point."

The day of the split arrived. Twenty-one ships headed west. Twenty-one ships headed east. The Command ship found a shallow to drop anchor so that they would not be floating helplessly with any current.

Thirty-two ships were now being disguised. Masts were disappearing. Portions of the hull were disappearing. Reebuck and Takar went further than any of the others. They made the top four decks disappear as well.

The 1,977 chosen sailors were all staring with awe, surprise and some horror at the changes to the ships. They went to places where they knew there should be stairs or a wall or a portion of the mast and waved their hands through it. They had originally thought that the parts would just be invisible. They never dreamed that the missing parts were untouchable and untraceable. Some were beginning to wonder if the ships would ever be intact again.

Every piece of the ships that disappeared made the people of Oosam even more respectful (and afraid) of the Owlamites.

They rechecked the calendar. Today was the day the census should be finished. All that was being done now was the final paperwork. The thirty-two ships set what few sails they had left and headed for the harbor. Some of the "crippled" ships were towed.

The Owlamites who were on the thirty-two ships all hopped to Spy. They were going to just be observers as the people of Malantroi got the shock of their lives.

Of the ships that headed east and west, only one of each flotilla got near the land. They dropped several longboats and those personnel rowed ashore. They kept themselves at a point in the road where no one in Malantroi could see them. They set up banners for anyone coming to Malantroi to see. The banners were a warning that there was a very nasty, contagious plague currently in the city. Everyone should keep their distance – no one in or out…and hope that there was no contingency of Healers in the area.

The other ships got closer to Malantroi. All of their invasion forces started disembarking and heading for shore. They were setting up all of the supplies for the complete takeover of the town and the imprisonment of all the citizens. They now, just needed to wait for a signal to advance toward the town with all of the equipment.

The thirty-two ships arrived in the harbor. The men on the ships did everything they could to appear very tired and very relieved to find a port. They had to have some rather strong discipline because in order to assist in the disguise, none of them had had anything to eat in two days. This way, when the people of Malantroi supplied them with a meal, they were ravenous.

All of the ships that were anchored in the harbor already

had every single member of their crews staring horrified at the spectacle they were seeing. The men on the "crippled" fleet saw from the reactions that their deception seemed to be working rather well.

A longboat was being rowed, rather rapidly, from one of the piers. A man on the longboat was waving a striped red and green flag. This was the international symbol at all harbors, this was the Harbor Master.

The ships started to drop their anchors. There were three ships where the anchor itself had been *disguised.* These three ships had to be tied to other ships in the broken flotilla.

The Harbor Master had his boat moved among the damaged ships so he could get a better look at the horrid sight. He signaled the man with the rudder to steer them to the closest ship. They came alongside the ship.

He looked up the side of the ship and called out. "I'm Harbor Master Hessmeth. Who…is in charge of this…mess?"

One of the men leaned over the railing on the ship. "There's no one in charge, Milord! All of our officers, navigators and any instructors were all killed in that hell-spawned storm. All washed overboard or died at their post…and were buried at sea."

Hessmeth closed his eyes and tried to digest what he had just heard. He looked up again. "Drop the ladder! I need to get up there and speak with you."

The crewman tried to keep from laughing. "We don't have a ladder anymore, Milord! Most of our equipment was lost as well…in the storm."

"Have you got…anything that I can climb?"

The crewman threw a rope over the side. "I have it tied off. You can climb this safely."

Hessmeth groaned and rolled his eyes. He grabbed the rope and used it to walk his way up the hull. He reached the railing and climbed over. He looked around in horror at how much of the ship was missing. "Some…storm…did all of this…damage?"

The crewman sneered. "You think we did this to the ship ourselves?"

Hessmeth looked around again. "Can you tell me what happened to your fleet?"

The crewman gave the story of how forty ships started out from Lower Oosam. The ships had been purchased by the government of Tabrow. The people who were on board were going to use the voyage back to Tabrow as a training voyage. There was no cargo, they were just supposed to get used to the handling of the ships. Once they were competent with the ships, then they would be used for commerce by the Tabrow government. On the way, they had gone through a storm, the likes of which, none of these experienced seamen had ever gone through and it had damaged all of the ships that had survived. They had started with forty. Eight ships had been sunk in the storm. The surviving ships had lost a lot of their crew, including *all* officers, and navigators. Each ship had started out with twelve officers and one hundred ten crewmen. They had been able to gather these damaged ships together and then do what they could to find land.

Hessmeth groaned after listening to all of their woes. "I have to report this to the High Council. Wait here, on your ships, until they decide what to do." He climbed back over the railing. They rowed back to the pier.

The High Council members of this wharf area were sitting in their office, both feeling rather bored. The wharf was Sector Seven of seven city sectors. Representative Biyaba Jop was the one in charge during peace time. Commandant Goroben Hebedissor would be the one in charge during war.

Biyaba was a tall woman with thick blonde hair, which she had probably not cut since she was born. All of her hair was pushed up and wrapped around her head in large, long braids. She was a very organized person who was a stickler for detail.

Goroben was a very dark-skinned and very tall man with thick, short black hair. He was normally very calm, even in the most traumatic situations, and always had a way of calming others in any of those situations with his demeanor.

Hessmeth came bursting in the office. "We have a huge catastrophe on our hands."

Goroben was momentarily startled at first. "Hessmeth! What is the matter with you? I haven't seen or heard any panic out there. What could possibly be so bad?"

Biyaba was rather upset over the man charging in. "Don't you know how to knock?"

Hessmeth was a little breathless. "Out in the harbor... ships...there are ships out there..."

Biyaba scowled. "Ships in the harbor? My, how odd!" She scoffed. "Where else would you find ships…in the mountains to the north?"

"No, Representative Jop, I'm talking about a fleet of ships that just came into the harbor. Several ships that…are very badly damaged."

Goroben stood up and looked down, sternly, at the shorter man. "Hessmeth, stop babbling. You need to calm yourself and tell us what is going on."

Hessmeth closed his eyes and got his heavy breathing under control. He then informed the two Council members of all the information that had been given to him.

Goroben headed out to the end of the long pier in order to get a good look at this dilemma. Biyaba was following as closely as possible. Goroben was able to take long strides and it was difficult keeping up with him. He looked around at the damaged ships and shook his head in disbelief.

Biyaba finally reached the end of the pier, puffing and panting slightly. "What do we do?"

Goroben hung his head. "I'll go inspect the ships and see if…or how bad the damage is to each one." He turned to his colleague. "Why don't you go to each ship and find out…exactly how many of these crew are involved."

Biyaba looked a little concerned. "How am I going to make sure that I don't go to the same ship twice?"

Goroben scoffed. "Take a look! Each ship has a number

on the side. They haven't been named yet, just numbered. Just don't go back to the same number twice."

Biyaba flushed in embarrassment. "Right. I'll get some paper and a quill and...I'll start the count immediately." She headed back to the office to get the papers.

Goroben looked out at the ships again. "Hessmeth, get my longboat ready. I'm going to have to inspect all of them." He shook his head in gloom. "This is not going to be pleasant." He snarled as he scanned the harbor again. "Get a longboat ready for Representative Jop as well."

The sun was going down as Goroben boarded the last ship. He was going through each ship looking over each deck, mast, hold, bridge and quarters. He carefully annotated every bit of damage that he could see on all of the ships.

Biyaba made three rounds of all thirty-two ships. She could not believe that there were still that many personnel on all of these wrecks.

Back out at sea, Zebyuro was getting rather impatient. "What is going on? They've had all day! What are we waiting for?"

Soolchakan closed his eyes. **"The royalty out here is getting restless. Can you give me any update on what is taking so long**?"

Jotsoom responded. **"They've got a man who is slowly and meticulously annotating all damage to all**

ships.  They have a woman who is counting souls.  She
has gone to every ship three times because she can't
believe the figures."

Soolchakan turned to Zebyuro.  "They're making sure
that everything is documented.  I can't see as how I blame them.
There's a couple of those ships that…we made them look so badly
damaged, the things just might be condemned.  In order to justify,
to Tabrow, the condemnation and scuttling of a ship belonging
to another nation, he has to have all of the paperwork done so
precisely that there is no doubt in anyone's mind that he acted
correctly.  Otherwise, they might hold him financially responsible
for the sinking of a reparable ship."

Zebyuro clenched his teeth.  "The longer we're out here,
the better the chance of being discovered and…that could be
disastrous."

Soolchakan smiled.  "Don't worry, Your Majesty.  We're
ready if something like that happens."  He snickered.  "If we do see
a ship coming in, I hope that it is a slaver's ship.  We'll take them
and let their…*cargo* go free.  Then we'll have a few more allies on
our side."  He grinned malevolently.  "Plus, we'll already have a
few slavers that we won't have to worry about in the harbor."

Zebyuro still looked worried.  "You're sure that you're
ready for something like that?"

Soolchakan just gave him a patronizing glare.

Zebyuro backed down.  He headed for the officer's mess
to get something to snack on, seeing as how his stomach was
growling a little.

They waited another full day while Goroben and Biyaba went over all of their information again. Soolchakan had to send mental messages to all of the people who were blocking the roads into Malantroi. He also sent messages to the Owlamites in the harbor asking them if they could speed up the process. They were informed that they would have to wait until Goroben and Biyaba reported to the full High Council. Zebyuro was learning about patience – through clenched teeth - whether he liked it or not.

Soolchakan made another call to the harbor. **"Do we know where those census binders are**?"

Tormino responded. **"There is no problem keeping track of those binders. There's one copy in the Office of the Governor, one copy in the Office of the Military Commander and one copy for each one of the Council members. Once the attack begins, we'll have all copies down at the piers**."

Two very fatigued members of the High Council called an emergency meeting and reported the calamity to the other fourteen members of the Council. There was a lot of yelling, panicking and general confusion. It was a normal situation when you get a pack of bureaucrats together with everybody yelling and no one paying any attention to what the others are saying. The meeting ended with no idea of how they were going to take care of 1,977 shipwrecked sailors – without a lot of help from the King and others in the Capital. They all headed to bed to sleep on it.

Dispatches were sent out to the capitol city and to some surrounding towns who might lend a hand, or money, in taking care of this disaster. All riders were "detained" by the Oosam personnel guarding the roads.

Soolchakan smiled as he turned to Zebyuro. "Tomorrow morning! The free citizens of Malantroi are going to get a very rude awakening."

Zebyuro stood there with his fists clenched. "When they take this…Aboreema Keldigin, I want to know immediately. I don't want to be on the same ship with her, but I want to know that she is in chains…on a ship."

"Don't worry, Your Majesty. There's a special brig set up for her on one of the ships to the west." He nodded. "She'll have a very uncomfortable trip back to Oosam."

Zebyuro looked toward Malantroi. "Tomorrow will be a good day," he muttered gravely.

The military guards for the evening were being relieved of duty. The night shift was taking their positions. The Owlamites were reading their minds for any kind of code words that had to be used. Once they had the code words, the night shift personnel were knocked unconscious and Oosam personnel put in their places. Before night was half over, Oosam had complete control of the night watch and the signal was given for the ones on the road to head inside the town gates to start the work.

All of the Oosam military that were to be the ones obtaining prisoners disembarked from their ships. They headed in with the wagons full of equipment for taking of the prisoners.

The night watch of the Constables offices were next on the list. Most of them were on duty in the area of the taverns. They were taken by complete surprise and silenced rather quickly. The ones patrolling the quieter areas were taken by even greater surprise. That night watch was now in custody of the Oosam military and no alarms were sounded.

The fishermen who went out at night for their catch cast off. They headed to their favorite spots, only to be met by the big Oosam ships and taken into custody. One ship in the east now had some prisoners and one ship in the west had prisoners (plus each had a few fishing boats loaded with equipment).

Zebyuro frowned at Soolchakan. "How do you know of all these things that are going on?"

Soolchakan smiled. "Haven't you figured it out by now? We can communicate telepathically. Saves a lot of time. Not to mention the fact that no one else can hear us."

Zebyuro swallowed hard and smiled weakly. No, he had not figured it out and he was now even more awed (and terrified) by these Owlamites.

The Oosam Army moved in to Malantroi. They sent some personnel directly to some thirty-three taverns that stayed open very late. Since all of the constables had been taken already, they were able to walk directly into the taverns and take everybody. Drunken patrons and prostitutes were easy to take. The sober tavern owners, bouncers and serving personnel were slightly more difficult, however, nothing that could not be handled.

Soolchakan once again turned to Zebyuro. "Now, you see why Vooshk and Teeveel were constantly asking questions. Everything is going rather smoothly so far. They questioned all of the plans because of the intelligence that we gathered and because of that there are no casualties of any type for our personnel." He smiled.

Zebyuro nodded. "A thousand questions they asked...a thousand answers we came up with. More and more I'm understanding why they seemed so pessimistic."

"Again, not pessimistic – realistic."

Next they went to the barracks of the Malantroi military. Most of them were either in bed, getting ready for bed or getting drunk after having just been relieved of duty. The Oosam military swarmed in and had all of them taken prisoner before most of them even realized what had happened. They did the same thing with the Constabulary.

There were some twenty-six wizards of varying capabilities. The Owlamites led the charge into their homes. At least one Owlamite was in Spy dimension when they went in. This way none of the wizards were able to get any of their gadgets, charms or any other magical toy in play. They were taken prisoner, knocked unconscious and gagged for the safety of all concerned. None of these wizards were up to the standards of joining the continental Clique, so they were rather easy to subdue.

Now they went from house to house, rudely waking up all of the citizens. As they moved into each house, they gave the promise that all of the slaves were to be freed (whether they wanted freedom or not). The vast majority of the newly freed slaves were more than glad to assist in helping their former masters being taken prisoner, and surrender any information on valuables.

They started in the slums and other lower class areas. Most of these people were very easy to take with very little violence. Once they saw that they were going up against armed personnel, they did very little in the way of resistance. The fact that they had just been pulled out of their beds and were still not quite awake helped immensely.

The invaders started working their way north through all of the homes. The further north they went, the more luxurious the homes and the more slaves that were there to assist in taking the owners…plus a few more of the Constables that had not been taken yet.

The city elite, who mainly lived on the north perimeter, were the last ones to be taken. They had the biggest homes along with the most slaves. For some absurd reason, they also had some very loyal slaves as well. Once those slaves got the message that all of the city had been taken and that their masters were now going to be imprisoned, the loyal ones seemed to lose a lot of that blind loyalty, in most cases. There were a few who had to be informed, no matter what their reluctance, they were now free.

Zebyuro was listening to the reports as Soolchakan got them. He still seemed a little impatient about one thing.

Bendarik suddenly appeared next to Soolchakan. "Grandfather, we have obtained the Lady Aboreema Keldigin.

She is currently in chains in the brig of ship number 21."

Soolchakan nodded and turned to Zebyuro. "Any questions, Your Majesty?"

"Uh…what is she wearing?"

Bendarik frowned at the question. "A long nightgown, that is rather filthy at this time, Your Majesty."

Zebyuro shook his head. "No! She leaves here with absolutely nothing. She left Sanyee and I with nothing…she gets nothing."

Bendarik shrugged. "As Your Majesty wishes. It will be done…immediately." He vanished.

Zebyuro looked rather smug. "Sanyee remembers nothing of the voyage to Malantroi. I don't remember anything either. This *Lady* Aboreema…will remember all of it. She'll be in darkness, in chains, alone, naked and cold…and hungry."

Soolchakan bowed his head. "As Your Majesty wishes." He went back to listening to the reports as the sun started coming up. He nodded. "The prisoners are being brought to the piers. We need to move the ships in to accept their (ahem) cargo." He chuckled. "We also need to get in there and repair some damaged ships."

Zebyuro yawned. "Been a long night." He sighed. "It has also been very successful in that…we didn't lose a single man." He smiled. "I *will* believe in the intelligence of those two High Military Commanders. They planned well with their *realistic* questions."

"You go ahead and go get some sleep. Your people can do all of the roll calls at the wharf area. They have the census books to assist them. My people will now go do our part to make it appear that there is nothing left of Malantroi for them to return to…ever again."

Zebyuro smiled and nodded. He walked away stretching and yawning again.

Soolchakan closed his eyes. "**All Owlamites in the Malantroi area! Now it is our turn. All Owlamites go to your appointed locations on the north side of the town**." He pictured his spot between a tree and a fence and Jumped. He looked to his right and left. The men who were here were placed at intervals where they covered the entire northern area of the town from east to west. "**Proceed**!"

All 150 Owlamites started forward heading south to the wharf. Anything they touched, they hopped into Ghost dimension. Soon every building in the town would be in Ghost dimension. None of the Malantroi citizens would be able to tell their town was not gone. Soon, there would be nothing but thick smoke covering all of the area.

Two hundred more of the Owlamite men Jumped to the northern area of Malantroi. They came with large barrels of some highly flammable liquid. They started tipping the barrels over. As the liquid became shallow and stopped flowing quickly downhill, it was set on fire. Large plumes of black billowing smoke went up from the area. Now, any Malantroi citizens would see the area in flames and would figure that all was lost.

The original 150 continued forward hopping everything to Ghost. The following 200 Jumped back to the gorge for more of the flammable liquids. Soon it appeared to virtually everyone that there was nothing north of the harbor that was not burning. There was enough of the liquids to keep the fires burning for several days. That way, each boat load of prisoners was able to look back and see nothing but thick black smoke where their town had once been. They all hung their heads as they turned away, hopelessly, from the horrible spectacle. The ruse was having the exact effect that had been desired.

Before the last prisoners were taken out to the large ships, the Owlamites secretly placed some platforms over the piers. They were going to dump the last of the liquids on those platforms to make it appear that all of the piers had been burned as well. In fact, nothing that belonged to any of the citizens of Malantroi was damaged - other than a few thousand doors that had been broken down by the Oosam military.

The very last longboat was filled with city High Council members. The Owlamites were the only ones in the boats with them. To keep the councilmembers confused, all of the Owlamites were talking in the Chokchakchok language. It worked. None of the Council was familiar with this language at all and therefore totally in the dark as to who these people were, what was being said and where they were being taken. Being Council Members, they were familiar with many different languages and dialects. Chokchakchok left them all baffled.

The last display was when a barrel of a tarry substance was dumped on the last pier. Ookalt of the Sixth had claimed that he was very good with a bow and arrow. It took two arrows before he hit the tar with a flaming arrow. Now the last of the piers was in flames as well (or that was the way it appeared). The actual pier itself was in Ghost dimension.

Soolchakan was even more amazed at the capacity of the giant Oosam merchant ships. There had been around 90,000 people, free and slave, in Malantroi. All of them had been loaded on the seventy-five ships. That was around 1,200 passengers per ship – plus crew.

The freed slaves were not complaining about the cramped accommodations. The thought of freedom and going back home was enough to keep them happy no matter what. The prisoners were not allowed to complain about their accommodations…or at least their complaints were totally ignored.

Zebyuro came up to Soolchakan as they set sail and left the Malantroi harbor. "Did you hear, my friend, did you hear?"

Soolchakan was confused. "Hear…what? What information are you familiar with that I am not?"

"There were thirty-three slaver ships anchored in that harbor when we attacked. We got *all* of them." He seemed to be bubbling with joy. "We didn't get all of the ship commanders and other slavers alive. The fools fought to the death. But we did get all of the ships and were able to free the slaves…at least the ones who were still alive." He scowled with clenched teeth. "Most of which were Oosam citizens."

Soolchakan smiled. "Then we're definitely off to a wonderful start."

# 15

The ship was going along very smoothly in the Metindonner Ocean. They headed due east around the northern part of the Ficara continent. They would turn southeast into the Dinelean Ocean and head directly to Lower Oosam.

While they were on this voyage, they were now taking a roll call of all of the ex-slaves. The Malantroi census consisted of only a head count for the slaves. It did not have names or places of origin – or status of genitals. Most of the men had been castrated so they would be good eunuchs. Now there was a question of what would happen to eunuchs when they landed in Oosam. Many of the women had been used as sex slaves. Many of the women had children that they did not want and did not want to care for because of who the fathers were. No one could blame them for their feelings and it seemed that there was going to be a rather large population abandoned in the orphanages.

Soolchakan secretly called Bonarain, Kiyalee and Chyning to his cubicle on the ship. "It seems that around 11,000 of these men have been neutered. They were wondering if there is anything that we can do for these men." He took a deep breath and sighed. "Since we were able to bring our people back to life with the stones...I was wondering if we could...restore...one organ...to all of these men."

Bonarain looked concerned – and horrified. "ELEVEN THOUSAND! You want us to…restore a set of testicles to…each of these men?"

He shrugged. "I'm sure that each of them would be happy with…just one. That's enough to do the job. It almost seems anticlimactic to let them go…with no future as a father or husband. What would they have to look forward to…in any job… or relationship?"

Kiyalee groaned. "Do you have any idea how long that would take? We were only able to do twenty-five resurrections per day. How long did that take?"

Chyning nudged Kiyalee. "That was twenty-five full scale resurrections *plus* the restoration of any and all guts that the Teltermak stole from them." She shrugged. "This is…just one small organ…per man."

Bonarain still looked rather concerned. "Should be simpler. All they need is just one *small* organ." She shook her head. "I don't see as how that would be as difficult or taxing as what we did for our own."

"So…when do we start?" Kiyalee looked perplexed. "They still have those questionings that they want to do on the slavers, once we get to Oosam. How long is that gonna take?"

"As long as it takes," said Bonarain sadly.

"What about the questioning of the higher ups from Malantroi," said Chyning? "When are we gonna get to that and... still hide that we're doing some mind messing with them?"

Soolchakan smiled. "I have an idea on...how it'll take less time...if we start here on the ship...without the slavers...or anyone else knowing about what we're doing."

Bonarain gave him a patronizing look. "And how are you going to pull that one off?"

He smiled. "Right now, we're off the coast of Grenboling, to our east, on the Ficara continent and to our west, Monokland on the Aerisau continent. Just south of that is Upper Oosam to our west and nothing but ocean to our east. Once we're off the coast of Upper Oosam, we let the elite of Malantroi and those elitists from the slavers, that were captured in Malantroi harbor, some time to run around the main deck and get some exercise to keep them healthy...healthy enough to be good slaves in Oosam. Once they're on the deck and mingling amongst each other – talking - we'll be doing some mind reading. I'll send any information I get to you and you three record it as quickly as possible. While we're here, on the ship, you can use some of the technology that we've been able to swipe from the Algothon and all of those outworlders. No one will see you doing that. When we get to Semoron, we'll have to use their paper and those messy quill pens. If we can get a lot of the information before we get to Semoron, think how much easier it'll be if we already have a lot of that information."

Bonarain sat there chuckling. "My, you really are getting smarter...and craftier."

He shrugged. "It happens with age…whether you like it or not. Not to mention the fact that I've been hanging around some very intelligent advisors for two monarchs for the last two years. You do pick up advice and tactics and other things when you keep your mouth shut and listen."

Kiyalee had a phony awed look on her face. "You? You, kept your mouth shut? You…listened? How?"

Soolchakan wrinkled his nose at her, showed his teeth and raised his hand as if he wanted to backhand her. Chyning sat there giggling. Bonarain looked off to the side to try to keep from laughing.

Kiyalee sniffed. "So…how long is it until we're south of Grenboling?"

Soolchakan sighed in despondency. "At least thirty-four days…if the weather is nice and the wind is with us."

Bonarain grinned. "We have an advantage there."

Kiyalee frowned. "How?"

Bonarain looked smug. "We still have several satellites from Algothon that have been repaired and are still working." She looked at Kiyalee. "You've been doing some wonderful things in keeping those relics in excellent working condition. We also have a lot of the outworld technology. We can steer around all of the bad weather while watching the wind patterns and get you in the strongest southerly winds. That might make the trip a little shorter."

Soolchakan smiled. "You're getting smarter as well."

Kiyalee sighed. "I wasn't there for a long time. It was Bikaropin and some of his students that did a lot of the work while I was..." She looked off to the side and cleared her throat. "I do have to give a lot of credit to him for keeping up with what I was doing at first."

Soolchakan nodded with a smile. "You kept some excellent notes on what you did and that was where he gained most of his knowledge of those satellites and all of the workings."

The navigators did not like being told where to steer the ship at times, however, they were so afraid of the Owlamites, they complied with those directions. The Owlamites were able to use their satellites to observe favorable ocean currents as well as unfavorable weather conditions. It became clear to the navigators that the Owlamites had some kind of incredible secret knowledge of the oceans, stars and the clouds because they were heading south to Lower Oosam at a pace that none of them had ever dreamed possible. The fear was changing to respect as well as awe (along with a few mega-tons of jealousy).

The crew of the ship was also taken by surprise when Soolchakan said that he wanted the elite of Malantroi up on the main deck. He wanted them washed and free to mingle around on the deck. Zebyuro was one of the main ones to voice a complaint against treating them humanely at all. Once Soolchakan explained that he needed to observe them while in a somewhat calm state of mind, he would be able to grab some of their thoughts and would be able to figure out some of the intelligence information that would be needed to battle the global problem of slavery. That explanation made Zebyuro and the officers of the ship a lot happier and ready to comply with the request. If they could obtain information out here, by stealth, that would mean a lot less time worrying about it back in Semoron.

They were now south of Grenboling. Now, to the west was Upper Oosam. To the east was open sea. To the southeast was their destination of Lower Oosam. It would still take a few weeks before they reached their destination so now was the best time to get the people on deck and start reading their minds.

Upper hold number 3 held all of the female elite of Malantroi. The women were pulled out of the hold first. They were brought up one at a time. Once they were on deck, they were completely stripped of all their clothing (most of which was nothing but very filthy nightgowns). They were led to large vats of clean water and instructed to clean themselves with the water. They were each given a large towel. The women did clean themselves, however, the towels were used more for modesty purposes rather than just drying off. After washing themselves, each woman was given a clean (what appeared to be) nightgown. Most of them had owned expensive nightgowns that covered almost everything except the head, the hands and the feet. These shapeless gowns only went down to the knees and left the arms completely bare.

Six of the women were on the High Council – three Civilian Representatives and three Military Representatives. There were ten women who were wives of the High Council members. There were seven slavers wives and daughters that had been taken from the slave ships in the harbor.

Soolchakan was on the bridge overlooking the main deck. From there he could observe all of the prisoners who were mingling around the main deck. He was trying to get their thoughts as they all looked around, gathered together and started doing some talking. He was very irritated over the fact that most of them were more concerned with their total lack of makeup, any form of decent of fashionable clothing, fine jewelry, the whereabouts of their children or what was going to happen to them once the ship reached…wherever.

Bonarain, Kiyalee and Chyning were in the cubicle that had been assigned to Soolchakan. They were waiting for some mental messages from him that would give them any intelligence information about the whereabouts of other slavers hideouts, sanctuaries, havens, ships, routes or schedules.

The slaver wives and daughters were worthless. They were brought along to cook, sew, and do other domestic chores for their husbands and fathers on the ships. They were very poorly educated and they geographically did not know Agrosha from Oosam from Tabrow. At first, it was difficult to tell which of the women were actually relatives of the slavers from slaves of the slavers, however, he eventually was able to distinguish which was which.

The wives of the council members were not any better. They were snobbish elitists who had only been worried about showing off their fancy dresses, jewelry, possessions and throwing lavish parties to impress their friends and try to influence votes for their ideas.

The six women who were actually on the council had nothing but some very vindictive thoughts towards all of the attackers who had placed them in this position.

Practically one entire day was wasted on the women. The actual Council women were the most intelligent, however, they knew nothing of the slave trade, other than the fact that they owned slaves. Very irritating.

The next day, the men were brought on the main deck for cleaning. There were nine from the Malantroi High Council, four Malantroi Grand Wizards (good enough to impress the High Council but not good enough to be elitists in any of the Cliques), five professional slavers and two professional slave auctioneers.

Soolchakan was a little confused over the lack of slavers. He remembered that there had been over thirty slave ships in anchor at Malantroi when the attack was executed. If there were over thirty slave ships – why were there only five slavers? He then remembered that Zebyuro had said that they did not get all of them alive. It must have been somewhat of a bloodbath regarding the slavers. Apparently a professional slaver was only proficient in fighting against an adversary that is basically helpless. If a professional member of the military comes after them, they do not seem to be very good at combat with an armed adversary who is very adept at using whatever weapon they have in their hands to fight back – a typical puerile bully – good with the whip against someone unarmed person, however, helpless against a trained soldier with sword and shield who is fully capable of fighting back – with lethal force. Also, rather stupid when it comes to facing an armed opponent by fighting to the death.

The two auctioneers were a complete waste of time. He could not understand what they were doing on one of the slaver raids. Unless they were going to inspect the "merchandise" while on the way to the market. They were to decide which ones were to be put on the auction block and which ones were to be given to wizards for experimental fodder.

The four wizards could only sit there complaining about the strange charm that had been placed on them that barred them from doing any kind of major spell. It had taken several days to convince them that they could not do the spells by having someone constantly sitting next to them in Spy dimension. Every time they attempted any major spell, they were given an electrical shock that destroyed their concentration and focus. One by one, they gave up any attempt at the major spells because of the pain that it was causing them. The real power being used against them was the power of suggestion, telling them that there was something magical about their special bonds that was preventing any form of spell casting. The only magic was the electric gadgets inside the charm. Certain words brought up an electrical shock.

The Council members were in a group trying to figure out what to do and figure out if there was anything that they could do. Soolchakan decided to have some fun with them. While they were discussing this mysterious (so-called) half-breed, he looked directly at them and grinned. This told them that he could definitely read their minds and that there were no secrets. They all were now feeling a massive amount of discomfort. If they did try to plan something, he would know immediately. They gave up on any plots after that. They were so upset over this revelation, they did not tell any of the other men in the hold about this new knowledge.

The slavers were a wealth of information. As soon as they had any conversation or thought about a safe haven, a refuge or their home port, Soolchakan mentally sent the information to his trio of wives. They were able to get a plethora of information without any torture or even asking questions.

"This is embarrassing," said Chyning. "All those women and all they could do is bellyache about their cosmetics." She looked at Bonarain. "Sound like anyone you remember?"

Bonarain just scowled.

Kiyalee giggled at first. "It is ridiculous. None of those women could give us anything that was in any way, shape or form, useful. The men have all of the information." She shook her head. "What a sexist world we live in. Makes me sick."

Bonarain sighed. "The sexist part comes from women who help the situation along. Why aren't they thinking of tactics and strategy of escape...no, they're just bellyaching about lack of makeup, fancy clothing, fancy homes, putting on a glorious party and showing off their ostentatious jewelry." She huffed. "I wonder what they do at the council meetings. Do they help in making decisions or do they just come up with grand plans for their special parties? Before they can do anything, politically, they have to have some kind of ambition or desire to lead."

Soolchakan mentally heard their complaints. **"Just be glad that you're not Heyyah or a slaver. You're Owlamites! That should mean more to you than all** of this information that we're collecting. You haven't really had to be subservient because of your gender. Remember that we did have a few females who were **Drey Sssorg**."

Chyning scoffed. "Yeah, we had a few women. Even though the men are only one fourth of the population, there were more males than females in that position."

Kiyalee shook her head. "Yeah, odd coincidence – but there still were some women in charge."

Soolchakan snarled. "**Did you get all of the information from those slavers**?"

Bonarain responded. "**Of course we did. All we have to do now, is write it down on the papers that these Heyyah supplied and we'll be able to forget about this mess until you get to Semoron**."

Soolchakan sighed. "**Right! We still have to keep sailing on this ship...for several more days before we can land and give the slavers a huge, nasty surprise**."

Bonarain snickered. "**The nastier the better**."

"**That means that this'll be the worst nightmare of their lives**," sent Chyning. She giggled with glee.

After all of the men had been herded back into the hold, Zebyuro walked up to Soolchakan. "Did you find out anything from them that we can use?"

Soolchakan smiled. "Yes, I did. Right now, my main

problem is that I'm going to have to go back and check on some geography. They were thinking about places that I've never heard of. I may have to dig a little deeper once we get to Semoron. I heard names of places and…I can't even tell you which continent those places are on." He gave Zebyuro an evil grin and cleared his throat. "Yet!"

Zebyuro nodded his head. "So there was some success in this endeavor."

"Yes," sighed Soolchakan. "I may have to just come out and ask the question: Which part of which continent is that place located?"

Zebyuro now looked worried. "What if they refuse to answer?"

Soolchakan shrugged. "If I ask the question, they'll still think about it. That is all I need to find out what we need to know. When I get the telepathic spell going full speed, there is nothing that they'll be able to hide from me."

Now Zebyuro looked even more worried. "That means that…there is nothing that anyone can hide from you."

Soolchakan just grinned. He left the bridge. He was wondering about a certain anomaly. If all of the female elite were in one hold, including the wives of the male Council members – where were the men who were the husbands of the female Council members? Why were they not in the same hold with all the other male members of the city elitists? He shook his head. If they were as useless as the wives, then it could not possibly make any difference to the issue. It was the Council members who had all of the secrets of the city locked in their heads. He did not need anything from any spouse...maybe.

They arrived in Semoron. When the elite were pulled out of their holds, each one was left a little confused as to where they were. Two of the female Council members recognized the Lower Oosam flag and had no doubt. When the male elite were pulled out of their hold and the slavers did not recognize the port, until one of them recognized the Lower Oosam flag, now the slavers were not so cocky. As a matter of fact, all of the men were rather distraught. The slavers had promised that they knew every port in the world and that there were very few places that could handle slaves in this volume. Now, the Council, like the slavers were all in uncharted territory.

The first ships that arrived were the ones carrying the lower class. They had no trouble breaking these people. They had been stepped on all their lives and this was no new situation for them. They gave in to the circumstances without any trouble. There were a few, however, that needed a few electrical shocks from the Owlamites and they were now obedient.

The second set of ships that arrived had most of the middle class and business owners. They took a little longer to break. Most of the business people tried to bargain their way out of the situation. They found that nobody was listening to their pleas because they had nothing left to bargain with. All of their belongings had been confiscated and reassigned to other people... like ex-slaves.

The elite had to be herded from one place to another, being treated like livestock. Dump them in one place for a while with no explanations. Move them somewhere else, again with no explanation. After they had been starved and stripped and were extremely hungry, they were taken in to a very large room in the local constabulary to witness the questioning and torture of the slavers. That was when they realized that they were not going to be rescued…especially after Zebyuro was able to reveal that their beloved Malantroi had been the refuge for a Monarch assassin, most of the slaves in Malantroi had originally been free born citizens of Oosam and the King of Agrosha was fully aware of the invasion before it took place. The King of Agrosha would not get involved because he would lose a great deal of diplomatic prestige with other nations regarding that wretched Monarch assassin.

Soolchakan wanted to know what the Malantroi wizards knew of what was going on and the magical stunts that they were doing during the questioning. Bikaropin and a few others stood near the wizards to read minds and hear what was said. They were able to find out that these men had heard of the Owlamites, knew they were powerful and now knew they were completely outmatched…because of what they had read in the Teltermak Chronicles.

Soolchakan was a little surprised to hear that anyone else knew of the Owlamites. He was also surprised to hear that they knew that the Owlamites were powerful wizards. Maybe he had been a little hasty in destroying any and all copies of the Teltermak Chronicles (that could be found…so far). Maybe there had been something that was very important in those tomes. Maybe there was another copy of it somewhere that had not been destroyed yet. The only relief was that no one had ever showed up at the gorge, so either no one guessed where they were now living or the dragons of High Country were doing their job better than expected.

The elite of Malantroi were also able to watch as Prince Zebyuro decided the punishment of his own mother, Aboreema Keldigin. Since she had attempted to use sex to change the mind of the late King Tooron, he turned her into a sex slave for the palace guards. She had a mind control put on her so that she could never harm any living soul again. She was now a nymphomaniac who would do everything she could to sexually satisfy any man, who touched her, without the capability of receiving any satisfaction or pleasure from the act for herself. It would be a lifetime of complete frustration.

The elite of Malantroi were then taken to the auction house. There, each one had their turn up on the platform. Other than an iron collar they were completely naked. Once they were sold, a leash was attached to the collar and they were led away, still naked, for their fate at the hands of their masters.

The people of Malantroi were told that they were going to spend the rest of their lives in slavery to the people of Oosam. None of them had a clue that this was actually a seven year prison sentence and that after the seven years was up, they were going to go back to Malantroi. By being told that they were now lifetime slaves, they had no hope of ever being free again under any circumstances. Welcome to a long life of bondage with no end in sight. You are a slave and you will submit to your master in all things in all ways without complaint - forever. Thus they will know what it is like to be a slave and what it was like for the people they abused as slaves.

The only way that they could keep other squatters from coming into Malantroi and taking over the town was to go back, hop all of the structures into Spy dimension and then scare the *piddleeyanks* out of anyone who tried to move in and build there. They had to have numerous excursions to Malantroi every month to keep the place clean. It did have a very nice harbor with a natural breakwater and was therefore very appealing to just about anyone who knew anything about harbors.

During 5480 while the male Owlamites were busy assisting with the capture and illusionary destruction of Malantroi, there were 381 new Owlamite babies born including a second member of the twenty-second generation. 2,179 new children from 5476 to 5480. The first real baby-boom for the Owlamites in many millennium.

In 5481 there were only seventeen new babies. In 5482 there were forty-one new babies. In 5483 there were fourteen new babies. In 5484 there were fifteen new babies. In 5485 Koshena of the Twenty-First was born. With her birth, the population count reached 9,000. In 5486 there were thirty new babies. In 5487 there were twenty-nine new babies…and time for the release of the citizens of Malantroi.

When the invasion had taken place, all of the women were back in the gorge taking care of the huge count of new babies. Now that the citizens of Malantroi were being released and taken back to their homes, the women were to be involved with this task. Nadiwi did not like it. If it had been up to her, all of the citizens of Malantroi would have been held in slavery for the rest of their lives. Soolchakan reminded her that the entire purpose of this endeavor was to end any form of legal slavery – permanently. The best way to do that was to show them how distasteful it was to actually be a slave.

Soolchakan, Bonarain, Kiyalee and Chyning went to Malantroi to supervise bringing the entire town back to Home dimension.

As soon as this job was begun, all kinds of looters came running out of the mountains and woodlands to see what booty they could find in the abandoned town. Shalam, Monaha, Loov, Jotsoom and Molkan suddenly became the head of the constabulary in order to imprison all of the looters. It was decided that the trial and punishment would be left up to the returning Malantroi citizens. The only reason the Owlamites would stay would be to act as witnesses for the prosecution.

They waited for the ships to arrive from Oosam where they were going to give the Malantroi citizens a few more surprises.

www.ingramcontent.com/pod-product-compliance
Lightning Source LLC
Chambersburg PA
CBHW060927030726
47503CB00003B/506